GRA

SECRETS

By

Melvin Foster

ISBN-13: 9798501638068

CONTENTS

Prologue

In one ghastly sweep of its icy hand, premature death had snatched away the artist's closest friend and her blithe creative spirit. She threw down her pencil and stared straight ahead. Beyond her studio window, it was summer, bright with colour, buzzing with bees, alive with birdsong. She slid her latest grizzly sketch into the shredder and turned to her easel. The cover remained down over the work she should have been completing. She stood, turned again toward the window and gazed out.

Summer scents finally drew her out through the French door. She stepped into her hillside garden, automatically unbuttoning her shirt as she ambled onto the lawn. The light cotton fabric billowed open. Soothing summer breeze stroked the artist's body. She kicked off her sandals to let the cool grass caress her feet.

Sudden screeching shattered the moment as birds dispersed to surrounding foliage. Stillness descended. The artist shielded her eyes and scanned out over the valley in search of a hovering kestrel or hedge-hopping sparrowhawk. The lichen flecked old table and chairs near the garden boundary briefly diverted her attention from the almost tangible silence. As the day cooled, she would sit there diverting her morbid thoughts with a little phone gossip, a glass of wine and a shared sunset, with her friend across the valley. She took the exquisitely personalized phone from her shirt pocket to check that the battery was fully charged.

The pleasant moment passed. Morbid thoughts loomed once again. I need a distraction, she thought, something pretty to think about.

She left her phone on the kitchen window ledge where it wouldn't fall into the dirt, collected her gloves, secateurs and bucket from beside the door and bent to begin nipping off dead heads in her flower border.

A shadow fell across her back. She dropped her gloves and secateurs into her bucket and turned. 'Oh, hello,' she said, fumbling to do up a few shirt buttons, as her cheeks flushed pink. 'I'm so sorry. I wasn't expecting company.' She nodded toward the chairs beside her table. 'Have a seat and I'll make us a cold dri…'

A lean yet powerful arm seized her neck, cutting off the blood supply to her brain. Terror surged through her slender body. Urine escaped and trickled a little way down her suddenly paralyzed inner thighs. Consciousness ebbed. The neck-hold switched instantly. The forearm pressed hard against her throat, closing her airway. Her breathing, then her pulse and finally her life, all ceased. Death froze her lovely face into an ashen mask.

Long fingers closed like talons, tearing into the artist's hair. The killer dragged her backwards to a nearby silver birch tree and casually discarded the body against its white trunk. The artist's ponytail slid down over her shoulder and hung like a stark exclamation mark on her left breast.

The killer quickly gaffer taped a small bottle to the tree trunk above the artist's head, pulled on clean gloves and disappeared into the cottage.

Minutes later, the kitchen door crashed open. The killer stomped out, snatched the artist's phone from the window ledge and sent a message to a number selected from the contacts list.

Pausing only to record a digital image of the corpse and confirm that no traceable evidence remained at the scene, the killer strode out onto the hillside.

*

A visitor hurried from the lane and disappeared in through the open kitchen door. A few seconds later, the French door burst open. The visitor lurched out and ran screaming across the garden.

'Cal, where are you? Are you okay? Are you there, sis?'

A shotgun-like discharge startled the visitor to an instant halt. She gasped and turned. Her face froze.

A tongue of flame leapt up, igniting a mist fine chemical spray above the artist's head. The flame curtain descended over her lifeless cadaver. Birds scattered in a black cloud across the sun. Frogs watched still as stones from the shaded margin of the garden pond. Tiny incinerated leaf fragments fluttered down, like soot black snow.

The visitor seized the artist's bucket, scattering tools and plant debris onto the grass. She lurched back and forth, whimpering and stumbling as she gabbled a call to the emergency services and hurled desperately inadequate splashes of pond-water at the flames. Steam hissed and dissipated to no effect.

The artist's skin blistered, then charred and peeled revealing underlying muscle and sinew, defiling and devouring her once unblemished body. The flawless face shrank and distorted. Her forget-me-not blue eyes stared unblinking, unseeing into the eternally frozen moment. A pair of yellow cotton gloves lay palm to palm on the grass, as if in silent prayer.

*

DCI Andy Nash and his partner, DS Alex Reid, wandered the garden until SOCO and the Home Office Pathologist had completed their initial on-site examinations. The sickly meaty metallic odour of burned human flesh wafted in their wake as they removed the charred remains.

The detective's shared first impression of the murder scene was the striking lack of obvious disturbance. No sign of struggle or skirmish. No damage to surrounding plants. No spilled blood. As Reid pointed out, except for the incineration, the killing appeared almost casual.

'Or professionally efficient,' Nash suggested. 'Burning will have obliterated defence injuries if there were any, along with a good deal of trace evidence and forensics.'

'There's pretty strong evidence of trashing inside the cottage,' Reid said. 'Could it have been an interrupted burglary rather than planned murder?'

'Why would a burglar bother to set the body up like that?' Nash wondered. 'She could have been topped and torched anywhere in the garden. And everything of obvious value seems to be still there in the cottage. Why would a burglar go to all that bother, then apparently leave behind everything you'd expect a thief to take first? There are too many odd similarities between this case and another recent job. I need to get back and have a word with the boss man.'

Chapter 1

Alistair Dawlish skirted Weaverston city centre and turned off the ring road into depressingly familiar side streets. Eight nights B&B, and twelve hundred fuel-guzzling miles had failed, yet again, to deliver a job. As always, the inevitable question had scuttled his interviews. *"Why exactly did you leave the Royal Navy, Commander Dawlish?"*

Alistair drove past the unkempt row of suburban shops, deserted but for a man watching his Jack Russell fouling the pavement. He turned into the service area and parked his cherished Mercedes Cabriolet alongside the crumbling concrete steps leading up to his flat. A glance up at the building left him still barely able to believe, even after two miserable years living there, that one infantile error had wiped out his career and plunged him into this social sinkhole. He stepped out and locked his car. 'Your insurance is due next month, babe,' he mused. 'Unless something changes p.d.q., you'll be going up for adoption. And if I don't find a job, it's looking like I'll be homeless too.'

He dragged his holdall up to flat 4A above the hairdresser's salon, whose tediously lustful proprietor was also his landlady. Alistair opened his door with all the enthusiasm of a man letting himself back into prison. A residual disinfectant smell wafted past his nose amid the sickening odour of burnt hair and bad eggs that permeated through from the salon downstairs. Several hot June days, sealed in from the outside world, had distilled the atmosphere to its vile essence. He grimaced as he stepped inside, gathered up his post and wandered toward the kitchen, sifting through the bundle. He dumped the junk into his pedal bin and tore open the single remaining envelope.

The letter, dated ten days earlier, carried the heading of Thomas, Nightingale & Thomas – Solicitors. A tide of shock rose as Alistair read the short correspondence.

Dear Commander Dawlish,

We regret to inform you that your uncle, Dr James Anderson Hastings, passed away on Sunday 30th May. As executors to your late uncle's estate, we would be most grateful if you would contact our office as soon as possible.

Sincerely,

Owen Thomas – Partner.

Three days before their shared birthday and, Alistair now realised to his shame, he had forgotten to send a card. He leaned against the worktop and reread the letter, feeling oddly detached, somehow denied the overwhelming emotion he knew should be gripping him. Failure to summon what he realised must be the appropriate response, left him shocked, saddened and deeply ashamed. Maybe the real bereavement had happened too long ago. All the same, James was there when Alistair needed him most. Common decency demanded that he showed up at the funeral, if it had not already gone off, during his fruitless job-hunt.

Five unanswered landline messages, all from Thomas Nightingale & Thomas, suggested that the solicitors were keen to get James dispatched and draw their fees. He picked up the handset and tapped redial.

A pleasant female voice answered after two rings. 'Oh hello, Commander Dawlish, thank you for calling,' the receptionist said a little breathlessly. 'I'll put you through to Mr Thomas.'

A male voice answered almost instantly. 'Good morning,

Commander Dawlish, I'm Owen Thomas. Please accept my condolences on your sad loss. Can you possibly come into my office?'

'Of course,' Alistair agreed. 'Whenever it's convenient to you.'

There was a brief pause. 'I fear we may be bound by expediency rather than convenience,' the solicitor finally replied. 'Your uncle's funeral is arranged for three this afternoon at St Michaels Church in Lowesley Pryor.'

'Excellent,' Alistair replied. 'I'm so relieved that I haven't missed it. I can be available whenever you wish to see me after that.'

'Do forgive me, Commander,' the solicitor said after another hesitation. 'Would it be at all possible for you to call in here on your way to the funeral? I shall be away from the office for the next few days. I need to complete certain formalities, routine documentation, verification of personal details et cetera. Our potential problem is that I have keys, which you may require, to your uncle's properties. Meadford is more or less en route to Lowesley Pryor. I'm sure we can complete matters in time for you to get to the funeral.'

'Very well,' Alistair agreed. 'It may leave me a little tight but I'll be with you as soon as I can.' Alistair rang off, deleted the stored messages and hurried to his bedroom. He quickly changed into a fresh blue shirt and black chinos and replaced the contents of his holdall with a selection of clean clothes. His favourite blazer joined the dark suit on a hanger from his wardrobe. With his minimal packing completed, he slid the necessary documents into his blazer pocket, grabbed his holdall and headed downstairs. A sparrow-like chirp greeted him as he reached his car.

'Hi, Alistair.'

Alistair turned, forcing a smile. His landlady, Kelly Taylor appeared from her back doorway. Between the top of her miniscule black skirt and the hem of a deeply plunging white top, a spray tanned orange midriff slumped out into the June sunshine. In the ten days since she and her tenant last met, Kelly's short-cropped hair had metamorphosed from its former tangerine tone to a colour similar to barbecue sauce and, in Alistair's opinion, at least as tacky. She teetered over in marginal control of her four-inch heels and grabbed Alistair's arm for support.

'You off again?' she said nodding toward his bag and hanger. 'I didn't know you was back.'

'Family funeral,' he replied as politely as he could manage. 'Forgive me, Kelly. I'm running a bit late. I'm not sure when I'll be back. Will you keep an eye on the place for me?'

She nodded. 'Sure, no prob. Mind how you go. Don't want no more family funerals, do we?'

Alistair stowed his bag, hung his suit, and draped his blazer over the front passenger headrest. He slid into his seat, closed the car door and turned, for the sake of politeness, to exchange waves with Kelly. The hairdresser's soot black eyelids blinked, like badly maintained awnings. Alistair shuddered, drove out to the road and accelerated away.

*

As Alistair set out on his journey, thirty miles away in the village of Lowesley Pryor, Rev Clive Chapman was preparing to lead the final farewell to a respected member of his flock.

Rev Chapman stepped into the church, closed the door quietly behind him and stood looking past the lone man sitting, head bowed, in a pew near the alter. An irregular, though increasingly frequent, visitor over recent weeks, the man's obvious health needs had now passed irrevocably from the hands of his doctors to the beckoning hands of God. Clive bowed his head and closed his eyes, to add his own silent plea for the man's peace and comfort, before stepping silently out, into the June sunshine.

The churchyard stood still and quiet, with the archaeologist and contractors working on the church car park extension respectfully absent for the day. Taking advantage of what had recently become rare moments of peace and solitude, Rev Chapman wandered through the churchyard toward his car, outside the gate. As he paused to look over the archaeologists growing excavation, the church door creaked open behind him. The man who had been praying alone, stepped out. He made no response to Rev Chapman's wave, and walked unsteadily toward the car park. Rev Chapman sighed and returned to his car, to drive home and complete his preparation for the approaching afternoon service. The vicar and his lone visitor left St Michael's and drove away in opposite directions.

Chapter 2

Alistair coasted across the river bridge into Meadford and sped on up to Saint Mary's Mews. He found a lone parking space at the end of the smart Georgian terrace and reread the letter yet again before stepping out of his car. An uneasy blend of shame and sadness stirred as Alistair retrieved his blazer and took a moment to brush away imaginary dandruff. He slipped the immaculate garment on and strode off to his meeting.

The receptionist smiled as Alistair stepped in from the street. 'Commander Dawlish?' she asked.

'Yes,' Alistair confirmed. The girl showed him into an office with the name, Mr O.J. Thomas, sign-written in gold lettering on its door.

Owen Thomas welcomed his visitor with a firm handshake across a large ash desk.

'Your letter came as quite a surprise,' Alistair admitted as he took his seat. 'How did my uncle die?'

The solicitor passed a death certificate across. 'A heart attack, quite sudden, and sadly common, I'm afraid,' he said, retrieving a file from his desk drawer. 'Surprises constantly lurk unseen in life's undergrowth.' He coughed. 'Best get on. You're obviously keen to be on your way.'

Alistair presented the necessary proof of identity, including his birth certificate, passport and the signed declaration section of his release papers from the Royal Navy. The solicitor examined the paperwork, scanned each item into his computer and returned the bundle.

'Thank you, Commander, everything is in order,' he said, sliding a formal looking document from his file. 'Our information is that your uncle had only two blood relatives, those being a sister – your mother – and yourself.' He placed the document down on his desk mat. 'In any event, this is a very simple will. We need not waste time on a formal reading. You are the sole beneficiary of your uncle's estate, which, as you probably know, comprises a house and its contents in the village of Lowesley Pryor and a bookshop in Oxton, together with all associated business assets and capital residues. I simply require a few signatures.'

Mr Thomas pulled a bundle from his file and pushed the documents across for signing and dating. The solicitor witnessed each signature and divided the bundle into two sets. He handed one set back and slipped the other into his file, drawing Alistair's attention to two dog-eared documents tied with ribbon.

'These are the deeds for your properties,' he said. 'Would you like me to retain them on your behalf?'

Alistair nodded. 'It may be a good idea to keep them handy,' he said.

The solicitor made no comment. In exchange for two further signatures, he handed over a letter of authority for Uncle James's bank, an invoice from Percival Hinchcliffe & Son, Funeral Directors and a sealed envelope, which, Alistair correctly anticipated, contained an invoice from Thomas, Nightingale & Thomas.

'We took full instructions regarding funeral arrangements,' Owen Thomas confirmed as Alistair gathered the items together. 'I believe your uncle's wishes have been properly carried out. I have settled the invoice from Hinchcliffe on your behalf, together with our charges up to today. As I said, we aren't aware of any surviving relatives, other than possibly your mother. Do you have any idea where she might be?'

'None,' Alistair replied.

'And your father?'

'Dead,' Alistair confirmed. 'My father was Australian, a First Officer on a cargo ship voyaging between Sydney and the UK. He died at sea, somewhere in the Pacific, before I was born. I don't know the circumstances.'

'So, you never knew him and yet you followed in his seafaring footsteps. Perhaps we might trace the details for you?'

'No thanks.' Alistair replied. 'I spent an entire childhood constructing the image of a brave master mariner. I'll stick with it.'

'What about your mother?' Owen Thomas asked.

'My parents lived in Australia,' Alistair said. 'When my father died, my mother returned to the UK, pregnant with me. She apparently stayed around until I'd been born, then left again.'

'Do you have any brothers or sisters?'

Alistair shook his head. 'There was just me.'

'You and your mother?'

'Just me,' Alistair repeated feeling and, he realised, sounding awkward. 'My mother's wanderlust apparently returned. She disappeared soon after I was born.'

'It should be possible to trace her. We could...'

'She doesn't want to be traced, Mr Thomas,' Alistair interrupted. The solicitor waited, holding firm eye contact. Alistair coughed and continued. 'I attempted to trace her myself, some years ago. My father was a skipper with an Australian shipping company. I approached them for contact details. They refused to release personal information to me, but forwarded my letter to my father's last known address. His parents had moved on, but were still living a few kilometres away. The new owners were able to forward the letter. Mr Dawlish eventually contacted me.'

'And your mother?'

'Mr and Mrs Dawlish never heard from her again. They knew nothing about her pregnancy or my birth.'

'Disappointing. Were you able to make progress?'

'I tried but my information was vague. I was born June 2nd 1981 and my mother left when I was a few weeks old. Airlines won't release passenger lists to the public, but I managed to make some checks via navy contacts. They found no record of my mother leaving the UK between my birth and the end of that year.'

'In which case, she may still be here.'

'Not under her own name. I've checked, or persuaded contacts to check, electoral roles, DVLA, HMRC, all the places where she might be on file. There's no trace. I suppose she may have remarried and changed her name.'

'Was foul play considered?'

'Not to my knowledge. I was a baby when she left, but I spent much of my childhood in and around Oxton. If there had been any suspicions, I'm sure they would have surfaced. Some people are able to set conscience aside, dump their baggage and start again. I believe that's what she did. My Uncle James more or less inherited me by default. I never heard from my mother again, nor did he as far as I know.'

'How odd,' the solicitor replied. Alistair broke Owen Thomas' penetrating stare with a glance at his watch. 'You haven't seen your uncle for some time, I understand,' the solicitor persisted.

'Almost twenty years.' Alistair hesitated. Hearing the words spoken aloud somehow stretched the span of time. 'My career regularly took me abroad. Communication was difficult. We continued to exchange cards and occasional emails, but I never went back.'

'Will you continue with the bookshop?'

Alistair shook his head. 'I can't imagine myself as a shopkeeper.'

'You don't share your uncle's passion for antiquarian books?'

'Sadly no. I owe my uncle a great deal and I'll do my best to honour his memory, but he and I were different people with our own horizons.'

Owen Thomas nodded and handed over a buff envelope from his

desk drawer. 'Your uncle brought these into the office quite recently,' he said. 'You may need them.'

Alistair raised an eyebrow as he read the neat handwritten italic aloud from the envelope. '*New keys*? These must be the first *new* things he ever bought.'

The solicitor smiled. 'They surprised me too. I imagine he'd upgraded his locks for security purposes.' He looked at his wristwatch.

Alistair slipped the envelope and other papers into his blazer pocket, wished the solicitor a good afternoon and hurried back to his car. Once inside, he tore open the envelope. Two sets of keys, labelled *'house'* and *'shop'*, fell into his moist hand. A note caught his eye. He slid it from the envelope, unfolded the single page and read.

My Dear Alistair,

Since you are reading this note, my estate is now yours. Bookworm has been my life. I hope you will at least consider retaining the business as your own. Should you choose this new path, as I hope you will, Bayeux is the password, let your memory be its key.

Eternal affection,

James.

Alistair gazed at the letter. 'Oh uncle, I want to do what's right,' he whispered. 'But your boots may just be too big for me to fill.' He stuffed the letter among the other documents in his blazer pocket and turned his thoughts to a sad and urgent family duty in Lowesley Pryor.

Chapter 3

Alistair swept over the pale wild summit of high top, and began his long descent toward the lush river valley. Oddly familiar hilltops punctuated the landscape, triggering images of a distant former life. A beautiful smiling face, with hypnotic forget-me-not eyes, blossomed from his memory. Perpetual childhood summers shone bright and brief, before the deep sadness of parting plunged them into shadow. *Where are you now, Caroline?* he wondered. *Did you stay in Oxton, become a teacher, marry, have children?*

Present reality nudged memories and questions aside as buildings appeared beyond trees to Alistair's left. Sunlight glinted on the rivers Oxburn and Corvdon gathering pace along Oxton's western and southern boundaries as they prepared to merge below the town.

Sat nav directed him into a narrow lane then over the river Oxburn by a stone bridge. Oxton receded in the rear-view mirror. The river tumbled away into rich greenery on Alistair's left. He glanced at his dashboard clock, accelerated up the steep incline into Lowesley Pryor, on past the church and through the deserted village.

James's lovely old timber framed home, with its beautifully aged herringbone brick panels, sheltered alone in a private cul de sac at the village's far perimeter. A garage sized building of similar age and style, stood among tall trees at the property's left-hand boundary. A path to the right of the building led, via a pleasant shrub garden, toward the rear of the house. Alistair parked alongside the building, gathered his belongings and hurried along to the front gate.

Small patches of sunlight penetrated the shadows cast by a compact mountain ash and a large copper beech, speckling the brickwork with cheery orange highlights.

Alistair's inner compass indicated that the rear of the house must command a lofty west facing view over the river. He stepped in through the front gate, already sensing the old man's elation at acquiring the house, steeped in history and blessed with a prime location. This lovely home was certainly a step or two up from the flat above James's bookshop in Oxton. Alistair recalled the old place and the omnipresent Nancy Lazenby, housekeeper to his uncle and proxy mother to him. Nanny Laze remained among the happiest of Alistair's returning childhood memories. If he had realised the finality of his goodbyes when he left for University and the Royal Navy, he would surely have made more effort to stay in touch.

The second of Alistair's new keys turned the front door lock. He stepped into the hall and closed the door behind him. Nancy Lazenby ran from the kitchen, drying her hands, and enveloped him in a tight hug. He surprised himself by returning the gesture. Nineteen years of separation instantly melted away.

Nancy stepped back with her warm smile undimmed by the years. 'Look at you,' she said, squeezing his firm biceps. 'Tall, strong, and you still have your mother's lovely dark hair. I've had some gangly youth in my head for nineteen years, where did he go?'

'Life took him away, Nancy,' he said. 'It would have been nice to come back in happier circumstances.'

'You're here now, that's what counts,' she said. 'I'm so pleased you've made it. I wasn't sure whether Mr Thomas had managed to get in touch with you.' Nancy glanced at her watch. 'We need to hurry along,' she reminded him. 'I've put on a buffet in the lounge for after the service. I hope you approve. Dr Hastings would have liked it, I think.'

Alistair smiled. 'You knew my uncle better than anyone,' he said.

'If you think a buffet is appropriate, who am I to disagree?' He turned to take his bag upstairs. 'I've parked my car outside that building in the lane. If it's in the way, I'll move it into the garage, if there is one.'

'It will be safe there,' Nancy replied. 'There isn't a garage. Dr Hastings thought of converting that old workshop when he bought the house. The planners refused permission, with it being listed. In any case, it stands on stilts so the floor wouldn't bear the weight of a vehicle. You needn't worry. This is Lowesley Pryor. Your car is perfectly safe.'

'I'll take your word for that,' he said with a smile. His brow creased. 'Do you really still address him as Dr Hastings after how long is it, nearly forty years?'

'Not quite that long,' Nancy replied, wagging her finger. 'It will be thirty-eight years, come the fifteenth of September.' She returned his smile. 'It wouldn't have felt right to address my employer by his first name.'

Alistair laughed. 'Does that mean you'll be addressing me as Commander Dawlish from now on?'

'Of course I will, when I'm in company,' she replied. 'That's called respect. There isn't enough of it about nowadays. You'll still be Ali when we're on our own, mind. You may call me whatever you decide, within reason.' She nodded at the hall clock. 'We need to get a move on, or we'll be late for the service.'

Alistair headed toward the stairs. 'What are the arrangements?' he called over his shoulder. 'All I know is that it's at St Michael's. Will the hearse be leaving from here?'

'I didn't see the point of having Warren Hinchcliffe struggle up here with that big car.' Nancy replied. 'I decided he might as well go directly to the church. There are only us two going from here. I didn't book a following car in case you... Dr Hastings never liked having too many cars cluttering the village. I'd decided to walk down but I can call Warren if you want me to.'

'No need,' Alistair called over the banister. 'I'll be happy to walk. Which is my room?'

'I wasn't sure you'd get here so... Anyhow, I got them all aired and ready. Choose whichever you prefer.'

He smiled. 'You shouldn't have been fretting over me. You had much more important things on your mind, but thanks very much anyhow. I appreciate it. I'll be down in ten minutes.'

With less than forty-five minutes to go before the funeral, Alistair barely had time to freshen up and change into his dark suit, a clean white shirt and a black tie. He returned downstairs, Nancy cast a final glance over her buffet, hurried to join Alistair and checked her outfit in the hall mirror. He opened the front door and followed her out into the quiet lane.

Nancy linked arms with Alistair and walked close beside him, occasionally stroking his forearm as if to confirm that he had actually returned. Her fingers tightened as St Michael's came into view. 'Everybody liked him, couldn't help but like him,' she said. 'I hope they'll make the effort to come and say goodbye.'

Alistair gave her hand a reassuring squeeze. 'They will,' he said. 'If my uncle was as popular as you say, people will want to share their loss. I'll miss him too, Nancy. I've been absent for a while, but I haven't forgotten how much he did for me. Nobody will miss him quite like you, of course. You must be devastated.'

'I couldn't believe he'd died, still can't,' she replied. 'It was so sudden, as if he'd just been cancelled.' She swallowed a tear. 'While I remember, Ali, on the night he passed away there was a bit of a break-in at the shop. I'm sure that's what caused... I've heard that Dr Hastings' heart gave out while he was chasing the burglar, or being chased. I'm not sure which really.'

Alistair looked down at her. 'Is there much damage to sort out?' he asked.

Nancy's attention had shifted to the church. 'I can't recall what the police said,' she replied without looking at him. 'I didn't pay much attention to anything, after they told me what had happened. Fred Reynolds has repaired it temporarily but I think you'll need to do something a bit more permanent.'

'Don't worry, I'll get it seen to.'

They hurried into the churchyard, where several people had arrived to pay their respects. Nancy gave a relieved sigh. 'Good turnout,' she whispered. 'I'm pleased for him.'

*

The lovely old church of Saint Michael the Archangel continued benignly dominating the village as it had for centuries. In front of the building, the old churchyard remained much as Alistair remembered it, though several of the older headstones now teetered on the verge of inevitable collapse. An ancient yew tree standing near the church door, and four mature oaks guarding the driveway, shielded the ground with islands of shadow.

Memory stirred the image of a February half-term holiday when he and Uncle James had visited to see the church's stunning annual display of snowdrops. Alistair smiled at tales of ghosts and ghouls, passed back and forth along the churchyard wall by eager young storytellers. His eye found the incongruous domino ranks of new headstones in a cemetery extension behind the church. A board alongside the churchyard wall announced the presence on site of County Archaeologist, Oliver T. Grainger M.Sc., a man no doubt blessed with a job for life in this historic area.

The garish yellow bucket of an excavator stood, like a huge praying mantis, a little way beyond the church. Alistair felt his jaw tighten. Would it have been so hard to park it out of sight for an hour or two?

An unaccompanied hearse drew up outside the churchyard gate.

The vicar, who seemed somehow familiar to Alistair, stepped out to meet the coffin at the church entrance. Nancy tugged at Alistair's elbow before he had time to trawl his memory and put a name to the face.

The vicar bowed and turned to escort James's pale casket inside. Alistair and Nancy followed. A lady churchwarden guided them into the front pew. They sat and bowed their heads, while fellow mourners filed in behind them.

Alistair raised his head and looked around. A tiny carved pulpit faced diagonally from the front right corner toward the centrally positioned altar. Three pure white arum lilies stood in polished copper urns at either end of the table. Their light perfume mingled with the comforting aged atmosphere. Stillness settled. Attention focused on the coffin at the altar rail.

The vicar turned to face his congregation and raised his arm, drawing the mourners into a symbolic embrace.

The heavy church door creaked. The vicar's eyes shot open. His obvious surprise triggered an irresistible response. Mourners, including Nancy and Alistair, turned toward the back of the church, where two men stood framed in the open doorway. The taller visitor beckoned to the vicar. His companion took a folded document from his inside jacket pocket.

'Ladies and gentlemen, I must apologise most sincerely,' the vicar said, not quite managing to disguise his sudden annoyance. 'It appears that our service is to be delayed for a little while. Please excuse me.'

He strode up the aisle and bundled the intruders outside. The door swung half closed against his broad back. Whispered discussion escalated into hissing discord. The congregation listened with rapt and deeply embarrassed attention.

Heated discussion and frantic paper shuffling riveted the congregation until silence slowly returned.

The vicar, his face now flushed deep crimson, strode back to address his congregation. 'Ladies and gentlemen, I regret to inform you that I… um… Our service cannot proceed today.'

A hum of disbelief circulated. All eyes focused on the slightly tongue-tied vicar, who finally managed to continue.

'The gentlemen who arrived as we commenced our devotions are police officers.' The officers lowered their eyes from the vicar's glare. 'In general, the police have no legal right to enter any church while a service is in progress.' The vicar beckoned the men forward to share in his discomfort. 'However, the officers have a Coroner's Order prohibiting our burial. In these exceptional circumstances, I am unable to proceed. I can only offer my sincere apologies to you all.' A brusque cough conveyed his mood to the entire gathering. 'If Nancy Lazenby and Commander Dawlish will please remain here, I must ask that the remainder of you leave the church. I'm very sorry.'

The mourners filed out, hurling barbed stares at the detectives as they passed. The taller officer closed the outer door. He and his colleague joined the trio waiting beside the front pew.

The senior officer introduced himself to Alistair as Detective Chief Inspector Andy Nash and his colleague as D.S. Alex Reid. 'Please accept our apologies for this intrusion,' Nash continued. 'Yesterday's murder on Redstone Hill has prompted us to reconsider the circumstances of Dr Hastings' death.'

'I don't live in the area,' Alistair said. 'I haven't heard about any murder. Perhaps you would like to explain.'

'We aren't releasing details at this stage,' Nash replied. 'All I can say for now is that our victim and Dr Hastings were known to be close friends.'

'Do you suspect foul play in connection with my uncle's death?'

'We need to check things out.'

'What things?' Alistair demanded. 'My uncle's death certificate clearly states that he suffered a tragic but uncomplicated heart attack. Are you saying that the doctor overlooked something?'

'At the time of death, neither the certifying physician nor the police saw anything suspicious. However...'

'Do you have fresh evidence?'

'I have a thread of common interest, Commander,' Nash replied. 'Two closely associated people, one of whom is your uncle, have died unexpectedly. The proximity of those deaths concerns me. Given the circumstances, I now have grounds for further investigation.' He paused briefly. 'Weird coincidences bother me, Commander,' he said quietly. 'I realise how this might appear to you, but by carrying out a post-mortem now, I am trying to avoid the far greater trauma of an exhumation at some time in the future.'

'When is the funeral likely to go ahead?' Alistair asked. 'I'm sure that my uncle's sudden death has shocked this community. I would like to see him respectfully laid to rest. I'm keen to dispose… settle the estate, so that things can move on for everyone.'

'I would prefer that you leave your uncle's estate exactly as it is for the time being,' Nash said. 'I'm sure we are all equally keen to see Dr Hastings properly laid to rest, and to have matters *settled*. You have my personal assurance that the burial will go ahead as soon as possible. I can't be more precise until I have the PM results.'

'Then I suppose you must do whatever you have to do,' Alistair conceded, 'but I would like to complete my business here as soon as possible.'

'As we all would, Commander,' Nash confirmed. He and his sergeant wished the trio good afternoon and left.

'What can I say?' the vicar murmured. 'This situation is unprecedented. The police are clearly facing a difficult task. I'm sure they share our distress.'

'I'm sure they do,' Alistair replied, as the bearers returned to collect their client. He turned to comfort Nancy whose expression confirmed that he had inadvertently revealed his intentions rather sooner than he might have wished. He opened his mouth to attempt an apology. Nancy turned away.

*

Nash and Reid sat talking in their car near the churchyard gate.

'Commander Dawlish seems keen to get his hands on the loot,' Nash said as Alistair followed Nancy out from the church.

Reid nodded. 'Aye, sir, an understandable reaction, maybe. We'd given him quite a shock.'

'Fair comment,' Nash conceded. 'Still, it won't do any harm to run a routine scan through PNC.'

Reid made a note.

*

Shock had scattered mourners into huddled, strangely disconnected, groups of two or three. A tall, skinny, elderly man stood alone. Vague recognition stirred again.

Attention turned to the church door. The bearers wheeled James out to the hearse. Mourners watched in silence as the vehicle slipped away, followed by an unmarked saloon driven by DCI Nash.

People began dispersing. Nancy stood with a handkerchief to her eye until a small group of friends ushered her away to the car park.

A woman standing outside the churchyard wall caught Alistair's attention. Their eyes met for an instant. She turned and walked away. June sunshine lit the soft waves of her pale golden hair. So, you stayed here, Alistair thought as his mind raced back once again to distant childhood, with its deeply cherished image of a spindly little girl already on the cusp of becoming a beautiful young woman; and of promises made and broken.

The sound of a quiet cough redirected Alistair's thoughts. He turned, also coughing to clear his tightened throat. The skinny man stood, smiling sympathetically, behind him. He offered his prehensile hand.

'I came to offer my sincere condolences and willing assistance,' he said, with cultured precision.

Alistair shook the limp, unnaturally lean, hand. 'Thank you,' he said, again sensing vague recognition. 'Have we met?'

The man appeared taken aback. 'My name is Aiden Gale,' he said. 'Your uncle and I were partners for many years.'

Alistair frowned. 'I wasn't aware that my uncle had a business partner.'

'Quite correct,' Gale replied. 'James is, or sadly was, the sole owner of Bookworm. However, he and I were very close. The unfortunate development in church just now has compounded what was already a tragic personal loss.'

Alistair nodded slowly. 'This delay will prolong everyone's agony,' he agreed.

'I also trade and have some experience in the world of books,' Gale continued. 'James called upon me when required and insisted upon paying an entirely unnecessary retainer for my services.'

'Forgive me, Mr Gale,' Alistair said. 'This isn't an appropriate moment...'

'I didn't mean to imply... Shock, I suppose. You have been plunged into a deeply unfamiliar environment. I merely wish to confirm that I will be happy to remain at your service until you have familiarised yourself with the many quirks and vagaries of your new profession.'

Alistair smiled. Thanks for the offer, but I'm not planning to continue with the business,' he said.

'That is very sad,' Gale replied. 'Bookworm has been with the Hastings family for two generations. I imagine James faced a similar dilemma when his father passed away. May I assume that you plan to remain in the Royal Navy?'

Alistair stared, barely managing to control a gasp. This man knew personal details about him. How much did he know? 'This isn't an appropriate time to discuss the business or my career plans, Mr Gale,' he replied coolly. 'If you will forgive me, I have pressing family duties.'

Gale bowed politely and handed Alistair a business card. 'Please feel free to contact me.' He began turning and paused. 'If you are intent upon selling, perhaps I might...' He coughed. 'As you said, this is not an appropriate time to discuss business matters.' Alistair watched until Gale disappeared past the excavator. A car engine started and faded into the distance.

The silence of the churchyard suddenly felt too deep, almost malevolent. Alistair shivered and hurried away through the deserted village to join the other mourners at the house.

Chapter 4

Alistair poured a glass of mineral water and attempted to mingle, feeling uncomfortably like a gatecrasher. Conversations withered on a bow wave of uneasy silence. Guests nodded and smiled politely but did not invite him to join them. Casual eavesdropping revealed stifled and quite unexpected whispers concerning a disturbed grave. Alistair found comments that James had recently become reluctant to discuss his work on some project at St Michael's church, still more surprising. He recalled his uncle as an implacable critic of religion. The notion of the old man having any role in church activities was quite astonishing. Maybe I've lost touch more than I realised, Alistair thought sadly. He left the gossips to their whispering and slipped outside.

As he had anticipated, the terrace commanded an impressive and appealingly private view over the steep river gorge. Far below, the River Oxburn weaved like a jewelled ribbon, stretching from the hills and mountains of Wales to Shropshire, the Bristol Channel and finally the distant Atlantic Ocean. The flow carried Alistair's thoughts back to his seafaring life and held him there, until a hand on his shoulder drew him back to the present.

The vicar from St Michael's greeted him with a firm handshake and a sympathetic smile. 'I felt I should call in to check that you have recovered from your dreadful experience,' he said. 'For such a thing to happen to anyone, and to James of all people, is simply shocking.'

'I agree.' Alistair replied, nodding toward the lounge. 'Speaking of shocks, people in there are gossiping about my uncle being involved with your church. I don't recall him as a religious man.' A smile flickered on his lips. 'Rather like me I suppose.'

'James had no formal religion, as he often reminded me,' the vicar acknowledged. 'However, your uncle was an active and highly respected member of our community. His death shocked us all. This afternoon's event will deepen distress, both in Oxton and this parish.'

Something in the vicar's eyes and his swarthy, slightly lopsided, features triggered a childhood image. 'Do forgive me, Reverend, but have we met?' Alistair asked.

The vicar nodded. 'I wondered when the memory would return,' he said. 'Do you recall your uncle's fondness for mature English Cheddar?'

'My uncle had a taste for all things mature and English,' Alistair replied with a wry smile.

Rev. Chapman returned the smile and explained. 'When we were children, my mother owned a dairy shop in Oxton. You went there quite regularly on errands for James.'

'Yes, I did,' Alistair confirmed. 'So, if your mother was Mrs Chapman, you must be… Cheesy? You can't be Cheesy Chapman. I don't believe it.'

'Most people know me as Clive, these days,' the vicar corrected, 'but yes, I was that wayward youth. I hope I can show you that I have changed my ways.' He smiled and nodded to Nancy, who was hovering near the French door. 'I think your housekeeper wants to speak to you, Alistair,' he whispered. 'Forgive me. I fear I've buttonholed you rather.' He gave Alistair's hand another warm shake. 'My door is always open,' he said. 'God bless.' With a parting wave to the guests in the house, he disappeared, via a path through the shrubbery, to the lane outside.

Nancy walked over and stood beside Alistair. 'Isn't this the most magnificent view?' she said. 'Your uncle loved to sit and look out there. Like an eagle in his eyrie, he used to say. I miss him so much.'

Alistair placed his arm around her shoulders. 'Nancy, I'm sorry I blurted out my plans in church,' he said. 'Today's news, hit me like a hammer. My first thought is that I'm inadequate. I know for sure that I don't have the expertise to take on the bookshop. It's too important, too precious for an amateur like me to bumble in and ruin it. This house is obviously gorgeous, but after years of wide-open ocean, I'm not sure I could cope with land-locked village life. So yes, my first thoughts are to sell both properties to people who will take better care of them than I could. Obviously, the police have put everything on hold for now. I promise that whatever I decide to do, I won't ignore what you have done, are still doing, for my uncle and me.'

'You need to think things through before you make any decisions about the future,' she said. 'That isn't important for now. I should have told you something. I didn't have time to explain when you arrived, with the funeral to attend and all.'

He felt Nancy trembling against him. 'What is it?' he asked. 'Calm down and tell me now. It can't be that bad.'

She looked up into his eyes. 'I'm afraid it really is very bad, Ali,' she murmured. 'I think you should sit down.'

Alistair guided her to a table. 'I'm fine, Nancy,' he said. 'Tell me what's wrong.'

'That murder yesterday, your uncle's friend.' She reached across and held his hand. 'It was Caroline Blackham. I'm so sorry, Ali. I know how close you once were.'

Alistair slumped onto a chair and looked up at her. 'It can't have been Caroline,' he said. 'I'm sure I saw her earlier on at the church. She stood over near the car park.'

'You saw Marcia, Caroline's sister. I noticed her there too. They were very much alike. Marcia works... worked for Dr Hastings at the shop. I'll get you some tea.'

'No, thank you, Nancy. I can't believe... How? I mean... murder. Have the police said what happened?'

'I haven't heard any details just yet. Poor Marcia must be devastated. She had already lost her best friend and now her sister too. It's awful.'

'Beyond awful I'd say,' Alistair replied. 'Poor woman. I'm surprised she's still around this area. I thought Caroline might stay, but her sister was such a high flyer. I assumed she would have disappeared to do something academic long ago.'

'She did go away to university, but she came back to work at the shop with Dr Hastings. The big wide world often tempts folk away, but an aching heart can always bring you home, if you listen to it. Marcia lives on a boat out at Stowe Junction.' She stroked his hand. 'Let me get you that hot tea.'

He shook his head. 'No really, I need a little time on my own. Perhaps I should check things out at the shop. Will you make excuses for me?'

'You don't need excuses, Ali. Everyone will understand. I'll see to things here and tidy up before I leave. Just take care in that car.'

Alistair ran up to his room, changed into chinos and shirt and made a quiet escape to the solitude of his car. His fingers trembled on the steering wheel. All thoughts of inheritance and the suspended funeral slipped from his brain.

His mind raced back through the years to his twelve-year-old self, sitting bored and forlorn on the bookshop window ledge. Shoppers and tourists bustled along the uneven pavement. Young Alistair sulked amid the musty dusty tedium of old books. A spindly little girl, a year or so younger than him, ran along the opposite pavement. She stopped, smiled and dashed across to the shop door. The old bell clanged as the girl burst in. What was that book she wanted so badly? Faded blue dust jacket... pinafores... He smiled. *Little Women* by Louisa May Alcott. The girl held a new one-pound coin in her hand. A million-pound smile lit her face. Although the book carried a price of three pounds, the child's single coin purchased it for her. As she left the shop, clutching her book, he and the girl exchanged mutually self-conscious smiles.

Late next morning, she reappeared. Alistair recalled Uncle James, inviting her in with an irresistible offer. "We have excellent lemonade. It's free to our readers."

Through the remainder of that summer holiday and several that followed, the spindly Caroline became Alistair's most treasured companion. She opened his eyes, opened his spirit. Boyish obsessions with sport and sci-fi became sprinkled with the sprites and spirits of Caroline's enchanted world. He remembered the heartache of separation through endless terms at boarding school and the thrill of rushing home to Oxton for each precious holiday.

A joyfully indelible memory reawakened. Alistair smelled the intermingling perfumes of grasses and wildflowers. He and Caroline were eighteen, poised on the threshold of life. He recalled her forget-me-not eyes, felt the warmth of her body as a deep and joyful tide overwhelmed them and they sealed their affection in the perfect harmony of innocent young love. As that magical day stretched toward its crimson sunset, they pledged to spend their lives together and meant every word, yet within a few short weeks, Alistair left and the spell lay broken.

The memory became unbearable. Alistair's thoughts crashed forward to the dreadful shock of Nancy's revelation. For the first time that day, he felt truly bereaved.

Chapter 5

Nine-hundred years of use and abuse, had seriously depleted Oxton's ancient fortifications, yet the town's character remained defiantly unchanged. Alistair drove through narrow half-forgotten streets. Old buildings gazed down on departing tourists, wearied by cobbled pavements and riverside walks.

James's bookshop enjoyed a prominent corner position linking Elizabethan terraces in Bishop's Hill and Radley Street. Bow windows, one facing onto each street, attracted customers to the shop door on the corner between them. A new looking sign above the door, identical in every detail to its predecessor, proclaimed *Bookworm Antiquarian Books*. The shop's interior currently hid behind closed blinds.

Alistair drove into Radley Street and turned beneath an archway leading to the private rear entrance in what had once been the carriage yard.

A marked police car and a grey saloon stood close together on the far side of the yard. Police crime scene tapes stretched across the rear of the shop. Alistair parked beside the saloon.

Chipped paint showed how easily the intruder had bypassed James's ancient security system by simply leaving the kitchen door locked and removing a panel. Fred Reynolds had replaced the damaged timber.

DCI Nash appeared from the Bookworm back door. 'I didn't expect to see you here today, Commander,' he said.

'My uncle's housekeeper mentioned that there had been a break in, Alistair replied. 'She said that Reynolds' had carried out some sort of repair. I thought I should check to see if I need to have more work done.'

'You were almost late for the funeral, I understand, sir,' Nash said.

'I was,' Alistair confirmed. 'I didn't know that my uncle had passed away until turned eleven this morning.'

'Quite a surprise then. How much do you know?'

'Just what's on the death certificate; heart attack. It's obviously tragic but seemed like natural causes. That's why I was surprised when you stopped the service.'

'Understandable in the circumstances,' Nash conceded. 'At this moment, Dr Hastings' death itself still appears routine. It seems that he was pursuing, or more likely attempting to escape from, his intruder when he died. We found him in his car. However, Ms Blackham's death is certainly murder. She and your uncle were very close, and both deaths occurred alongside break-ins with nothing apparently being taken. I need to identify and explain any common factors before either case can be closed. I'm sorry for the inconvenience, sir. We're almost done here for now. You should have access to the property by morning. The office is in a bit of a state.'

'In that case, I'll walk over and pay for that repair while I'm in town,' Alistair replied. 'I'll come back here tomorrow.'

*

Reynolds & Son, DIY & General Contractors had been on hand to solve Oxton's domestic emergencies for three generations. Despite Alistair's long absence, the current owner, Fred Reynolds, recognised him immediately. He came over to offer a handshake and an apology for his absence from James's funeral. News of the forced suspension had already filtered through the grapevine.

Alistair confessed his shock at both the police intervention at St Michael's and the whispered comments of mourners at the house.

Fred didn't speculate, though he shared the observation that

James had seemed unusually quiet for a few weeks. 'Not chatty,' he said. 'That was very unusual for James. Something was definitely troubling him.'

'Any idea what it might have been?' Alistair asked.

'Not a clue,' Fred replied. 'He worked too hard, of course. The old ticker can only take so much.'

'Something we should all remember, I guess,' Alistair agreed. 'Thanks for putting the kitchen door right, Fred. What do I owe you?'

'Nothing for that. I've only done enough to tide you over. You need a new door on there.'

'I appreciate your help, Fred. Can you sort the upgrade?'

'Course I can, but you need to concentrate on James and whatever the police want to sort out first.'

'I'd rather not set sail on a leaky ship,' Alistair said. 'If the old place needs attention, I'd best get things rolling.'

'In that case, you'll need to replace the kitchen door and frame with something more substantial.' Fred thumbed through a catalogue and slid it across the counter. 'This is the best one,' he said. 'It's fully reinforced, bolted front and back, and it satisfies listed building regs. I can have it made and fitted in around four days. I'll use the existing lock. James had all the door locks replaced a few weeks ago. He wouldn't replace the door, said it would spoil the character. If I were you, I'd think about upgrading your security too. That intruder bypassed James's old system pretty easily.' He punched a few digits into his calculator and turned the display to Alistair. 'That will cover everything,' he said. 'I've knocked a bit off for trade. Shall we go ahead?'

'Fine,' Alistair agreed. 'It was my Uncle's pride and joy. I don't want any harm to come to it on my watch.'

The streets felt eerily quiet as Alistair walked back to Bookworm. He sensed that traders had retreated inside their shops to avoid him. Discomfort quickened his step. He arrived back in the carriage yard feeling uncomfortably like a fugitive seeking sanctuary. The police had left. Only their crime scene tapes remained.

Alistair slid into his car. His gaze wandered up the external metal stairway to the mezzanine, James's minimal outdoor space, adjacent to the flat. A wave of sadness swept over him. Everything has gone, he thought, first mom then the navy, now Caroline and you James, all lost. There won't be any more, silly games at the kitchen table or coded notes to wind Nancy up. We laughed a lot in those days, didn't we? Why did we let it go? Why did *I* let it go?

His gaze slid to the ground floor. An unwelcome, though not altogether unexpected feeling of melancholy crept over him. Although books were never likely to become his passion, he would be saddened to see the shop in the hands of strangers.

A movement in his rear-view mirror caught his eye. A man peeped from the archway, made brief eye contact and stepped back into the shadow. Alistair stepped out of his car 'Can I help you?' he asked.

The visitor, a man of perhaps similar age and once similar physical stature to Alistair himself, crept out. Bright sunlight revealed features prematurely aged by sagging skin and pain-laden eyes. His once strong frame now appeared stooped and sapped of vigour. A quite disturbing aura of emptiness seemed to surround the man. 'I saw the police leaving,' he said. 'Is James around?'

'I'm afraid not,' Alistair said hoping the man had enough strength to cope with news of James's death. 'I'm sorry to tell you that he passed away several days ago. I assumed that everyone knew. I'm sure you will be shocked.'

The man's gaunt features registered no emotion. 'We weren't close,' he said. 'Not in a personal way. I don't live in Oxton. I call in for coffee and a chat when I'm in town.' He glanced toward the building. 'I'll miss those chats.'

'I'd normally be happy to make coffee,' Alistair said, 'but, as you saw, the police are working here. There was a break-in.'

'Never mind,' the man replied flatly. He turned and disappeared into the archway as silently as he had appeared.

A faint almost, but not quite, medical odour wafted past Alistair's nose. He shuddered and turned his thoughts elsewhere.

He had only met Caroline's sister, Marcia, once and recalled her as a snappy unpleasant teenager. Almost twenty years had passed since those adolescent days. He and Marcia now shared a double bond of tragic bereavement. The impact of losing a close friend and now her sister, in such a cruel way, was unimaginable. At the very least, he thought, he should offer his condolences. He punched a few details into his sat nav and postponed his reunion with Bookworm to another day.

Chapter 6

As Nash headed for his office, Reid beckoned him to the CID room. 'I've turned up an interesting log entry,' he said. 'Caroline Blackham reported a mugging, or attempted mugging as it turned out, a few weeks ago.'

'Details?'

'Not many, sir. She was walking home from the pub on Redstone Hill. She heard a movement behind her, turned and hefted the guy with her handbag before he was able to grab her. Then she kicked him in the nuts and ran home. Left him gasping on his knees.'

'Good for her. Did she give a description?'

'Nothing useful. Average height and build. Dressed head to toe in black, including a black ski mask. And he didn't speak.'

'Did we follow up?'

'We did sir, but Ms Blackham didn't report the attack until several days later. There were no witnesses, so by the time we investigated it had all gone cold.'

'Why did she finally report?'

'Dr Hastings had mentioned to Marcia Blackham that he suspected someone might be watching the bookshop and possibly him too. She persuaded him to report to us, although he had no firm evidence and agreed that he might have imagined it. Caroline was present when Dr Hastings was interviewed. She got a bit shirty because she thought the PC was treating the old man's report too lightly. She reported her own attack at that point.'

'It doesn't seem quite so trivial now, does it, Alex?' Nash commented.

Chapter 7

Three miles south of Oxton, the sat nav directed Alistair into a tiny lane hemmed between tall hedges. Gingerly nursing the Mercedes over humps and potholes, he wondered if the unkempt byway could actually be a road to anywhere. A plume of dust in his driving mirror indicated another vehicle some distance behind him. Alistair had no intention of speeding up and risking damage to his car. If the other driver caught up, he or she would just have to be patient. The gap had not closed noticeably when the sat nav announced *destination reached*.

The screen map showed the rivers meeting a hundred metres or so to Alistair's right, but no road in between. He rolled along to a gap in the hedge. Barely visible tyre tracks stretched up over open pasture before disappearing down toward tall trees. Alistair swung in and followed the tracks, over the brow and down between two horse chestnut trees. He parked alongside a blue Mini, stepped out of his car and listened. There was no thrum or gurgle of running water among the birdsong cascading from nearby woodland.

A tall man, presumably a bird watcher, stood scanning the area with binoculars from a hillside a little way beyond the clearing. Alistair called over to confirm that he had found the right place. The man turned and walked away over the hill.

Alistair cringed. *Sorry*, he thought. *I suppose my shout disturbed whatever you were watching.*

A narrow path alongside the two cars led down into the woodland. Since downhill seemed to be the most logical route to a river, Alistair set off between the trees to check it out. The trail threaded like a discarded bootlace for forty or so metres before emerging back into daylight. A little way ahead, down a grassy bank, a narrowboat with the name Gaia written in elegant gold script on her port bow, lay at her riverside mooring. Half-shaded ripple reflections danced along the intricately decorated aquamarine superstructure.

The woman Alistair recognised from his brief glimpse at St Michael's sat cross-legged on the saloon roof facing the afternoon sun, with her back to him. He coughed to announce his arrival. The woman glanced at him then turned away to dab her eyes with a handkerchief. She stood up, drew in a long slow breath and turned to face him.

'I'm Alistair Dawlish, James Hastings' nephew,' he said.

'Marcia Blackham,' the woman replied. 'I saw you at St Michael's this afternoon. I guessed who you must be. Why were the police there?'

'They had some sort of order to suspend my uncle's funeral. They suspect a link between his death and what happened to Caroline.'

Marcia's eyes narrowed. 'There must be a link, surely,' she said. 'Don't you think so?'

'All I know about what happened to Caroline, is that the police are involved,' Alistair replied. 'They wouldn't give any details. I didn't know my uncle had died until this morning. This is all quite… Well, you know what it's like, far better than I do. You sound fairly certain that their deaths are connected.'

'It seems too much of a coincidence, that's all,' she replied. 'To be frank, my head isn't really functioning at full capacity right now.'

'I'm sure it isn't, I didn't mean to challenge.'

'I know, forgive me, I'm a bit edgy. James and Caroline had been researching some story for the parish magazine. The vicar is relocating an old grave to make way for a car park extension. People are sensing a connection between that grave and...' A tear welled in her eye. 'James's death kicked off the usual wave of whispering. Now that Caroline has been...' She paused and blinked. 'I can hardly bear to talk about it. I was there, you see. I found Caroline and then...' She caught her breath. 'I had a text from Caroline's mobile, obviously sent by whoever killed her. That's why I was there. The killer apparently wanted me to witness what happened to my sister.'

'How callous,' Alistair replied. 'Did you say my uncle's death triggered some sort of speculation?' He asked to redirect Marcia, at least a little.

She nodded. 'It doesn't take much to set gossip rolling when the graveyard is involved.'

'I've already heard some of it,' Alistair said. 'There were murmurs about a disturbed grave, at the house after the funeral.'

'It's inevitable, I suppose,' Marcia conceded. 'Caroline had a slightly unconventional view of the world. When details of her death leak out, they'll set more tongues wagging.' She blinked slowly. 'I don't want my sister branded as some sort of crank.' A tear escaped onto Marcia's cheek. 'I feel a little dizzy,' she said. 'Can we walk please?'

'Maybe you should sit, sip some water,' Alistair suggested. Marcia stepped down and set off along the riverbank as if she hadn't heard him. 'Yes of course,' he agreed.

They walked for a few quiet minutes, before Marcia stopped at a flat, slightly raised, circular area of grass with standing stones set around its edge. The two largest stones, approximately two metres tall, at the far side, gave an impression of a gateway. Fifteen stones, each around a metre high, marked the ten-metre perimeter. Perfect in construction, weathered by countless millennia, yet all still upright.

Marcia dried her eyes and stood gazing into the space. 'This is our place,' she said, directing her words toward the circle rather than Alistair. 'We come, or used to come here, to sit, to think, just to be.' Colour drained from her face. She swayed.

Alistair reached out. Her shoulders stiffened just enough to discourage physical contact. 'I'm fine, really,' she said.

'Sorry, I shouldn't have barged in like this,' Alistair admitted turning to look along the river. 'This is a remote spot,' he said. 'Are you sure you ought to be out here on your own? Shouldn't you be with your family, or a friend?'

'Probably,' she agreed. 'Unfortunately, I don't have any family. There was only Caroline. I'm sure you're right, about needing company. The trouble is everybody will want to talk about the same thing and…' Her eyelids creased. 'It's just too painful. He strangled her and then…' She looked at Alistair barely able to force out the words. 'He'd already taken her life. And then he destroyed her body, her beauty, all of her; he burned her. What sort of monster could do that?' Tears erupted again. 'Why?'

Alistair stared into her eyes, saw and felt the intensity of her pain. 'I don't know,' he admitted. 'I felt I had to come and talk to you, but now I'm here I have no idea what to say.'

Marcia turned back to the circle. 'What are you going to do about Bookworm?' she asked.

'I have no idea,' he gasped. 'I didn't come to talk about business. Please don't think…'

'I brought it up, you didn't.'

'It seems bizarre to discuss a bookshop at a time like this. I really haven't given it much thought. My immediate reaction is to sell both properties. I'm not really a book person.'

Marcia's gaze fell to the ground.

'I'm sure whoever takes over the shop will be keen to keep you on,' he said.

'That isn't why I asked.' She looked at him and forced a trembling smile. 'I know how much the place meant to your uncle, that's all. I'd be more than happy to give you the benefit of my limited expertise, if you want it.'

'And I'll be more than happy to accept your offer, when you feel

40

able to face things again,' Alistair replied. 'That really isn't why I'm here.'

'The shop has been closed since James died,' she said. 'I couldn't face going there alone. It's going to be a thousand times worse now that Caroline has gone too.'

Alistair saw fresh pain about to erupt. 'Forget the shop,' he said. 'Are you sure I can't drive you to stay with a friend somewhere?'

Marcia shook her head. 'I mustn't give in. I'll be fine on Gaia.' Her tone did not invite debate.

Alistair accepted her decision with a nod. He turned to leave.

'Tomorrow,' she said from behind him. He turned. Marcia nodded slowly. 'Honestly, I need to face the shop. Delay won't make it any easier.'

'There's been a break in,' Alistair said. 'DCI Nash says there's a mess. I ought to tidy up before you go there.'

'I know about the burglary,' Marcia replied. 'I'm the registered keyholder. The police phoned me on the night James died. I should have gone over but they had his keys. The body was still to be moved, so they said I needn't go. I have to go back now so I'll come in with you. I'll know if anything's missing.'

'Are you absolutely sure about this?'

'Absolutely not,' she admitted. 'I just know I have to do it. I'll meet you at the house in the morning.'

Alistair accepted the offer with a nod and walked back to his car.

*

As promised, Nancy had restored order to the house before leaving. The post-it note, stuck to a cling-filmed selection of buffet leftovers in the fridge, reminded Alistair to eat. He opened a bottle of Cabernet from the small wine rack, poured a glass and sat gazing out over the gorge. In a few short hours the world had changed completely.

Chapter 8

When Nancy arrived for work, she found Alistair standing at the terrace railing, gazing out over the gorge. 'Well, this is quite a surprise,' she said with a wry smile. 'My young Ali Dawlish used to stick to the mattress like a bedbug. I remember…'

'He lived in a previous life,' he said. 'This Ali is an early riser. and he just discovered that Lowesley Pryor is a great place for his morning run. There are no choking traffic fumes, no bratmobiles cluttering the pavements, very few pavements to clutter really and no people at all, as far as I could see. I've just run for over forty-five minutes without seeing anyone.'

'The village has been quiet since your uncle passed away,' Nancy replied. 'So has Oxton. There's plenty of whispering going on, mind, especially now that Caroline has been… I can't bring myself to say the word.'

'What sort of whispering?'

'Silly superstitious nonsense about a witch. You have much more important things to think about.'

'We all do,' he replied. 'You, Marcia and me are all grieving for two very important people. I haven't been close to them for years and I'm feeling a huge impact. I can't imagine the pain you two must be suffering.'

'We're all reeling from these shocking losses, Ali, but something else is troubling you. I see it in your eyes.' She waited for a response.

'We all collect baggage as we go through our lives,' he said quietly. 'Memories, good and bad. Things we should have done but didn't, stuff we did do but shouldn't have. I don't have any recent memories of James or anything else here. Coming back has wound my head right back into my past. I turned up as an abandoned stray and James took me in. He gave me a home, an education. Caroline brought light into my life. Those two, and you, gave me everything. Memories are all that's left of them now, I'm just pleased that *they* are all happy ones. There's a big blank space in my head, where my mother should be. I've never even seen a photograph of her. I guess Uncle James thought it best to let her go, but there should be something in that empty hole. How well did you know her, Nancy?'

Nancy walked over and linked arms. 'I don't know much more than gossip,' she said. 'I didn't come to work for Dr Hastings, Mr Hastings as he was then, until after Kate had left. Your mom was younger than Dr Hastings, so I think he felt responsible for her after they lost their mom and dad. When Kate left, it seemed to take all the stuffing out of him.'

'But what was she *like*?'

'As I said, Ali, I don't know much. People rarely mentioned her and certainly didn't have anything good to say after what she did. She was beautiful, of course, everybody agrees on that, adventurous, always looking for a new life. I suppose that's why she married your father and shipped out. When she came back widowed and pregnant so soon after being married, everybody felt sorry for her until she did what she did. Folk said she still hankered after the new life, but nobody thought she'd go back to Australia without you. What kind of mother would do that?' She gave Alistair's forearm a squeeze. 'Hurry along for your shower. Your breakfast will be on the table in twenty minutes.'

*

Alistair returned wearing a fresh blue shirt and black chinos. Nancy stood loading a tray at the kitchen worktop. 'I thought you might like to eat on the terrace,' she said. 'It's fresher out there and it seems a shame to waste this gorgeous weather. I can serve up in here, if you'd prefer.'

'The terrace will be perfect,' Alistair agreed.

The toast popped up in the toaster. Nancy fumbled in her bag and produced a part used jar of lemon marmalade. 'Dr Hastings always had lime,' she said. 'I know you prefer, used to prefer, this. Old memories you see, worth their weight in…'

'Lemon marmalade, apparently,' Alistair said cringing slightly. 'I'm happy to eat whatever comes,' he said. 'But I appreciate the thought, thanks.'

'It's no trouble,' Ali,' she replied. 'It's what I'm here for, and you strike me as a man who needs a bit of looking after. Go and enjoy the sunshine. I'll be out with your breakfast in a minute.'

He left her fussing over her tray. If only a few good meals and a spot of sunbathing could make everything right.

Nancy had moved a table over to the terrace edge. It stood, laid up with a white linen cloth and gleaming cutlery, commanding a perfect view over the gorge. Alistair smiled and strolled over to look down into the rising mist. A half-obscured figure was moving among the trees near the riverbank.

Nancy appeared from the French door, carrying her fully laden tray. 'Takes your breath away, doesn't it?' she said. 'Just wait until you see it in the autumn.'

'If I'm still here. We'll see.' He sat at the table. 'I thought the land between here and the river belonged to James,' he said. 'I'm sure I saw someone down near the river just now.'

'It possible,' Nancy replied. 'The land does belong to… well it belongs to you now of course. There shouldn't be anyone down there but your uncle turned a blind eye if people from the village came to fish from his jetty.'

Alistair frowned. 'Anglers, from the village are welcome,' he said. 'Unfortunately, I don't know the locals like James did. Everyone is a stranger to me. There's a killer on the loose and possibly press people looking for a story. We need to be careful.'

Nancy shuddered. 'I'll mention it in the village hall,' she said. 'I'm sure people will understand.'

'Thanks. I'm expecting Marcia in a little while,' Alistair said, quickly changing the subject. 'We're going to the shop.' Nancy frowned. 'It was her suggestion, not mine. The thing is, she's finding it difficult to talk about Caroline or James. If you could try not to mention either of them, I'd appreciate it.'

'Trust me,' Nancy replied with a sympathetic smile. 'I'll bring fresh coffee and leave the two of you alone.'

*

Marcia arrived at a few minutes after eight-thirty wearing a dark business suit, perfectly complimented by a charcoal grey silk blouse. She stood tall and elegant.

Alistair stared.

'I thought I should at least try to look the part,' Maria said. 'Is something wrong?'

'Not a thing,' Alistair replied. 'I was just thinking I should have made a bit more effort.'

Nancy reappeared with fresh coffee and cups. 'I'll just move the debris, my dear,' she said, welcoming Marcia with a warm smile. 'Then, if you'll excuse me, I must go out for a few things.' She cleared the breakfast crockery and left.

Marcia joined Alistair at the table.

'I couldn't believe James had left the flat,' he said. 'Now I'm here, it's easy to see why he made the move.'

'He loved this place,' Marcia said gazing out over the gorge. 'As Bookworm expanded it became obvious to everyone, except James, that he'd have to move out.' A fleeting smile lit her face. 'Bookworm and that flat were his personal universe. He clung on there like a limpet. I can still see him, clambering over boxes of books insisting that he could manage.'

'What changed his mind?'

'Caroline heard that the old lady who lived here wanted to move into sheltered accommodation closer to town,' Marcia explained. 'Nothing much escaped my sister's ear. Anyway, James came out, charmed the owner and hey presto. Caroline was convinced the house had been waiting for him. Nancy lives in the village and the property is stewed in history. Even the name is perfect, it's called The Bookbinder's House.'

'I hadn't noticed the name,' Alistair admitted. 'Maybe Caroline was right.' He poured coffee and slid the cup over to her.

Marcia added a little cream to her coffee and stirred slowly. 'Those two were like father and daughter,' she said. 'Caroline filled his life, all our lives, with light and laughter.' She paused and stared into space. 'Now all that's left is dark silence and that awful blaze. James and my sister released something creepy and now…'

Alistair coughed uneasily. 'Look,' he said, 'I think it might be too soon for you to tackle the shop. I'll drive over and tidy the place up. Nancy is going out. Why don't you hang on here and enjoy the view for an hour or two? Stay as long as you like.'

'That's a kind offer, Alistair,' Marcia replied. 'I must face up to things and the sooner I do it, the better.'

'You really don't need more stress. I can manage on my own.' He stood to leave. 'Enjoy.'

Marcia gulped down the last of her coffee and shot to her feet. 'I said I'd be going to the shop with you,' she reminded him. 'I've spent half the night psyching myself up. I need to do it. Please, Alistair.' She forced a smile onto her quivering lips. 'Would you mind calling in at the cemetery? It's on our way.'

Alistair nodded. 'Of course, but why?'

'I have a wreath for James. Caroline and I made it. That's why I was at St Michael's yesterday. I wouldn't normally go near the place. When everyone had gone inside, I thought I'd have time to lay my wreath and leave before the service ended. As I ran past the church, everyone started coming out. I panicked and left.'

'I'm willing to take you, if that's what you want,' Alistair agreed. 'Do you think it's wise to go there while your emotions are so raw?' Marcia blinked and turned away. 'James isn't there,' he reminded her. 'Why not lay your wreath here? This was his favourite place. I'm sure he'll stick around, for a while at least.'

Marcia considered briefly nodded and ran out to her car. She returned carrying a floral sculpture of wildflowers and herbs, arranged with great precision into the shape of an open book. There was no written message. None was necessary.

A lump rose in Alistair's throat. 'Lay it there,' he said, pointing to the terrace edge near the table. 'I'm sure that's where he'd stand.'

Marcia placed the arrangement carefully, paused for a moment, then raised a tissue to her eye and strode out to the road.

Chapter 9

Reid stepped into Nash's office carrying a computer printout. 'Your guess turned up trumps,' he said.

'I'm a detective, I don't guess, I deduce,' Nash corrected with a grin. 'What have you got?'

'Commander Dawlish has a record, ABH, three years ago. There's just the one matter recorded.'

'Well, well, violence eh?' Nash took the printout. 'Do you have any more details?'

'No, sir. The Navy took jurisdiction. They'll have any trial and sentencing details.'

'That sort of conviction might have been enough to get him booted out of the Navy,' Nash said. 'If he's been living on benefits, he could be strapped for cash by now. Maybe that's why he's arsy with me for keeping his inheritance locked up.'

'Shall I look a bit deeper, sir?'

'Not until we have more reason to,' Nash replied. 'It was ABH, not attempted murder. Caroline Blackham's death was a planned slaughter. There are no common features in how her and Dr Hastings were killed, but I'm sure the deaths are connected. We need to find the connecting thread. Any thoughts?'

'That incendiary device had to be detonated at the right moment, so the killer would need to stick around until Marcia Blackham turned up,' Reid suggested. 'She reported no other vehicles near the cottage or on the road up the hill. Therefore, the killer left on foot.'

'Unless Marcia Blackham is the killer,' Nash replied. 'What else have you got?'

'PM report on Caroline Blackham, sir. No breakthroughs or surprises. Death resulted from manual asphyxiation.'

'Why?' Nash asked. 'What's the motive, Alex? We now have two deaths and neither candidate has any obvious reason to be targeted. The killer is almost certainly looking for something specific. He may have found whatever it is now. Who knows? But that something, is what connects our victims. None of the obvious stuff went missing in the Hastings burglary. We can deduce that our killer didn't find what he was after. That's why he went for target two. Let's go take another look at Caroline Blackham's cottage. We need to finish off there, anyhow.'

Chapter 10

Alistair drove into the carriage yard and parked near the bookshop's back door. Marcia dried her hands on her skirt.

'I'm fine,' she said fixing her stare firmly on Bookworm. 'Let's do it.' She sprang from the car, flung the door shut behind her and headed for the building. Alistair followed in her wake as she unlocked the door, strode across the kitchen, along a short passageway past the stairs and cellar door and into the dark showroom.

They stopped.

Marcia stood, panting. 'Made it,' she said.

The scent of books stirred embedded memories of haphazardly stuffed shelves, a tiny though rarely overburdened counter and reading tables where books often lay untouched for days. Alistair smiled as he recalled tourists blundering in after mistaking the shop for a cafe. James's contagious enthusiasm would often hold them enraptured for an hour or more before they left, always wiser and, more often than not, carrying a book or two.

Marcia tugged the front of her jacket straight and switched on the lights. Alistair gaped. A sleek electronic till and laptop computer had replaced the battered old cash box on the counter. Each reading table now had a covered shelf, to protect books that would once have littered its surface. The entire showroom had an impressive and completely unexpected sparkle.

'It doesn't look as if the intruder gave this area much attention,'

Alistair said looking, still wide eyed, around the showroom. 'This is nothing like I remember. I can't believe it's the same place.'

'I'm so relieved,' Marcia replied. 'This was your uncle's territory and he loved it. I've dreaded finding the place ransacked. My desk is upstairs. I only worked down here when James was away.'

'You are the expert here,' Alistair reminded her. 'I'm suddenly responsible for all this. I have to get it right, for James, for you, for Bookworm. I mustn't mess up.'

'Would it matter, if you're planning to sell the business?'

'I have no relevant expertise,' he said. 'Bookworm might fare better in the hands of someone who does. I'm not here to destroy anything. I don't actually have a *plan* yet.'

'Okay, your decision is none of my business. Bookworm is definitely yours right now. It's perfectly reasonable for you to be interested in how it works and what it's worth. I'll do my best to explain. There's a complete inventory of the showroom stock and backup, on our database. I can't give you an overall total until I've totted up and checked that everything on the stock list is still here. Your uncle sometimes forgot to delete books when he made a sale. He knew every millimetre of this showroom, but organised and conventional were not among his strongest skills. There's no way around the big slog. We also have some stock that isn't in the general catalogue. I'll tell you about that later.' She smiled and turned toward the stairs. 'We know there's a mess up there. And there's bound to be a backlog of orders,' she said. 'We'd best get that sorted before we start thinking about anything else.'

Alistair followed her upstairs and along to what had once been James's lounge. A wave of sadness fluttered as he stepped in. The drawers of the two desks and a bank of filing cabinets hung open along with the glass doors of book cabinets lining the two longest walls. Papers, files, and a sea of books, littered the floor.

'I should have cleared this lot up before you came back,' Alistair said. 'The police didn't tell me there was this much mess.'

They have much more important things than books on their minds right now, to be fair,' Marcia replied.

The phone rang on her desk. She picked up. 'Hello, Bookworm. Marcia Blackham speaking.' She stopped, stared briefly at the handset and replaced it on its base. 'He hung up,' she said, turning back to Alistair. 'Never mind. Let's get on with what we're here for. You can check for size ten boot prints and get the books back onto their shelves, if you like. It doesn't matter what order they go in for now. As long as they're safely behind glass, I can arrange them later. I'll try to sort out the rest of the mess first.'

In a little over an hour, they had cleared the floor. Marcia finished up at the filing cabinets. Alistair closed the glass doors on the refilled bookcases and looked around. The former lounge was now a stylish office, fitted throughout in pale, almost disturbingly modern, maple. James's desk stood end on to the window alongside the door leading out to the mezzanine. They and the upstairs kitchen, beyond a short passageway to Alistair's right, were the only recognisable landmarks from his former life there.

'It could have been worse, I suppose,' Marcia said as she closed the final drawer. 'The computers and all the stock seem to be here. I hope you like the layout. It took the carpenters days to fit this place out. The floor is so twisted by age, the fixtures will only stand up straight where they are.'

'I remember,' he said with a smile. 'My old room had the same problem. This arrangement looks fine to me.'

'Why don't you have a browse downstairs, while I do the orders?' Marcia suggested.

Alistair sensed that she needed to reclaim her space. He nodded and left her to it.

A few minutes in the showroom confirmed to Alistair that he had intruded into a deeply alien world. He retreated to the kitchen, opened the back door to refresh the air and began clearing an old desk beside the sink. James's spirit imposed its disapproving presence. Alistair grabbed a bucket from beside the sink, filled it with hot water and disinfectant and mopped the kitchen floor as if performing some sort of antiseptic exorcism. He had completed the task, checked use by dates in the small fridge and tidied the dresser, when he sensed eyes behind him.

Marcia stood in the passageway carrying two filled bin liners. 'Orders are done,' she said. 'All except one. There was a call from some uppity man on the evening James died. He was going on about being kept waiting for something. He didn't say what it was, so I can't follow up. It was the same number as that call earlier on. Maybe he'll get back. Anyway, nothing is missing.' She stepped into the kitchen and dumped her bags of parcels on the old desk. 'If you put the kettle on, I'll make coffee.'

Alistair began filling the kettle 'Have there been any calls from that number between James death and this morning,' he asked.

'No,' Marcia confirmed. 'I suppose word has spread.'

'If it was someone who was anxious to get something, but didn't know James had died, why has he not kept on phoning?' Alistair asked. 'If it's someone who knows about James, they must also know that the shop is closed, so what would be the point of phoning this morning?'

'I have no idea,' Marcia replied, clearly not following Alistair's logic.

'Perhaps the caller just wanted to know if there is anyone here,' he suggested. Marcia stared. 'Sorry, I have a suspicious mind,' Alistair admitted. 'I've begun making space for you to put stuff if you want to declutter the showroom,' he said, nodding toward the old desk. He switched on the kettle.

Marcia stood gazing at the dresser. 'It hasn't taken you long to move things around,' she said with a sad smile. 'James wasn't so orderly. You look tidy and organised, are you?'

He reached over her shoulder and picked up the coffee. 'I try,' he replied. 'Have a seat, I'll do it. I think you've done enough for today.'

She sat at the kitchen table. Alistair made coffee and joined her. 'I spent a few years aboard naval submarines,' he said. 'Personal space was pretty limited. It's important to keep things tidy.'

'You don't have to explain.'

'I'm not trying to erase James,' he said. 'Bookworm will always be his place to the folk around here, no matter what happens in the future. I've already had some pushy character offering to help. Handshake like a dead herring, I didn't like him much.'

'You were probably wise,' Marcia replied. 'There are some fly characters in the book trade. Did he give a name?'

'Adrian something, I think.' He retrieved the card from his blazer pocket and handed it to her.

She smiled. 'He's fine,' she said. 'It's Aiden Gale. Ignore the haughty exterior. Aiden is a lovely man, a dealer in rare books, a real expert. He and James worked together for years. I'm so pleased he's come back.'

'Back from where?'

'He and James were, *very* close,' Marcia replied. 'A few weeks ago, I arrived for work and found them arguing. I'd never seen them so angry at one another.'

'What were they arguing about?'

'Something to do with James's project at St Michael's. I didn't catch the details. When I walked in and the doorbell clanged, Aiden stormed out. I haven't seen him since and James refused to discuss the matter. I'm so pleased Aiden has offered to help.'

Alistair frowned. 'I'd prefer to see how we get on by ourselves if possible. I'm not sure about Mr Gale.'

'Aiden would be a fantastic asset to you,' Marcia insisted. 'James trusted him and so do I.' She paused and held him with her eyes. 'I rarely give advice and something tells me you may not take it all that often, but in my opinion, if Aiden is offering his assistance, I think we should haul him back in here right now. Bookworm isn't how you remember it. The shop is a relatively small part of the business these days. James brought me in to extend our reach onto the internet and we've done well. We're selling worldwide these days.' She walked over and swung the dresser aside to reveal a two-metre-high strongroom door. Alistair's jaw dropped. 'This is where James keeps the really valuable stuff,' she said. 'It couldn't be installed upstairs, due to the weight.'

'May I take a look?' he asked, stepping over to join her.

Marcia laughed. 'That should be okay. It's your strongroom.' She called out the combination. Alistair tapped the digits into a keypad beside the door and turned the large handle. Marcia pressed a finger to her lips. 'Forgive me,' she said. 'No one except James ever opened that door. It feels strange to see someone else doing it. I'm sorry, go ahead.'

The four-inch-thick door swung open. Air hissed in. LED light filled the stainless-steel interior. Shallow rectangular boxes, plus a few items wrapped in silk cloth, lay neatly arranged on strong wire shelves.

'Isn't this a bit over the top, for a few old books?' Alistair said.

Marcia gave an exasperated huff. 'Those are the non-catalogue items I mentioned,' she said. 'There are currently twenty-six books, each worth several thousand pounds. I think they justify the security.'

'These too?' he asked, pointing to three dusty cardboard cartons beneath the bottom shelf. 'They don't look particularly valuable to me. What's in them?'

'I've never seen them before,' Marcia replied. 'I don't get to look in here very often. I can tell you for sure that James wouldn't store rubbish in his strongroom.'

As Alistair began closing the door, he read some familiar words engraved inside on a small metal plaque. *Every precious thought is recorded somewhere in a book.* He smiled. 'If I had a pound for every time my uncle drummed that phrase into my head, I'd be a wealthy man,' he said.

'You will be a wealthy man if you sell this place,' Marcia reminded him. 'Lock up and I'll show you the rest of your business.'

Alistair closed the heavy door and followed Marcia back up to the office. 'I haven't touched James's desk,' she said. 'It seems like trespassing.'

'I'm sure it does,' Alistair agreed as he walked across to the desk. 'This entire place feels like foreign territory to me.'

James's computer and keyboard stood, flanked by an empty in-tray and a landline phone, on the pale desktop. 'All very modern and entirely incongruous,' Alistair said, running a finger along the edge of the screen.

'Bookworm changed,' Marcia replied, 'James didn't.'

Alistair reached down and retrieved a handwritten list of figures from between the desk and the wall. The torn off bottom of the page was missing. 'What's this?' he asked.

Marcia took the page and glanced at the details. 'James's notes, they're ISBN's.'

Alistair frowned. 'They're what?'

'International Standard Book Numbers. It's a unique book identifier; virtually all published books have one. I suppose he was working on some project or lecture.'

'Or trying to find whatever that man on the phone was looking for,' Alistair suggested. 'What's wrong with titles?'

'This makes it harder for people to crib your notes. It would be easy enough to identify the books.'

Alistair pointed to the letters, Xjqnr, scribbled alongside several numbers. 'Do you know what this means?'

'I'm afraid not,' Marcia replied. 'People who seek out rare books tend to be slightly paranoid about their sources. James sometimes disguised details of special items. He had many quirky qualities.' She contemplated briefly. 'He'd been working up here just before he died. He often worked here alone in the evenings. The insurance company insisted on having a silent alarm between the showroom and this floor. The police seem to think the intruder triggered it as he approached the stairs.'

'It seems odd that James would set the alarm when he was working in here,' Alistair said.

'I wouldn't read much into it,' Marcia replied. 'James triggered the thing himself a week or so before he died. Your uncle tended to be single tracked when he had a project on his mind. He may have set the alarm intending to leave, then had a sudden thought and carried on working.'

'That's odd too, isn't it?' Alistair said. 'Why would an intruder break in, when it must have been obvious that someone was here.'

'I'm sure the police would like to answer that question too,' Marcia replied. 'Just like they want to know who killed my sister. I think we should let them solve those problems, while we concentrate on Bookworm.' She glanced at the list in her hand. 'I'll check these out and get the titles, if you're interested.'

'Don't make it a priority,' Alistair replied. 'We have quite enough on our plates right now.'

Marcia dropped the page onto her desk and led Alistair along to the larger of the two bedrooms. Heavy blinds cast the room into darkness. When Marcia flicked on the light, Alistair gasped.

Old books filled floor to ceiling shelves all around the room. Stuffed boxes littered the floor. 'There must be well over a thousand books in here,' he said, sounding almost mesmerised. 'Those plates I mentioned seem to be piled higher than I realised.'

Maria gave a casual nod. 'Then I hope you have a healthy appetite,' she replied with a smile. 'Your old room is stuffed too.'

'Please tell me you're kidding.'

'I'm afraid not, and it all needs to be sorted. Shelf prices depend upon condition, rarity, provenance, many things. Forgive the cliché, but you can't judge these books by their covers. I'll have a go at valuing everything, but my skill is no match for your uncle's.'

'Did you say there's more?'

Marcia nodded. 'For the book fair at the Meeting Rooms in town next week. It was Caroline's brainwave.'

Alistair followed Marcia to his old bedroom. Boxed and stacked books covered most of the floor. The entire collection appeared to comprise titles on new age spirituality and the supernatural.

'This doesn't seem like stuff that would interest my uncle,' Alistair said.

'He wouldn't normally touch it,' Marcia confirmed. 'Caroline suggested having an esoteric book fair to coincide with the summer solstice. I suppose James felt a moral duty to support her.' She paused. 'When he died, Caroline thought Bookworm should withdraw from the fair as a mark of respect. I disagreed. She's worked hard to organise the event and we need to move this stock.'

'How do you feel about it now that Caroline can't be there?'

'She's spread the word and sent out flyers. It may look as if I'm snubbing people if I don't make the effort. You will obviously decide for yourself.'

Alistair frowned. 'This place is already overwhelming,' he said. 'An event like that might be a challenge too far.'

Marcia smiled. 'Leave it with me,' she said. 'If you're content for Bookworm to attend, I'll try to round up a few helpers.'

A floorboard moved beneath Alistair's foot. He stepped away. 'I don't imagine there's anything valuable among this lot,' he said to divert Marcia from the flush of embarrassment colouring his cheeks.

'Price and value are different things,' she replied. 'You might not value this material but people will fall in love with some of these books. A few pounds might put something priceless in their hands.'

'Sorry, foot in mouth,' Alistair replied. 'I'm a chronic case. Is it possible that those odd scribbles on James's note are code, to hide a valuable find?'

'It's certainly possible,' Marcia replied. 'James had a nose for the rare and desirable. If he had found something interesting, he wouldn't want to reveal any clues until he had the item in his hand, that's for sure.' They went downstairs. 'Alistair, if you wouldn't mind taking me back to Lowesley, I need to pick up my car,' Marcia said as she gathered up her parcels. 'We'll drop these at the post office then I want to drive over to Caroline's cottage. The police haven't let me near the place since she died. I need to clear up the mess.'

'You mustn't go there alone,' he said. 'I'll drive you.'

'I'm perfectly capable.'

'I'll drive you,' he repeated firmly, taking the bags from her.

Marcia nodded and strode out to Alistair's car.

Chapter 11

A marked police car stood, blocking the narrow road, near the top of Redstone Hill. A second patrol car and a familiar saloon stood inside a cordoned area a few metres further on.

A uniformed officer approached the Mercedes. Alistair lowered his window. 'Constable Walsh, sir,' the officer said. 'May I ask if you're here officially? Press statements are being issued through the incident room.'

'Let them through, Bryn,' someone called from inside the cordon.

The officer reversed his car onto the verge. Alistair drove up and parked outside a small red sandstone cottage.

Nash emerged from the gateway. 'It's a bit soon for you to be visiting here, Ms Blackham,' he said as Marcia stepped out of the car. 'Things are still too fresh in your mind.'

'I'd like to tidy up and put things back as they should be,' she replied. 'I also need to find my sister's phone index and diary, so that I can contact her friends.'

'I have them,' Nash said. 'I'll get them back to you. How often did you normally visit your sister, Ms Blackham?'

'Once or twice a week, I suppose. We used to meet fairly often at the shop too of course.'

'When was the last time you met prior to her death?'

'We hadn't seen each other for around five days, here or at Bookworm.'

'Why was that?'

'We'd had a bit of a spat, as sisters do.'

'Serious?'

'Sisterly. It was never serious.'

'But you didn't visit here for a few days, so you wouldn't have noticed if anyone, a stranger perhaps, had been around the cottage.'

'I'm afraid not.'

'I understand that your sister and Dr Hastings, sometimes worked together. Were they involved in anything like that recently?'

'Not really. It was all pretty informal anyhow.' She thought for a moment. 'There's that grave at St Michael's Church. It's being relocated to extend the car park. James was writing pieces for the parish magazine. I suppose Caroline could have been searching out bits of background.'

'Nothing else?'

'Not that I'm aware of.'

'Thanks for your help. Don't let me keep you. Are you sure it's a good idea for you to be here?'

'I had to come, Chief Inspector,' Marcia replied. 'May I go inside, please?'

'Of course, if you really want to. Our crime scene team has finished. I'll see that you aren't disturbed.'

'Have you made any progress with my uncle's matter?' Alistair asked.

'Not so far, Commander,' Nash replied. 'The post-mortem is arranged for tomorrow morning. We'll move things along as quickly as possible.' He smiled. 'Most visitors like to linger in our lovely area. Is there a reason why you're so anxious to leave?'

Alistair's jaw tightened. 'Keen, Chief Inspector, not anxious,' he corrected. 'I'm keen to see my uncle properly laid to rest.'

'Yes, of course,' Nash agreed.

Marcia ducked under the crime scene tapes and led the way around to the back of the cottage. She lifted the latch, pushed open the kitchen door and paused for a steadying breath before stepping over the threshold. Alistair followed her inside. Lingering aromas of paint thinners, linseed oil and rosemary rushed to greet them, like a welcoming hug from Caroline herself. They stepped carefully into the small kitchen. Marcia looked around at the scattered saucepans and crockery littering the floor.

'Where to begin,' she murmured.

'Why don't you take care of things upstairs?' Alistair suggested. 'It's too personal for me up there. I'll make a start down here.'

Marcia brushed away a tear as she disappeared through a door at the far side of the kitchen and along the hall to the narrow staircase.

Alistair cleared and swept the kitchen floor, then washed the dishes and saucepans. An open doorway to his left led to what might once have been the dining room but now served as a studio. A double French door provided excellent light and a perfect view, over the garden to the valley and hills beyond. Incomplete works stood awaiting the artist's return. A soft black cotton cloth covered Caroline's easel, as if in mourning. The studio felt intensely personal. Much too personal for a bumbling stranger, Alistair thought. He found a bin liner and stepped out along the hall. The room beyond turned out to be a cosy lounge, occupying the remainder of the ground floor. Its low beamed ceiling sat on unevenly rendered white walls. Paintings lined the room. The distinctive touch of a single artist gave each canvass an individual voice while adding subtle harmony to the entire collection. Alistair began tossing broken fragments of the few ornaments into the bin liner. He stopped. Each item would clearly have sentimental value. He carefully removed the fragments, placed them on a coffee table and lay the bin liner over to protect them.

Marcia returned from upstairs. Alistair followed her into the studio and watched as she browsed, resting a feather light finger here and there as if gently touching her sister, exchanging unspoken words, mourning and remembering.

'I'll leave you to it,' he said. 'Just call if you need me.' He went out into the garden. 'Flowers, birds and butterflies reawakened memories of the nature loving little girl who had blossomed into a beautiful teenager. Her bright laughter once again skipped through Alistair's brain.

He wandered across to the silver birch, its pure white trunk now mutated by fire into an austere soot-stained monument. Fine leafless branches formed a black veil against the blue sky. At the front of the tree a drift of crumpled star-like pink flowers, their flattened foliage curled crisp by the flames, lay pressed into the earth. Pained screams replaced the laughter in Alistair's head.

Marcia emerged from the French door carrying a thick portfolio. Alistair walked away to the garden table and sat looking out across the valley. Marcia sagged onto the chair beside him. She tossed her leather-bound folder onto the table.

'Some of Caroline's work,' she murmured. 'I thought it might help to keep her close.' She shook her head. 'It can't bring her back, can it?'

'Perhaps in time,' Alistair replied. 'May I look?'

'Of course.'

Alistair opened the portfolio and began leafing through the drawings. 'These are beautiful,' he said.

'I haven't looked,' Marcia replied. 'I'm not sure I can.'

'Let's try together,' Alistair suggested.

Marcia looked but did not touch.

Each picture proclaimed Caroline's impressive skill. The precision of her hand and eye were stunning. Alistair slowly leafed through immaculate studies of birds, insects, wildflowers and trees, each, to his eye, a work of art in its own right.

His stare froze as he turned over a lovely illustration to reveal a desolate pencil drawn scene, like the grim setting of a horror movie. Two figures stood, lashed to posts, before a heavily shaded gothic manor house, thrusting their pale bodies, empty black eye sockets and gaping tongueless mouths into stark relief. Flames licked over them. Alistair flipped the sketch over in search of a gentler image. The following sheet and several beneath depicted similar grotesque scenes.

'This isn't right,' Marcia gasped. 'Caroline's world was a beautiful, enchanted place. These dark things had no business there.'

'She was an illustrator, a brilliant one from what I've seen,' Alistair said. 'Maybe these are some sort of commissioned work.'

'I've watched her work for years,' Marcia reminded him. 'She's never produced anything like these. They're horrible and...' Alistair waited. 'Those people are burning,' she murmured. 'Just like Caroline was burned.' She bit onto the knuckles of her clenched right hand. 'What does it mean?'

'Right now, it means we pass this lot to Nash and get you away from here,' Alistair said, slamming the folder shut.

A small copy of an old photograph fluttered out onto the grass. Alistair picked it up. 'Do you know who this is?' he asked.

'No, and I really don't care,' Marcia replied. 'I don't want to see anything else from in there.'

'Fine,' Alistair agreed slipping the photograph back inside the portfolio. 'Let's go.'

They stumbled out to the road. Nash ran over from his car as Alistair bundled Marcia into the Mercedes.

'I knew it was too soon for Ms Blackham to come here,' he said. 'Is there a problem?'

'You decide,' Alistair replied flicking through Caroline's grotesque sketches before thrusting the portfolio into Nash's hands. 'I need to get Marcia away from here, that's for sure.'

Without lingering for further discussion, he spun the car in an almost impossible U-turn, floored the accelerator and shot off down Redstone Hill spraying a hail of dust and debris in his wake.

*

Nash spent several minutes examining the sketches before he phoned

Reid. 'Get on the database now, Alex,' he said. 'I want anything you can dig out that has similar features to the Blackham murder.' He described the images in Caroline's portfolio. 'Work quietly. If the locals get wind of this, were going to have a full-blown pandemonium to deal with, as well as a murder.'

'Those drawings sound kind of religious,' Reid observed. 'I've been hearing whispers about that disturbed grave up at St Michael's. I had it down as the usual tittle-tattle. Do you think it might be relevant, sir?'

'To be honest, Alex, I'm not sure what might be relevant,' Nash admitted. 'All I know for sure is that something or someone around here is definitely disturbed.'

Chapter 12

The atmosphere in Alistair's car had become uncomfortably quiet. 'Would you like to call in at The Crown for a late lunch?' he said. 'You need to chill and so do I.'

'No, thanks,' Marcia replied, sharply.

'You shouldn't have gone to the cottage,' he said, glancing across at her grim profile. 'Try not to get hung up on those sketches. There's bound to be a rational explanation.'

Marcia turned and looked at him. 'I'm sorry I snapped,' she said.

'Forget it? You're obviously upset.'

She pushed damp hair back from her face. 'I really didn't mean to bite your head off,' she said. 'I'm just not all that keen on pubs.'

'Or churches.'

She smiled. 'Or churches.'

Quietness returned and hung like a light veil of unease between them until they drew up at The Bookbinder's House. 'You don't know me yet, so I can see how trust might be an issue,' Alistair said. 'I know you don't have family and you'd rather not rely on friends just now. Those are your choices and they're fair enough.' Marcia's gaze remained fixed straight ahead. 'Maybe this is a time when what you really need is someone you don't know and have no need to impress with your gritty resolve.'

She looked at him and blinked. 'I'm probably about to stick both feet into the usual place again,' he said cautiously. 'I admit that I came here to claim my inheritance and ship out. Nash has put that agenda on hold. I'll have to stick around for a while and, to be honest, a bit of thinking time may not be a bad thing. After that, who knows? Your pain must be almost unbearable; maybe too hard to handle by yourself. What I'm trying to say is, I'm here and I'll be around, as and when required. No strings. Okay, speech over. Do I need to change feet?' Marcia shook her head and stepped out of the car. 'If you need to get yourself together, I can still offer a sandwich and a good view,' Alistair offered.

Marcia smiled. 'I'll be fine, really,' she replied. Alistair stepped out of the car and turned to engage central locking. 'I could bring over a takeaway later if you like,' she said from behind him.

'That would be very nice,' he replied. He pressed the fob button and walked over to her. 'Are you sure you're okay to drive? I'd be happy to give you a lift.'

'I'll be careful.'

'Okay.' He reached for his wallet, pulled out a couple of banknotes and pressed them into her hand. 'I'm old fashioned,' he said with a warm smile. 'Indulge me.'

'Seven-ish?'

'Fine.'

She walked to her car.

Alistair saw the unsteadiness in her legs, the unnaturally defiant angle of her head. He watched her car disappear toward the village and wandered off along the shrubbery path.

*

Nancy appeared from the French door as Alistair arrived on the terrace. She had been crying. 'Will it just be yourself for dinner this evening, Ali, or is Marcia joining you?' she asked.

'Marcia is bringing food later, thank you Nancy,' he replied. 'You're obviously upset. Why don't you go home and try to relax?'

She pulled a tissue from her sleeve. 'If you're sure you don't need me.'

'I didn't say that, Nancy.'

She turned and walked away. A few seconds later, the front door closed with a thud.

The phone rang in the lounge. It stopped as Alistair approached to answer. He did not hear the faint rustle in the shrubbery or the footfall receding down the gorge side.

The lounge, with its comfortably well-used furniture, felt like the space James would have chosen to relax. A large bookcase crammed with volumes on history and philosophy, occupied the longest wall. Alistair scanned briefly with his uncle's presence close at his shoulder. At eye level on their own shelf, Alistair's old school sports trophies, from the junior cross-country cup to the sixth form rugby shield, still gleamed as they had when he brought them proudly home. He wandered to the dining room and recalled cosy relaxed mealtimes, free from the unyielding formality of school dining halls, in the flat above Bookworm. Such happy times. He turned and went to take a look around upstairs.

Beyond his bedroom at the front of the house, Alistair wandered into the larger of the two rear bedrooms, with its spectacular view over the terrace and gorge. Scattered personal items showed that this had been James's room A small, framed photograph with the printed inscription, *Commander Alistair K. Dawlish – Royal Navy*, stood alongside an ageing clock radio on the bedside table. Alistair recognised the standard publicity portrait, printed from the Royal Navy website. That person doesn't exist anymore, uncle, he thought. Perhaps it's better you don't know what happened to him. A crude pastel drawing of James smiled from the opposite wall. Memory transported Alistair to a lazy August evening on the mezzanine above Bookworm as he sketched that portrait, while his uncle made faces across the tiny table. Nothing dented your confidence in those days did it, Uncle? he thought. What changed? The portrait gave no answer.

The small third bedroom housed a computer of rather older vintage than the shop's modern equipment, along with various items of luggage. Three framed photographs of James receiving honours from his University leant, discarded, against the wall. Alistair smiled, and remembered his uncle dismissing such things as *'fuss and fluff,'* while providing a place of honour for his nephew's school sports trophies, as he had continued to do.

Alistair turned his thoughts back to the present and ran downstairs.

The terrace basked in golden afternoon warmth. Alistair laid two places at the table, put plates to warm in the oven and turned his attention to wine. Nancy had produced a bottle from somewhere so, since the house had no cellar or garage, Alistair found a clean cloth and went to look in the outbuilding.

Nancy had stacked and covered the patio tables and chairs used the previous day. A large barbecue, also draped in a dust-cloth, stood ready for its next outing. Alistair noticed a wooden trapdoor in the far corner of the floor. He lifted the hinged cover expecting to reveal additional storage space, and was surprised to see a vertical ladder, linking the building to overgrown steps cut into the gorge side all the way down to a small jetty. Intriguing bit of history to be uncovered there, James, he thought. I'll bet you couldn't resist.

A fleeting movement, down near the river, caught Alistair's eye. The figure, male he thought, disappeared among the thick riverside foliage. Probably another local angler, he decided. He began closing the trapdoor, then changed his mind and stepped down onto the ladder. He reached the cut steps and made his way carefully down to water level, checking every few steps to see if the figure emerged. All remained silent and still. Alistair reached the jetty and scanned in both directions along the river. There was no sign of a boat. A search of the waterside shrubbery revealed nothing. 'You're getting paranoid Dawlish,' he admonished himself. 'Imagining spooky strangers.' He climbed back to the workshop, and closed the trapdoor. As he turned to leave, he spotted the wine rack in a shadowy corner of the building. A tiny window, covered in cobwebs and screened by summer foliage, kept out most of the light, creating a near perfect cellar above ground. Alistair selected a Shiraz, which would suit him, plus a bottle of Sauvignon Blanc in case Marcia or the food preferred white. He dismissed thoughts of riverside strangers and returned to the kitchen, dusting his bottles as he went.

Chapter 13

Marcia returned, carrying a white paper bag decorated with the name and yellow orchid logo of the Thai Dreams Takeaway, at a few minutes after 7.00 pm. She had changed into fresh linen trousers and a light top. Alistair realised he should have made the effort to freshen up.

Marcia selected the Sauvignon to go with their food. Alistair took the wine and James's battle scarred cooler out to the terrace, while Marcia transferred their food to warm plates. She joined him a few minutes later. Alistair opened the wine and poured two glasses.

'I found a trapdoor in the floor of that outbuilding,' Alistair said, searching for a neutral topic. 'I can't imagine why it's there.'

Marcia smiled. 'That building was the original bookbinder's workshop,' she said. 'James had a theory that the old craftsmen used the trapdoor to smuggle illegal books down to the river. The original steps are still there, apparently. When James first moved here, he used that route down to fish in the river. The climb became a bit of a drag after a while. I think he preferred to cast around for books. They were his real passion and he had an uncanny gift for searching out rarities.'

'So those book numbers I found in the office might mark a trail to something valuable.'

'Almost certainly *of value*, not necessarily commercial,' Marcia cautioned. 'He may just have been researching for that phone query or a lecture.'

Alistair held up his hands. 'Okay, I admit I can't appreciate books as you do. All the same, if he had stumbled across something, it would be a pity to miss it.'

'That has to be your decision,' Marcia replied. 'I wasn't happy about Caroline and James getting involved at the church from day one. James began having second thoughts himself. He tried to dissuade Caroline in the end too.'

'I hadn't given a thought to the church,' Alistair admitted. 'I just wondered if he'd found a rare book. Do you think those references might be linked with that grave he'd been messing around with?'

'Who knows? He had been digging out the history. Something spooked him. Now he's dead and so is Caroline. I'd certainly like to know why.'

'Me too,' Alistair agreed. 'I'm a definite fish out of water here, but I have a responsibility and I'd like to do what's right.'

'I'd say you're more like a fish in a perfect pond,' Marcia insisted. 'Bookworm was your home for half your life.'

'My so-called *homes* were a series of boarding schools,' Alistair corrected. 'My memories of Bookworm and Oxton are almost entirely of school holidays with Caroline. She was my life. We met as kids and did all of our important growing up together. Yet we split up. It seemed impossible, even as it was happening. I never dreamed it would, or could, end like this. It hurts, Marcia. It hurts like hell.' He looked into her eyes. 'I'm an outsider, a misfit in my own life. All I really have are a few dog-eared memories of a dim and distant past. James was my only link to who I am. I'm suddenly realising how little I actually know about him, his world, or myself.'

'That's truly sad,' Marcia replied. 'I think James adopted Caroline as his family, because he missed you. Those two made an unlikely team, like magnets; opposite poles bound together by an invisible force. She must have driven him crazy at times, yet they were inseparable.'

'Didn't you want to be involved?'

'I'm happy with the books and the business,' she said. 'Caroline was inquisitive, insatiably curious.' She stood, turned to face the sunset and wrapped her arms around her body. 'My sister was so scatterbrained in some ways, yet her work was totally disciplined. James instilled that pin-sharp observation. *Look and see,* he would say, *Consider and connect.* He must have regretted those words more than once.' She smiled. 'Caroline would dig out all sorts of odd bits and pieces. James opened up trails into the past and my big sister littered them with folklore and fables.'

'Where did you fit into the picture?'

'In many ways, I didn't,' Marcia admitted. 'I'm quite a private person. I never got involved in anything beyond the shop. Now that James and Caroline are both gone, I wish I'd looked a bit deeper, taken more interest in their other stuff.'

'The last time you sat at this table, you suggested that those two had disturbed something creepy,' Alistair said. 'Were you talking about the St Michael's project or something Caroline had been up to?'

'It doesn't take much to set folk speculating,' Marcia replied. 'Especially when that particular grave is involved.'

'What's special about it?'

'It's just folklore really. The headstone shows the name of a man called Samuel Rosemont but, for some reason I can't explain, it's always been known as Nellie the witch's grave. All the local kids used to come up here each year to see the snowdrops. We were told that if we touched the flowers, Nellie would catch us and steal our souls.' Alistair bit his cheek too late to suppress a sceptical smile. Marcia's eyes narrowed. 'You're laughing at me, aren't you?'

'No, of course not. I heard similar tales myself as a kid.'

'And you grew out of them, right?' Marcia replied. 'So did I. All I'm saying is some people don't.'

'Let's not squabble over that nonsense. My uncle was writing a piece for the parish magazine. It wasn't important. Sit down and finish your wine.'

She sat and took a sip from her glass. 'Maybe the old tales of Nellie the witch are just superstitious twaddle, but there's no denying that things haven't been right around here since her grave was disturbed. That's plain hard fact, not folklore.'

'James and Caroline didn't disturb the grave.'

'They did go digging into the story,' Marcia reminded him. 'Something persuaded James to abandon that project. He was worried, Alistair, I mean seriously twitchy about something. Your uncle had a touch of angina but he definitely wouldn't strike me as a heart attack candidate. Now he's dead and so is Caroline.'

'Sorry I dragged it up,' Alistair said. 'Those two are why we're here. They're bound to keep turning up in conversations.' He lifted the bottle to top up her wine.

She covered the glass with her hand.

A twig snapped out on the gorge-side. Marcia gasped and shot to her feet.

Alistair stepped over and stood beside her. 'I heard it too,' he said. 'Sit down, stay still and keep your eyes peeled.' He vaulted over the fence.

'It's probably a fox,' Marcia suggested peering down into the deepening shadows.

'Best to be sure,' Alistair said as he gingerly descended the steep slope He crouched and listened. The gorge-side remained silent.

Marcia stood as Alistair reappeared beside her. 'It probably was a fox,' he said.

'I'm sorry,' Marcia replied.

'Don't be,' he said. 'We need to stay alert. Two very special people are already dead.' She nodded slowly. Alistair sensed a question in her eyes.

'Something on your mind?' he asked.

She looked into his eyes and hesitated for a moment. 'You really seem to care, and yet…'

'And yet what?' he prompted.

'What happened between you and Caroline?' she asked.

Alistair gasped. 'Marcia, please don't go there.'

'She never stopped thinking about you,' Marcia said. 'Would it have been so difficult to write, pick up the phone, send a text?' Her lip quivered. 'It's too late now, Alistair.'

'I had my place at Oxford,' he said. 'Caroline was going off to Art College.' Marcia shook her head. 'I loved Caroline and I worried about her,' Alistair continued at last. 'Your sister actually seemed to seek out odd people with strange ideas. She would never leave things alone. She was really switched on in many ways yet totally gullible in others. I asked her to be careful.'

'Asked?'

'I said she needed to choose between me and the weirdos.'

'An ultimatum? She'd love that.'

'I can't handle that mystical stuff.'

'So, you dumped her and headed off over the horizon?'

'It wasn't quite like that. We'd both gone away to uni, so I didn't have a contact number any more. We didn't have mobiles in those days. I called your parents several times. They said they would pass on my contact details, but I never heard from Caroline. Then your parents number went unobtainable.'

'Our mom and dad were killed in a car accident,' Marcia said. 'They were on their way to visit Caroline.'

'How tragic,' Alistair replied. 'I'm so sorry. I didn't know.'

'At least you tried to set things straight.'

'Not hard enough, obviously,' he admitted sadly. 'James didn't have contact with Caroline in those days. I suppose that got going after she came back. I graduated and went straight into the Navy. My work took me all over the world and I couldn't talk about it with outsiders. I knew James would press me for information, so I avoided contact. The split got wider and longer until I was out of the picture altogether. He never chose to have me around in the first place. I suppose he decided he'd done his job.'

Marcia shook her head. 'That doesn't sound like the James I knew,' she said. 'Your name didn't come up very often, but when it did, James certainly didn't speak about you like a reluctant guardian.'

'In many ways, James was a better father than the real thing might have been,' Alistair said. 'I'm not ungrateful, far from it, but I could never stop wondering what it would have been like to have real parents.'

'Do you know much about your real father?' Alistair shook his head. 'I'm sorry. I shouldn't have asked,' she said. 'It's none of my business.'

'I don't know a thing about my father,' Alistair replied.

'I thought he was a merchant seaman.'

'Captain Iain Dawlish was my mother's husband,' Alistair said. 'He wasn't my father.'

'But James always said...'

'He told me the same story. I guess that's what my mother told him, but it isn't true. Captain Dawlish married my mother in June of 1980. He died at sea in September that year. That much is true. Kate left for England a few days after the funeral.'

'So, your mother must have conceived around the time her husband went to sea.'

'Iain Dawlish was a long-haul skipper. He'd been at sea for seven weeks when he died. Unless my mother had the longest pregnancy in history, there are only two possibilities. One obvious scenario is that she had been up to something while her husband was at sea. That might explain why she left so soon after the funeral. The other possibility is that she came back to an old boyfriend here and fell pregnant straight away.'

'Either is possible,' Marcia agreed, 'but why did she leave you here with James?'

'Nancy says my mother always hankered after a new life,' Alistair replied. 'Australia hadn't worked out. Maybe she came back to give it another go here. She travels fastest who travels light and I was excess baggage.'

'I don't know what to say,' Marcia admitted.

'What's to say?' Alistair replied. 'I can't change what my mother did to me or what I did, intentionally or not, to Caroline.'

'If it makes you feel any better, you weren't the only one to worry about some of the company my sister chose,' Marcia said. 'Caroline was an open book, a totally trusting individual who simply didn't understand that most people aren't like that. I warned her to be careful, like you did. She didn't appreciate my advice either. We argued and she'd gone before I had time to say sorry.' Marcia looked down into the gorge and shivered. 'I can feel eyes looking at me,' she said, stroking the goose bumps on her forearms. 'It's just stupid paranoia. Sorry.'

'Don't apologise, it is a bit creepy out here. Let's go inside.'

Marcia glanced at her watch. 'Time to go,' she said. 'Thanks for the food.'

'Your mooring is very remote,' he said quietly. 'Please don't misinterpret what I'm about to say. I have a spare room. You're very welcome to stay.'

'Too welcome, perhaps,' Marcia replied. 'I'll meet you at Bookworm in the morning.'

'Why not here?'

'Bookworm is where I work, if I still have a job. I want to try and sort something out first thing. I'm sure you do too. I can press on with checking the showroom stock by myself.'

'Fred has only done a temporary repair since the break-in,' Alistair reminded her. 'Security isn't brilliant. I'd rather meet you here and go in together.'

'I appreciate the thought, Alistair,' Marcia said, 'but please don't mollycoddle me. I'll meet you at Bookworm.'

'Of course, if you're sure,' he replied. 'I have a couple of chores too. I need to deliver a letter of authority to the Bank Manager, so that I can access the business account. I'd also like to keep the vicar on the boil with James's funeral. Promise you'll phone me before you go into the shop.'

She smiled. 'I promise.'

They exchanged mobile numbers. Marcia said goodnight and disappeared along the path to her car.

Chapter 14

When Nash returned from James Hastings' post-mortem, Reid was already at his desk. His stare begged the burning question.

'Hastings died from a heart attack,' Nash said. Reid gave a disappointed sigh. 'Brought on by an assault,' the DCI added. 'Dr Sangha found two bruises on Hastings' back. They are consistent with the victim being kicked down those metal stairs behind the office. It was a hot evening, so Hastings was wearing shorts, as he regularly did when he wasn't working in the shop. Grazes on the calves and backs of the thighs were most likely caused by him being dragged. Dr Sangha is satisfied that James Hastings was deliberately kicked down the stairs, triggering the fatal heart attack. He was then dragged to his car and set up to create the impression that he had died naturally. The Doctor has concluded that Dr James Hastings was murdered.'

'So, we were right to suspend the funeral,' Reid said. 'That's a relief at least.'

'We did the right thing,' Nash agreed. 'I'm not exactly relieved. One murder was almost unheard of around here. Now we have two to solve. There are no obvious common factors in the actual killings, but I think it's safe to assume, for now, that they are linked. What do we have so far?'

'Not much, sir. They were both involved in that Church grave thing, of course.'

'And they both went a bit cool on the idea,' Nash added. 'Hasting was pretty agitated apparently.'

'So was Caroline Blackham,' Reid added. 'Those drawings in her folder are more gruesome than her own murder. Her victims have their eyes and tongues missing, which she did not. However her images depict bodies burning, as she did. Something triggered her to make those drawings. The nature of the mutilation suggests the victims were killed because they had seen, or said, something they shouldn't have. If Caroline and Dr Hastings had been looking into the same stuff, she might have been scared that something similar could happen to them.'

'Those sketches show ritual killings,' Nash said. 'There's no obvious ritual element to the James Hastings or Caroline Blackham murders.'

'Agreed, sir. She may still have been afraid that whatever they'd found, if anything, might be dangerous enough to put them at serious risk. I suppose there's a chance she could have talked about her concerns with a friend. Unfortunately, her communication history is all on her stolen phone.'

'Nothing on her computer?'

'Nothing relevant. I've copied her address book. I'll keep trying her friends, but they're a pretty tight-lipped bunch.'

'It would be helpful to know what the killer was looking for. Hit the phone, Alex. Shake something out of somebody. The killer may not be done yet.'

Chapter 15

Alistair returned from his run, showered and went down to the terrace. Far below him, the treacle black river flowed through the gorge and vanished into morning mist. A few invisible miles further downriver, Marcia would be alone on her narrowboat. Alistair wanted to pick up his phone and check that she was okay, but knew she would prefer to make the call herself.

The phone finally beeped at a few minutes before eight-thirty. Marcia's voice brought a huge wave of relief.

'I'm going to try my luck at cajoling some help with the book fair, first thing,' she said. 'I'll meet you at Bookworm when I'm done, if that's okay.'

'Fine,' he agreed. 'I want to sort out the bank and see the vicar. If you get to the shop ahead of me, don't go in until…'

'You're mollycoddling again,' she said. 'Sorry, Alistair. I'm not used to… Thanks for bothering.' She disconnected.

*

A few minutes into her walk along the riverbank, Marcia heard a woman's voice. She turned and saw Caroline's friend, Dawn Tyler, standing at the edge of the stone circle. Dawn's two German shepherd dogs, Sheba and Cleo, were sniffing inside the circle, ignoring her agitated pleas to come away.

Marcia waved and walked up from the river. 'Hi, Dawn,' she said brightly. 'You're just the person I'm looking for. Is everything okay?'

Dawn mumbled a reply and continued calling to her dogs. 'I was just on my way over to your cottage,' Marcia said. 'I'm looking for some help at the book fair. To be honest it isn't my kind of gig, but Caroline had put a lot of effort into it and people will be arriving.'

'People are already arriving,' Dawn said. 'There are tents and vans all over the hill. I can't help.'

'I just need a bit of moral support really,' Marcia continued. 'It's a huge deal for me, in the circumstances. Your smile will help me a lot and it's guaranteed to pull in a few punters.'

Dawn turned and stared. 'I said no,' she snapped. 'I can't say it no plainer.'

Marcia gasped. 'You and Caroline were friends,' she said. 'I thought you'd be keen to…'

'Look, Marci, I'm sure you mean well but you don't understand.'

'Then explain for me.'

'No point explaining to them as don't want to listen. Caroline was my friend right enough, a good friend and I loved her to bits, but she should have kept her nose out of…' She left the sentence hanging in the air.

'Out of what?'

'The kind of things people didn't ought to mess with. Caroline should have known when to stop. She's brought something nasty here, Marci, real nasty.'

Sheba and Cleo abandoned their sniffing and ran over to Marcia. 'Hello, girls,' she said, scratching behind their ears. 'I don't see you over here very often.'

'They dragged me all the way over the hill,' Dawn said. 'I reckon they've come looking for Caroline. They probably mistook you for her.'

Marcia nodded. 'This was Caroline's place,' she said. 'She'd been getting more and more excited about her big get together here. You'll find it strange celebrating the solstice without her.'

Dawn shook her head. 'You're not listening, are you?' she

snapped. 'There isn't going to be any celebration. We've decided to leave it be. I can't even bear to set foot inside the circle.'

Marcia gaped in disbelief. 'Are you serious?' she asked. 'Summer solstice is the biggest event of your year.'

'Not this year,' Dawn confirmed. 'Caroline had been messing around with that grave, teasing us about revealing something at that book fair of hers. Ever since she mentioned it, tales have been buzzing around. Then Dr Hastings died, and now… Just look what's happened to Caroline. People are too scared.'

'What was the thing she planned to reveal?' Marcia asked.

'I don't know,' Dawn insisted. 'Nobody knows. We don't want to know. None of us wants anything to do with the book fair, or the solstice now. I'd like to help but I'm too scared. I'm sorry Marci but… I'm sorry.'

Dawn turned and dragged her dogs away over the hill.

Chapter 16

Alistair drove into the carriage yard, and hurried over to the kitchen hoping to check the shop over and be on his way before Marcia arrived. He was about to unlock the kitchen door when an incoming call chirped on his phone.

'Change of plan,' Marcia said.

Alistair detected a tremble in her voice. 'What's wrong?' he asked.

'Someone's been on Gaia. My stuff is all over the place. I was only out a few minutes. I've called the police.'

'Good. Don't touch anything. I'm on my way.'

*

The Mercedes slid to a halt behind a grey Volvo. Alistair leaped out as Sergeant Reid approached along the path 'Good morning, Commander,' Reid said. 'Ms Blackham is unhurt and she has assured me that nothing appears to be missing. I've finished here. May I ask where you will be later on, sir?'

'Ms Blackham and I had planned to be at the bookshop. Why do you need to know?'

'DCI Nash will need to speak to you.'

'About what?'

'You have enough to deal with for now, sir. I won't bother you with more.'

Alistair ran down between the trees and onto the boat. He stumbled over pots on the floor of her small galley and through into the saloon. Despite the disarray, Gaia's long slender form felt strangely comforting. Pale maple panelling gave the space an air of uncluttered good taste. Two large windows provided a panoramic view up the grassy riverbank to the woodland. A matching pair faced in the opposite direction, across the river to the west. Alistair noted a TV, mounted between the west facing windows, plus a corner desk complete with small bookshelf and a PC, in the saloon's far starboard corner. Contents of the shelves and drawers littered the floor together with two sage green leather chairs, one upside down the other on its side against an upturned circular coffee table. Marcia appeared from a narrow passageway leading forward from the saloon along Gaia's port side.

'Everything was fine when I left,' she said. 'I was away less than half an hour.'

'Did Reid say it's okay to tidy up?' Alistair asked.

'Yes.'

'Good. I'm sure it looks worse than it is. If you carry on with what you're doing, I'll get this lot sorted?'

Marcia returned to continue putting her strewn clothes away.

Alistair set the chairs on either side of the coffee table, facing out over the river. He returned the books to their shelf and stacked the remaining items from the floor beside the PC.

When Marcia returned Alistair had tidied the galley and was putting the final pots back into the cupboard beneath the two-burner hob. 'This is a lovely boat,' he said stepping through to join Marcia in the saloon. 'I've guessed where things were supposed to go.'

'It looks fine to me. Thank you,' Marcia said with a smile. 'I'm glad you like Gaia, she means a lot to me.'

'Nice gear, too,' Alistair said. 'Is anything missing?'

'Not a thing, as far as I can tell,' Marcia replied.

'That's odd,' Alistair said. 'This must be like Aladdin's cave to a burglar. Why would anyone come way out here, go to the bother of breaking in, then clear off without taking any of this stuff?'

'The burglar didn't have to break in,' Marcia admitted. 'Gaia wasn't locked, she hardly ever is.'

'Is that sensible?'

'No, it's bloody stupid actually, considering what's happened,' Marcia admitted. 'Unfortunately, I don't have the gift of prophecy. The TV is bolted to the wall and my PC is well below the latest specs. Maybe the thief decided it was too bulky and not worth humping out. The clearing is as close as anybody can get in a vehicle. That's one of the attractions. Anyway, I haven't lost anything so let's just be thankful for that.'

'I'd agree, if this was down to some opportunist, but it obviously isn't,' Alistair said. 'It's the same as the burglaries at Caroline's cottage and Bookworm. Scumbags don't normally break into places and leave empty handed. Your intruder came looking for something. If he didn't take anything, it means he didn't find whatever it is. These burglaries are connected. So, what's the connection?'

'Search me,' Marcia replied. 'I wasn't involved at St Michael's. Caroline and James were certainly close, but she wasn't hugely involved with Bookworm. Maybe something will tick a box while we're sorting the stock. I'll get over there now. I'll see you later.'

Chapter 17

Marcia drove into the carriage yard and stopped beside the Mercedes. Alistair stepped out of his car.

'Why are you here?' Marcia asked as she joined him. 'I thought you had things to do.'

'There's no rush,' Marcia stared. 'Okay,' Alistair admitted. 'I don't want you here on your own. I know how difficult this must be for you, even without this morning's upset.'

'It will keep on being difficult until I get through it,' she said. 'I appreciate your concern, honestly, but I need to do this by myself, Alistair. Go and do your chores, please. I'll be fine. I have your number.'

'Lock the doors.'

'You're mollycoddling,' she said with a smile.

'I know,' he replied. 'So hate me for it. Just lock the doors.' He climbed back into his car and looked up at her. 'Promise you'll call if you need me.'

She pushed his car door shut. A smile flickered. She walked away to the kitchen.

*

Marcia hurried through the kitchen and along to the showroom. She hugged her body for comfort and wandered the dark aisles, desperate to reclaim the space before rapidly retreating courage deserted her completely. Fragments of muffled conversation crept in from the world beyond Bookworm's covered windows. Heels clicked on cobbles. A van door slid shut. Everything out there seemed normal. Things felt anything but normal to Marcia, alone inside Bookworm for the first time since her world had crumbled. James would never again clutter and disorganise. Caroline's free spirit had swept through for the final time. Her tinkling, occasionally annoying, laughter would tinkle no more. How could two people with such boundless presence, be so suddenly and utterly gone? A burning lump formed in Marcia's throat. Her fingers tightened on the phone, which had somehow found its way into her hand. She stared at it for a moment then stuffed it back into her skirt pocket and ran upstairs to her workstation.

An uneasy chill gripped the office like a clammy hand. Marcia shivered. Things had seemed familiar yesterday, almost normal in some ways, with Alistair downstairs. Today, her familiar haven of peaceful solitude felt cold and alien. The torn list of ISBN references, still lay discarded on her keyboard. Maybe tracing a few authors and titles, a little normal activity, would restore the stolen warmth. The computer booted up. Marcia stared at her screen. As her hand reached toward the mouse, normal activity suddenly felt entirely inappropriate. She logged off and slipped the list into her bag.

Her phone signalled an incoming text. She pulled it out, opened the inbox and gasped.

The message was short: *I just could not resist telling you how much I like that ivory blouse you're wearing this morning.*

Marcia stared at the screen. The phone trembled in her hand. She almost dropped it as another message arrived.

You are very brave to be there at work, all alone. Good thing I'll be here, silent as a shadow, keeping an eye on you.

Marcia stabbed the off button, tossed the phone onto her desk and lurched over to the office window. The carriage yard appeared deserted. She ran to Alistair's old bedroom, crashed past the book cartons and stumbled headlong against the window. The sash rattled.

She snatched the blind open and stared out into Bishop's Hill. Shoppers browsed. Tourists ambled along pavements. No one showed any interest in the pale figure gaping down from the first-floor window.

'But you are out there, aren't you?' she whispered. 'Watching, waiting, or...' She gasped. 'What if I forgot to lock myself in? What if you're already here?' She careered downstairs and gave the kitchen door a frantic shake. It was locked. Salty perspiration trickled into her eyes. She rammed the bolts across, turned and slumped back against the door.

Chapter 18

Alliance Bank's branch manager, Mark Weston, a rotund man wearing a dark brown suit, cream shirt and unattractive green silk tie, which Alistair thought gave him an oddly appropriate toad-like appearance, welcomed his visitor with a limp handshake and transparently bogus condolences. Alistair retrieved the letter of authority from the bundle in his jacket pocket, rescued his uncle's farewell note, which had somehow found its way in there and handed the letter over. Mr Weston accepted the document and launched into a depressingly predictable recital of the bank's services. Alistair sidestepped the sales pitch with an excuse that he had to meet someone else. Mr Weston stood. Alistair wished him a polite goodbye and left.

*

Rev Clive Chapman lived in the small village of Franley, a little over two miles from Oxton. The vicarage occupied a modest plot with a short well-tended, though sparsely planted, garden at the front of the property and a parking area at the rear.

Alistair pressed the front door bell. The sick looking man he had met on his first visit to Bookworm appeared from the back of the property. He seemed to notice Alistair, but left without acknowledging him.

Rev Chapman greeted Alistair with a warm, slightly nervous, smile and ushered him along to the study. 'Do sit down Alistair,' he said indicating a well-worn leather swivel chair facing the cluttered desk. The vicar stepped round and attempted to restore order to his litter-strewn workspace before flopping down to face his visitor.

'Sermon preparation,' he said a little breathlessly. 'I can't seem to hold a coherent thought, with all that's going on. I wish I could report progress on James's matter.'

'Do you have any idea how long we'll be stuck in this limbo?'

'None,' the vicar admitted. 'The burial cannot take place until I have police clearance. We must be patient and pray that the PM confirms natural death.'

The study door opened. A tall figure entered, wearing a cassock and carrying a tray. 'Coffee, gentlemen,' a chocolate smooth female voice announced.

Alistair looked up with enough surprise to raise a smile from a tall woman with large brown eyes. She placed a tray on Clive's desk.

'I'm Amanda Chapman,' she said warmly. 'That dreadful affair at Dr Hastings' funeral is the talk of all the parishes. Everyone is in shock, as I imagine you are. Let us all hope the situation can be resolved quickly.' Amanda placed a china cup and saucer in front of each man. 'I'm sorry I can't stay and chat,' she said. 'I have to conduct a funeral myself in little over an hour. Let's hope I have a better experience than you did. I want to squeeze in a visit to the gym first so, if you'll excuse me, I'll run along. She grabbed her shoulder bag from the desk.

'Laptop,' she said. 'How did we ever keep track before we had them?' She kissed her husband's cheek and left.

Alistair refused the offer of cream, prompting a slightly guilty look from Clive, who proceeded to add a generous amount to his own cup. 'Old habits die hard, I'm afraid,' he said.

'That's very true,' Alistair replied. 'So how on earth did you become a vicar? I recall the old Cheesy Chapman as a real pain in the stern quarter.'

The vicar nodded. 'Guilty as charged. Chances are I would have ended up in a prison uniform rather than a cassock if I hadn't met the lady who just left.'

'Just joking,' Alistair replied. 'I didn't mean to pry.'

'There's no secret to it,' the vicar said. 'Amanda is as close as I can imagine to an earthly angel. She is completely incapable of considering herself ahead of others. No needy soul ever leaves this home uncomforted.'

'I saw a visitor leaving as I arrived,' Alistair replied. 'I think I met him at the book shop on the day I arrived.'

'That would be Peter Christy,' the vicar replied. 'Peter isn't a member of our regular congregation. He arrived in Lowesley Pryor several weeks ago. You must have noticed that he is not a well man. All he asks of us, and asked of James too I believe, is a little conversation and companionship. Amanda has an inexhaustible supply of both. She is a very special person.'

'Is she an Oxton girl?'

'No. She came to Oxton as a weekend tourist and, miraculously, we hit it off. I was in a real rut at the time. Mom had handed the business over to me when I turned twenty-one. She retired to live with her sister in Canada. It was all planned, but never what I wanted.' He paused and smiled. 'To be frank, I didn't see an alternative. My reputation had slammed the door shut on any sort of decent job. Amanda convinced me that I had potential to do something better. It's odd how fate guides you sometimes. Can you imagine my shock when I met the family and discovered that her father was the local vicar? If she had told me beforehand, I doubt whether I'd have gone. And if her family had known anything about me, I'm quite sure I wouldn't have been invited.' He smiled. 'As it turned out, that visit set me on a quite astonishing journey. Amanda's father convinced me that I had the ideal life experience to reach out and redeem other troubled souls. He presented my one and only opportunity to become a decent useful person. I escaped the shop, left Oxton and here I am with my collar turned.'

'So how did you end up back in Oxton?'

'When this parish became available, Amanda persuaded me that God had called me home to show people I'd changed and perhaps right a few wrongs. I had left Oxton with a trail of ill will and broken bridges behind me. Some regrettably remain. With the help of God and my earthly angel, I'm attempting to make repairs as best I can. Amanda is my strong right arm. I'm extremely lucky to have her at my side. Life delivers many surprises, as I'm sure you can confirm.'

'It does indeed,' Alistair agreed. 'I'm still a bit stunned by the rumour that a super smart guy like my uncle died chasing an intruder. Why would he take such a risk?'

'Stress often triggers an irrational response. That rumour is quite rational, compared to some currently circulating gossip. No doubt you've heard about our notorious grave and the dire consequences of disturbing the local witch.'

'You're surely not suggesting that a witch scared my uncle to death?'

'Hardly. Perhaps I should explain. Our car park extension couldn't proceed until we had relocated that grave. Thanks to the generosity of our community, funds began accumulating more rapidly than I had anticipated, before I'd had time to prepare the way so to speak. I approached James to write a series of articles about the grave's history and surrounding myths, for the parish magazine. I thought it might calm a few superstitions, spark a little interest and perhaps swell the congregation. It seems that Caroline Blackham already knew about the car park work and grave relocation. She had begun searching out information on the site and stimulating James's interest. I understand she could be quite persuasive.'

'So, if the old boy was on board, why did he abandon the project?' Alistair asked.

'I can't say,' the vicar admitted. 'James could be quite secretive at times. He seemed perfectly happy with the project until he came back from a research trip.'

'Where to?'

'I really have no idea. He flatly refused to discuss the matter. I wish I had more information to offer you, about that and the current situation. Sadly, I do not.'

'I'm sorry to have taken your time, Clive,' Alistair said, glancing at his watch. 'Let's hope we can sort everything out soon.' He swallowed his coffee and stood to leave. 'I'm joining Marcia Blackham at Bookworm, for a little housekeeping. I'll probably be more hindrance than assistance, but being there alone must be really difficult for her. I don't want to leave her for too long.'

Clive stepped over and opened the study door. 'What will you do when this is over?' he asked. 'You have inherited a lovely house and a thriving business. Will they tempt you home from the sea?'

'The house is lovely,' Alistair agreed. 'Unfortunately, I don't see myself as a bookseller.'

'Back to the navy, then?'

Alistair confirmed that he and the Royal Navy had said their goodbyes.

The vicar raised an eyebrow. 'I'm surprised,' he said. 'James seemed to think you were in for the long haul.'

'Me too,' Alistair replied with a rueful nod. 'As you said, life comes up with all sorts of surprises.'

Chapter 19

Several minutes passed before Marcia summoned enough courage to leave the kitchen. More heart pounding minutes, peeping and creeping like hunted prey along showroom aisles, followed until she felt satisfied that her mysterious caller was not inside Bookworm. She attempted to divert morbid thoughts by selecting and weeding shelf stock. The awful chore felt like dismantling Bookworm and soon became too distressing. She sank onto a chair at the kitchen table.

Each creak of the old building squeezed the knot of fear tighter in her throat. Her hand edged into her skirt pocket and, tentatively at first then more urgently, fumbled for the phone. She finally remembered that she had left it upstairs on her workstation. A few steps toward the passageway, were enough to dissuade her from leaving her safe space. She stepped back and shuddered. 'Hurry back, Alistair,' she whispered. 'Please.'

The sound of a car engine finally jerked Marcia's attention to the carriage yard. She held her breath and waited. The kitchen door rattled. A key turned. The door shook again. A fist hammered outside.

'Marcia!'

'Alistair?' She sprinted across and slid back the door bolts.

Alistair opened the door and stepped into the kitchen, carrying a brown A4 envelope. 'I found this under your windscreen wiper,' he said, handing over the package. 'Are you okay?'

'I'm fine,' she lied, examining the envelope. 'It's addressed to me personally. I haven't ordered anything.'

'I'm pretty sure the postman didn't leave it there,' Alistair said as he noticed tiny beads of perspiration on her forehead. Unconcealed fear glared from her eyes. 'You don't look fine,' he said. 'Something's happened hasn't it?'

Marcia looked at him and gave a tiny nod. 'I've had a couple of texts,' she said.

'What sort of texts?'

'He... I suppose it's a man, wants me to know he's watching me.'

'Have you kept the texts? The police can trace where the messages were sent from.'

'There wouldn't be any point.'

'How can you be so certain?'

'Because...' She cleared a sudden thickening in her voice. 'The texts were sent from Caroline's phone. Whoever sent them, knew I was here alone and what I'm wearing. It obviously came from somewhere very close by.'

Alistair stared into her eyes. 'Have you told the police?'

'Not yet.' She swayed slightly, held onto the sink and turned to splash a little water onto her face. She blotted with kitchen towel and looked out through the window.

'You have to tell them right now,' Alistair insisted. 'Where's your phone?'

She shook her hair straight. 'It's upstairs on my desk,' she said. 'I don't need it. The police just pulled into the yard.'

*

Nash and Reid stepped into the kitchen as Alistair opened the door. 'Marcia was just about to phone you,' he said. 'She's had some disturbing texts.'

Marcia stared at Nash for a moment and swallowed. 'They were sent from Caroline's phone,' she said.

'I see,' Nash replied. 'Did he make any threats?'

'Not exactly. He knew my name and what I'm wearing this

morning. He called to let me know he's watching me.'

'He also wanted you to make the obvious link to your sister,' Nash said. 'He knows we can't identify him from her phone. Can you think of any reason why he might be targeting you?'

'I really have no idea,' Marcia replied.

'It must have something to do with this place, or the stuff Caroline and James were digging into,' Alistair said. 'If he knows, or believes, that those two found something he wants, he may think you have it or know where it is.'

'But I don't,' Marcia insisted.

'He doesn't know that,' Alistair replied.

'The commander is correct,' Nash agreed.

'Okay, I admit that the texts frightened me,' Marcia said. 'They would have scared anyone, but it's surely best to keep things as normal as possible until we know who he is and what he wants. I intend to get on with what I have to do here.' She tore open the envelope. Instant horror gripped her face as she pulled out the single photograph. She threw it onto the table and staggered back against the dresser, wiping her hands on her blouse. The image, a full-face portrait, showed Marcia smiling broadly. The outer area had been burned removing most of the hair and some of the face, while carefully preserving enough to leave the subject recognisable.

'I have… or had that photo on Gaia,' Marcia said. 'It must have been taken yesterday. I hadn't missed it.'

'Have you seen anyone in the yard this morning?' Nash asked.

Marcia shook her head. 'He was right here, watching me, and I didn't see a thing.'

'I found the envelope under Marcia's wiper blade, just now,' Alistair said.

'You didn't see or hear anything?'

'No. I've been away doing a couple of chores.'

'But you were here earlier this morning.'

'Along with Marcia, yes.'

'How long were you away? Where did you go?'

'Just to the bank, then over to see Rev Chapman at the vicarage. I didn't bring that thing here, Chief Inspector. And neither of us called you, so why are you here?'

'Dr Sangha carried out the post-mortem examination on Dr Hastings this morning,' Nash replied.

'Does that mean you are able to release my uncle's body?'

'Sadly no,' Nash confirmed. 'During his examination, Dr Sangha found evidence that Dr Hastings died from a fatal heart attack, after being kicked from the mezzanine stairs. He was manhandled into his car, post mortem, in order that his death would appear natural, as it initially did. I'm sorry to report, that we are now treating your uncle's death as murder.'

He turned back to Marcia. 'That photograph is sending a very clear message,' he said. 'I need to arrange protection for you. Your mooring is much too isolated. Do you have anywhere safer to stay?'

'Not really,' she replied, 'I'll manage on Gaia.'

'No, you won't,' Nash insisted. 'It's likely that the person who texted you, and sent that photograph, is the same person who murdered your sister and Dr Hastings. He thinks you have something or know something important to him. You mustn't be alone. Do you have family or friends who would...?'

'I prefer my own space,' she said. 'I don't have family any more. I have friends, of course, but several people who would normally phone me, have stopped. I'm getting loads of texts and emails, but nobody wants to talk. There's only one topic and they don't know what to say. I understand how they must feel.'

'You and I are trapped in the same mess,' Alistair said. 'The fact is we are probably safer together. The Bookbinder's House seems the obvious place for us to be right now. It's your choice.'

'Sticking together is a very good idea,' Nash agreed. 'You can look after one another and we can keep an eye on both of you.'

'If you and the chief inspector believe it's absolutely necessary,'

Marcia finally said to Alistair, 'I suppose I could impose on you for a few days, if you're willing to have me.'

'I certainly don't think you should be alone on Gaia,' Alistair confirmed. 'You will be very welcome at my house. There's a spare room. Stay as long as you like.'

'Thank you, Commander,' Nash said. 'Take no chances and don't accept phone calls unless you know the caller. If we need to contact either of you, we'll use the password, Archangel. We'll take the photograph. There may be some forensics.'

Chapter 20

Marcia stood, watching from the kitchen window until Nash's car disappeared beneath the archway. 'Thanks,' she said, turning to look at Alistair. 'I'll try not to clutter your house or get underfoot.'

'It's obviously the best solution for both of us,' he replied.

Marcia nodded. 'The only one, I suppose. Thanks anyway. Did you get your chores done?'

'Bank yes, vicarage no. Clive obviously had no progress to report on the funeral. He didn't know about the PM result at that stage. We know there won't be a funeral for a while now. I tried to squeeze some information out of him about James's parish magazine thing. He doesn't seem to know much.'

'Or won't say much.' She coughed. 'I mean, vicars are bound to keep secrets.'

'I suppose so,' Alistair agreed. 'Forget the vicar. I should have been here with you.'

'I didn't do much,' she said, with a half-hearted nod toward the books on the old desk. 'James and Caroline are steeped into the fabric of this place. I felt them following me around, disapproving of every book I took down. Things have to change they've already changed massively. Everything I've loved here has been snatched away. I know Cal and James can't ever come back, but I want it all to be the way it was.'

'It hasn't *all* gone,' Alistair replied. 'Like you said, they're in the fabric of Bookworm. They'll stick around, in one way or another.'

Marcia coughed to clear a lump from her throat. 'I thought about looking up those book references,' she said. 'I couldn't seem to get going. I have the list. I'll call a few of James's contacts later, if you like.'

'Maybe we should keep the list quiet for now,' Alistair suggested. 'If James or Caroline did make an interesting find, I'd rather not go public, until we know what it is. Yesterday, I thought it might be a welcome diversion to track down a rare book. We have no choice now. Whether you have what that psycho wants or not, he believes you do. Our only chance may be to find whatever it is. We have to pick up James's trail and try to retrace his footsteps. We definitely can't just sit here waiting to be picked off.'

'Actually, I think Caroline and James may have been on to something,' Marcia replied. 'Dawn Tyler said Caroline had been promising a revelation at the book fair.'

'Do you have any idea what it might have been?'

'Possibility a rare book, with James involved and looking for a crowd puller,' Marcia speculated. 'It could have been anything, obviously. Whatever Caroline had up her sleeve has definitely put the wind up her friends. My sister and your uncle occasionally stirred murky waters. There could be any number of explanations.'

'We might stumble across whatever it is, if we could find James's notes or get into the computer,' Alistair replied.

'I found his desk appointments diary among the floor debris upstairs, if you're interested,' Marcia said. 'It's written in that private gibberish of his, so I'm not sure it will help much.'

'No harm in looking, I suppose,' Alistair replied. 'A slim chance is better than no chance.'

Marcia nodded and followed him upstairs.

Alistair stepped over to James's desk and switched on the computer.

Marcia's lip curled as she slipped the phone from her workstation into her skirt pocket. She brushed her hand clean on her skirt and took the desk diary over to Alistair. 'There's a contacts list on the computer too but it's bound to be password protected,' she said.

Alistair thumbed through the apparently meaningless strings of letters. 'I feel I should understand this,' he said. The screen glowed and requested the password. Alistair stared for a moment and smiled. He retrieved James's farewell letter from his blazer pocket and handed it to Marcia. 'Read the bottom line,' he said.

'*Bayeux is the password,*' she read aloud. 'Thank you, James.'

Alistair typed in the word Bayeux. The computer did not respond. 'So much for that theory,' he mumbled.

'What does this mean?' Marcia asked pointing to the final words of James's letter. '*Let your memory be its key.*'

'I really don't know,' Alistair said turning back to the desk diary and flipping irritably through several pages. He began closing the book then stopped. A smile blossomed onto his face. 'Do you have paper?' he asked.

'Top drawer.'

Alistair found a pad and began writing out the alphabet.

'What are you doing?' Marcia asked.

'James's gibberish, I think it's plus five.'

'Say again.'

'As a kid, I invented a code to prevent anyone reading my diary. James cracked it in no time. He and I would exchange notes, written in the code, to wind Nancy up. It's very simple, as you'd expect from a twelve-year-old. You just move each letter five places forward. A becomes F, B becomes G, C becomes H and so on. Let's take another look at those book references.' Marcia handed over the list from her bag. Alistair wrote down the letters five spaces back from the string, Xjqnr, written alongside several of the ISBNs. Xjqnr became Selim. 'Sounds Arabic,' he said. 'That sequence is in the appointments diary too. Do you have any Arab customers called Selim, Salim, Saleem, Salima?'

Marcia shook her head.

'James had regular contacts with whoever it is.' Alistair pointed out several appointments with the letter sequences, *Xjqnr Phtyxwjafg*, written alongside.

'What's the translation?' Marcia asked.

Alistair scribbled, *Selim Kcotsrevab*.

'He or she sounds like a Lithuanian Arab,' Marcia said. 'There can't be many of those around.'

'It could be plus or minus anything,' Alistair conceded. 'The basic pattern is definitely familiar. I'm sure the solution should be obvious.'

Marcia smiled. 'Maybe it is,' she said running her finger backwards over the name Alistair had written on his pad. 'James used your code and reversed the result,' she said. 'The person you're looking for isn't Selim Kcotsrevab, it's Miles Baverstock. I don't know Sir Miles personally, but James has dealt with him for years. What a lovely simple code.'

'Simpler the better,' Alistair replied. 'Makes it easier to write. He wasn't trying to fool GCHQ after all. So, password Bayeux, coded and reversed becomes…' He scribbled, *Czjdfg*. 'Fingers crossed.' He tapped in the sequence and the screen opened. 'Excellent,' he said, selecting *"contacts"* from the file list. The un-coded list appeared. 'I'll download it to my phone,' he said. 'James also had a recent appointment with Rty Djqtk, which decodes to… Hang on.' He scribbled quickly. 'Tom Foley. He's on this list too, do you know him?'

'Sorry, no.'

'Never mind,' Alistair said clicking down the file menu. 'Everything is open now, accounts too.'

Marcia patted his shoulder and turned to leave. 'That file isn't for my eyes,' she said.

'I'd like you to stay,' Alistair replied, scrolling on with obvious approval. 'I'm the amateur. You've worked a miracle with Bookworm.'

'Not me,' Marcia replied from the landing doorway. 'James's expertise drove Bookworm.'

Alistair continued scrolling. 'I'm surprised at the amount of cash dealing,' he said.

'It's that kind of business,' Marcia confirmed. 'Most of our quality stock comes from private collections. Those clients often prefer to deal in cash.'

'We purchase a lot of quite expensive stuff from some outfit called ABCo. Who are they?'

'The Antiquarian Book Company, it's Aiden Gale's business,' Marcia replied a little uneasily. 'I really don't think I should be looking in there, Alistair. Why don't you carry on browsing while I go down and make coffee?'

'If you'd rather,' he agreed. 'I'll join you in a minute.'

*

Marcia disappeared downstairs. Alistair logged off, crept across to his old bedroom and slid a few boxes aside. He knelt over the loose floorboard he had rediscovered, to his embarrassment, on the previous day and took a deep breath. The board lifted easily. Alistair peered down at the small, tied bundle, still in the dusty void where he had hidden it a lifetime earlier. He reached, in and lifted out the memory.

A sudden intense scream yanked Alistair's attention downstairs. He stamped the board back into position and charged down to the kitchen. Marcia stood pressed back against the sink. Sheer horror etched her face. Her ice firm gaze was fixed on the phone lying at her feet.

Alistair slipped his bundle into the kitchen table drawer and ran to Marcia. She stared into his eyes and pointed her trembling hand to the discarded phone.

'It's from Caroline's number again,' she said. 'Look at it.'

Alistair picked up the phone, opened the message and gasped. The image of Caroline's corpse, slumped against her silver birch, loomed onto the screen, followed by the text: *You have what I want. She did not deliver and she burned. Contact this number for handover instructions.*

'This is vindictive cruelty,' he murmured. 'Do you have any idea what this means.'

'Not a clue.'

Alistair texted back: *Cannot deliver what I do not have.*

The response was instant. *Deliver or burn. I AM WATCHING.*

Alistair switched off the phone and handed it back. 'Let's get away from here,' he said.

Marcia nodded and walked, a little unsteadily, out into the yard and over to her own car.

Alistair locked the kitchen door. 'Where are you going?' he asked.

'I'll need a few things from Gaia,' Marcia replied.

'Obviously,' Alistair agreed. 'I'll take you.'

Marcia stared. 'I have to be strong,' she said.

'But not superhuman,' Alistair replied quietly. 'You've had your home turned over, and a day of hassle from some psycho. You aren't in any state to drive. Please let me take you.'

'If I crack now, I'm sunk,' she said. 'I'd like you to come with me, but please let me try.'

Alistair nodded. Marcia slid into her driver's seat. 'You are one tough lady, Marcia Blackham,' Alistair said as he climbed into the passenger seat beside her. 'Take your time. If you can't manage, I'll drive. You have nothing to prove.'

She sighed and drove steadily out through the archway.

Chapter 21

Marcia's hands were clearly gripping tightly onto her steering wheel. Concentration etched her face.

'Neither of us chose this situation,' Alistair said. 'We've landed together, but we arrived here from opposite directions. You've lost people you knew and loved and have always been close to. I hadn't stayed close, so in a sense I don't really know what I've lost. I would appreciate your help. It might do you good to talk and I need to do a lot of listening.'

'Caroline would dive headlong into all sorts of oddities,' Marcia said after a long pause. 'She spent her life searching out myths and isms. My big sister was driven by deep curiosity and it sometimes beguiled her, clouded her common sense. A few weeks ago, something sparked an obsession with Nellie the witch and that grave they were researching. To be frank, I wasn't very interested at the time. She wouldn't stop gushing about it for days. Then she suddenly switched and refused to talk about it at all. Something had obviously scared her. I mean seriously.'

'Did your falling out have anything to do with that stuff?'

Marcia nodded. 'She kept harping on about what she called ancient secrets, then suddenly clammed up about it.'

'Do her friends have any idea what it was all about?'

'I only know Dawn Tyler and she's in no mood to disclose anything, not to an outsider like me at any rate. Caroline trusted people too easily. That inquisitive streak of hers could have led almost anywhere.'

'I remember,' Alistair said. 'Are you sure she didn't mention who might have been feeding her that nonsense?'

'I never got names,' Marcia replied sadly. 'Caroline's friends like to preserve their silly mystique. I advised her to be careful. She told me to mind my own business.' A tear rolled onto her cheek. 'I loved my sister so much and now it's too late to tell her so.'

'Sorry, I didn't mean to rake things up. Caroline is everywhere, isn't she?'

'In a sense she is, I suppose, and I want her to be,' Marcia said. 'I've never imagined not having her around, noisy, nosey, sparkling, annoying, beautiful... and real.' She drew into her parking space at Stowe Junction and reached for her seatbelt. She didn't release the buckle. 'Cal burned, like those bodies in her sketches,' she said turning an imploring gaze to Alistair. 'It's as if she'd seen her own death.' She swallowed. 'I've tried so hard to see the world through her eyes. Maybe if we'd been more alike, I'd understand, but I don't, Alistair; I just don't.'

'Me neither,' Alistair admitted, 'but I know that every riddle has a solution, and two heads are better than one. Remember what James instilled into Caroline. *Look and see. Consider and connect.* Is there something... anything you haven't told me or the police?'

'Not a thing.' She released her seatbelt, stepped out of the car and walked away down the path.

Alistair followed her to the river. She stood looking at Gaia.

'Would you like me to check her over before you go aboard?' he offered.

Marcia shook her head. 'I just need a moment to prepare.'

'She's beautiful,' he said, gazing along the superstructure.

Marcia nodded. 'The artwork and the name are down to Caroline.' She smiled. 'I asked her to paint a kingfisher for me and ended up with an illustrated British wildlife encyclopaedia. That was Caroline.

Put a brush or a pencil in her hand and she couldn't stop.'

'That was no bad thing if Gaia is an example,' Alistair said. 'It's stunning. Come on. Let's get your stuff together.' He followed her up the short gangplank onto Gaia's aft deck.

Marcia fumbled to unlock the galley doors. She led the way through to the saloon and flopped down onto a chair. 'I love my gorgeous old girl,' she said.

'She's a fine craft and this is a great location,' Alistair replied. 'How did a canal boat end up on a river?'

'Canal to Stourport, low loader as far as Oxton then up the river to Stowe.'

'That isn't what I meant.'

'I know.' Marcia gazed into his eyes. 'Uni didn't pan out as I hoped it would. I ditched my physics course and found a job in a bookshop. The boat belonged to the girl I worked with. When I had to leave my student place, I moved in with her. We lived on board at Gas Street Basin, until Kathy decided to sell up and move in with her new boyfriend. I still needed a place, so I made a puny offer and Kathy, bless her, accepted it.' She hesitated. 'I'm not a city girl. I got homesick by myself, but I couldn't afford the gentrified property prices around here. Caroline suggested bringing the boat home with me. She spoke to James and he knew the farmer who owns this stretch of riverside. The mooring is perfect and it costs peanuts. Make yourself at home. It'll only take me a few minutes to pack.' She disappeared along the passageway.

Alistair admired the river view until perfume caught his nose. Feeling suddenly like an intruder, he wandered out through the galley and up onto the aft deck.

Marcia obviously heard his footsteps. 'Are you okay?' she called from somewhere toward the bow. 'The loo is next to the shower.'

A flash of reflected sunlight drew his attention up the grassy bank. A figure standing a little way back in the woodland put away binoculars and disappeared among the trees. You're tall, Alistair thought. Dressed like the chap I saw last time I visited here. Was that you? He jumped down onto the grass and ran up to the trees. The man had disappeared. Alistair searched without finding anyone, until Marcia appeared on Gaia's aft deck. He ran back to the boat.

'I've just seen somebody watching the boat,' he said.

'He's probably a twitcher,' Marcia replied dismissively.

'Or someone who saw your car and thought you were here alone.'

'There are several quite rare birds in the area,' Marcia explained. 'Peregrines, ring ouzels, little egrets, an occasional red kite. They pull birders in from all over.'

Alistair looked at her, standing fragile and isolated against the whale-backed hills of the Marches. 'There's another rare and dangerous species out there too,' he reminded her. 'Head down, eyes peeled. Okay?'

She conceded with a nod. 'I'll get my things,' she said. 'Could you break out the covers? You'll find them in the hatch under the tiller.'

Alistair retrieved and fitted the bow cover, while Marcia lowered the window blinds. She locked the galley doors, stepped down onto the riverbank and waited while Alistair fitted the stern cover. He picked up her holdall and they walked back to her car.

'Shall I drive?' he asked.

Marcia smiled. 'I need to do it,' she said. 'And you'd scare my little car. I'll drop you in town.'

*

She parked in Radley Street, a few metres from the archway and turned to look at him. 'I know that guy might not have been a twitcher,' she said. 'I love my boat, but at the moment, I admit I'll feel safer in a house, with company.'

'Good,' Alistair replied as he stepped out onto the pavement. 'Just hang on while I get my car and I'll follow you to Bookbinder's.'

'I'll see you there,' she said. The Mini pulled away and disappeared around the corner onto Bishops Hill.

Chapter 22

The sun slid like a giant peach toward the horizon. 'I think we should eat?' Alistair said to break the mutually self-conscious, silence that had somehow crept up on them. 'I'm reasonably well house-trained. I can probably knock something together.'

Marcia nodded and smiled. 'I'll do it if you like,' she said. 'I ought to earn my keep.'

'Of course, if you'd rather. I'll show you...' he paused and grinned. 'I don't have a clue where Nancy keeps anything,' he admitted. 'I'm sure you can hunt things out for yourself.' He followed her to the kitchen, collected cutlery and went back to lay the terrace table.

A few minutes later, Marcia joined him carrying a tray. 'I found some leftover smoked salmon in the fridge,' she said. 'I didn't want to mooch, so it's just omelettes and salad. Is that okay for you?'

'It looks delicious,' Alistair replied. 'You were wise to avoid my efforts.'

'Your kitchen felt a bit strange,' she said. 'It's as big as my entire boat.'

'I know the feeling,' Alistair replied. 'I've spent half my life on cramped fighting vessels of one sort or another. I suppose we need to adjust.'

'Is the sea calling you back?'

Alistair shook his head. 'I miss it, but there's no going back. We make our plans; circumstances make the decisions. This arrangement might feel a bit awkward to begin with, it wasn't part of *our* plan,' he said. 'We'll need to adjust.'

'I can leave if I'm making you uncomfortable.'

'I said slightly awkward, not uncomfortable,' Alistair reminded her. 'And I meant for both of us. I want you here and it's where you need to be. You're stuck with me until the police sort this mess out. Who knows how long that might take? There's no apparent logic to what's going on. Somebody wants something that James or Caroline may or may not have found. He killed them before he had it. Now he's demanding that you hand it over, and you have no idea what it is.'

'Like you told him, I can't deliver what I don't have.'

'So, what *do* we have?' Alistair asked. 'Let's assume that James's and Caroline's activities at St Michael's somehow triggered this insanity. If we could find out why James abandoned the project, we might get a handle on what this is really about. Clive Chapman seems to think Caroline may have persuaded the old man to get involved in the first place. Can you think of any reason why she might do that?'

'Anything could have triggered her interest,' Marcia replied. 'I doubt if it was purely the church. She had a deep spiritual side and she had taken an interest in the history of St Michael's for a while, but neither Cal nor James was a fan of conventional religion.'

'Is it possible that James found some commercial reason for wanting people to *believe* he'd dropped the project?'

'I suppose anything is possible, but what sort of commercial motive would cause a simultaneous personality reversal?' Marcia asked. 'James was a bookseller, a shopkeeper. He's lying murdered in a mortuary, along with my sister, for heaven's sake. Things like that aren't supposed to happen to people like them.'

'Those things aren't supposed to happen to anybody,' Alistair acknowledged. 'I'd like to know why they've happened.'

A tiny crease squeezed the bridge of Marcia's nose. 'You still think there might be a book in the mix, don't you?'

'I think it's possible, with James involved.'

'Okay, so let's say you're right,' Marcia suggested. 'A pristine rarity might bring in a few thousand pounds. If the deal comes with the murders of two wonderful people, and maybe more of the same still on the killer's agenda, the price is way too high for any book.'

'I agree,' Alistair replied. 'The problem is, we didn't kick this deal off and we aren't being allowed to back out. The other two have already paid their price. You have become his prime target. I won't leave you on your own, like a lamb waiting for the wolf to turn up. We can't just hang around until it happens; we have to do something.'

'And what if nothing happens, or we don't solve it?' Marcia asked. 'Will you let go and walk away from Oxton again?'

'I know I got things wrong in the past,' he admitted. 'I try not to repeat my mistakes.'

The sun had disappeared beneath the treetops. Alistair cleared the table debris away to the kitchen. When he returned, Marcia stood gazing out at the inky black sky. Alistair walked over and stood behind her.

She turned, took a step toward her chair, and shivered. 'It is getting cool.' Alistair agreed. 'Let's go inside.'

They went into the lounge, locked the French door behind them and continued upstairs. Alistair stood at his bedroom door and watched Marcia walk along to James's old room. They exchanged smiles from opposite ends of the landing and said goodnight.

Alistair closed his bedroom door and walked over to the window. A three-quarter moon had painted the hills and fields in pure silver blue. The world appeared perfectly at rest. Recent woes seemed like visitations from a distant alien dimension, a dark and hostile place, another time. His eye turned toward the village with its old church, old houses and old tales. Have James and Caroline somehow resurrected ancient horrors, he thought, or is this area trapped in its own history, like me? Maybe one day we'll all wake up looking forward instead of back, just maybe.

Marcia returned to his thoughts. Why had such a brilliant student abandoned the education she craved above all else, to while away her life in a small-town bookshop?

Instinct pulled him away from the window as a marked police car swung into the lane and turned in front of the workshop.

*

Marcia stood, for a moment, with her back against the bedroom door then walked over to the window. Beyond the gorge, moonlight bathed a picture-perfect landscape. Despite her recent nightmares, she dared to imagine a beautiful future, so near, so tempting and yet somehow beyond her grasp.

Headlight beams slithered over the shrubs. A long shadow swept across the terrace. Marcia gasped and jumped back from the window. Had the light revealed, or merely conjured, a transient human silhouette? She stood panting, gathering her courage before creeping forward for another peep. The shape, real or imagined, had gone. Icy perspiration trickled down the nape of her neck. She snatched her curtains shut, turned her back to the terrace and ran from her room.

*

Alistair was climbing into bed when he was startled by rapid knocking on his door. He reached for the trousers on the hanger beside his bed and scrambled into them as he stumbled over and opened the door. Marcia's wide eyes startled him.

'The terrace,' she gasped. 'Someone's down there.'

'Probably the police,' Alistair said. 'I saw the car arriving a few minutes ago.'

'It wasn't the police,' she gasped. 'The police don't wear hoodies in Lowesley. Anyway, he was already there when the car arrived. The headlights showed him up.'

'What does he look like?'

'A shadow. It was definitely a man. He stumbled and I heard a man's groan.'

'Wait here and try to calm down,' Alistair said as he pulled on a dark T-shirt. 'I'll go down and take a look.'

He crept downstairs and through to the French door, sensing Marcia very close behind him.

Her hand touched his shoulder. 'Be careful,' she whispered.

He slipped out onto the terrace, silent as a cat, and disappeared into the shadows.

Marcia waited, staring into the blackness for several silent minutes.

Alistair reappeared and opened the door. 'I didn't see or hear anyone out here,' he confirmed.

Marcia stepped outside to join him. 'I'm sorry,' she said.

'Don't be,' he replied firmly. 'I'd rather chase a hundred false alarms than miss the real thing once.'

Marcia gasped. She ran to the terrace edge and fell to her knees. Tears rolled onto her cheek. 'This is cruel,' she said.

The floral book wreath she had made for James lay crushed in front of her. Fragments of limp foliage fluttered on the light breeze. Marcia picked up the wreath and stood, stroking the broken leaves.

'Maybe the Constable tripped over it,' Alistair suggested.

Marcia shook her head but did not reply.

Alistair took the wreath and returned it to its place. 'No-one can stamp out the love,' he said. 'James will know.'

They returned upstairs and lingered briefly at Alistair's bedroom door. He smiled said goodnight again and watched until Marcia's bedroom door closed behind her.

Chapter 23

Alistair abandoned his morning run as he reached the lane. He turned and began searching back along the shrubbery path for evidence of the intruder. Tiny dew beads glinted on undisturbed spider webs. A close visual check revealed no trampled soil, damaged foliage, snagged cloth fibres or any other sign of human intrusion. He strolled across and scanned down through wisps of morning mist to the river and along its banks. It would be tricky but not impossible even in moonlight, he thought, for a determined intruder to climb up to the terrace. The wreath remained limp and broken at his feet. He looked up sadly at Marcia's closed bedroom window. The curtains separated. Marcia smiled, down at him and stepped back.

*

Alistair went to the kitchen and emerged, carrying a tray, as Marcia ran down the stairs. She followed him out to the terrace table.

'Scrambled eggs and toast,' he said, setting a plate in front of her. 'The eggs would have been poached if I hadn't broken the yolks.'

'Not a problem,' she said. 'I prefer them this way.' She began eating, though her thoughts plainly lay elsewhere.

'It might be a good idea to stay away from the shop today,' Alistair suggested.

Marcia put down her fork and gazed across at him. 'If he's still watching me, I'd rather not show any sign of fear,' she said.

'I'm not suggesting you should,' Alistair replied. 'He targeted you at Bookworm. Why let him keep control. A predictable routine is an open invitation. I thought we could try to start picking up the thread of James and Caroline's project?'

'I'm not so sure,' Marcia said. 'Look where it got them.'

'Fair point,' Alistair agreed. 'I just thought it might be a diversion from things here and what happened to you yesterday. I could have a word with Sir Miles what's-his-name. James visited him recently. He may shed some light on what the old man was up to.' He hesitated briefly. 'I'd like to colour in a few personal gaps about my uncle too, if I can.'

'I like *that* idea a lot,' Marcia said. 'You should get to know James better. Do it now, while it's in your mind.'

Sir Miles did not answer. Alistair rang off and returned from the hall as Nancy appeared on the terrace.

'Good morning, Alistair,' she said. 'Hello, Marcia. I see I'm too late to make breakfast.'

She strode off to answer a knock on the front door and reappeared a few seconds later followed by Nash. He handed Marcia a large brown envelope and Caroline's portfolio. 'Your sister's work file, diary and phone book,' he said. 'We found this among the drawings.' He handed Marcia the small photograph Alistair had hurriedly slipped back into the portfolio. 'Do you have any idea who he is?'

'Sorry, I don't,' Marcia replied. 'It looks quite old, though it's hard to tell from a photocopy. I suppose it might be from someone who wanted Caroline to make a portrait of a dead relative.'

'Possibly,' Nash agreed. 'You don't need to concern yourselves with the book fair for now. The council has decided to call it off, until things have settled down.'

'We have stock ready,' Marcia protested. 'Caroline's passing should be marked in some way.'

'In due course,' Nash agreed. 'I don't want too many strangers in town until the current situation is resolved.' He wished them good morning and left.

'Inevitable, I suppose,' Marcia conceded. 'It's still a pity. Did Sir Miles shed any light?'

Alistair shook his head. 'No reply. I'll give Clive Chapman a call when I've had a word with Nancy. I have a feeling she wasn't happy to see you here.'

Marcia smiled. 'Girl job,' she said. 'I'll do it while you stress the vicar.'

*

Clive Chapman insisted that he could add nothing to what Alistair already knew.

'It seems odd that my uncle wouldn't keep you up to speed,' Alistair said. 'You commissioned the project at St Michael's after all.'

Clive laughed. 'I wasn't at all surprised,' he said. 'James was a master magician when it came to pulling rabbits from hats. He was unlikely to reveal anything until he could guarantee maximum impact. He had delivered a light-hearted piece, portraying Nellie the witch as an invention to dissuade inappropriate nocturnal activities in the churchyard. I understood he was gathering information for more when he phoned to say he would be away for a day or two.'

'He didn't say where, or what for?'

'No, he simply teased me with a typical James pun, that I should be patient until he revealed some *grave secret*. He returned from wherever he had been and submitted a piece, quite enthusiastically claiming that he hoped to reveal some major discovery soon. I assumed he was drumming up interest ahead of the book fair. The local press picked it up too. It turned out to be his final word on the matter. I was astonished when he pulled out, particularly after he had accepted the task so eagerly.'

*

Nancy stood, producing more noise than strictly necessary, ironing Alistair's shirts and T-shirts. Marcia hesitated briefly in the open kitchen doorway then stepped inside. 'I think you may have made a wrong assumption, Nancy,' she said.

'I'm just the housekeeper,' Nancy replied. 'You and Ali are free to make your own arrangements.'

'You are much more than *just* the anything around here,' Marcia said with a smile. 'Someone disturbed my boat and we've had a couple of unpleasant incidents at Bookworm. The police are a little concerned for our safety. They thought I should move in here temporarily so that they can keep an eye on both of us.'

'I see. I made assumptions when I had no right to,' Nancy said. 'I'm sorry. Please forgive me. Shall I make us some tea?'

'That would be nice,' Marcia replied with a smile.

*

Alistair finished his call. Sounds of tinkling teacups and friendly female voices indicated peace in the kitchen. He left the ladies to chat and retreated along the hall, scrolling through James's contacts on his mobile. Tom Foley's name, rolled into the window. Alistair recognised it from his uncle's appointments diary and punched in the number.

A pleasant female voice answered. 'Vicarage, Ruth Foley speaking.'

'Would it be possible to speak with Mr Tom Foley?' Alistair asked.

'*Reverend* Foley isn't here at the moment,' the woman replied. 'I'm Mrs Foley, can I help?'

'I'm so sorry, I didn't realise,' Alistair said. 'I believe my uncle, Dr James Hastings, may have visited your husband recently. He'd been working on a project for his local church. His visit may have had nothing to do with that, but he has passed away and, if possible, I'd like to complete the work on his behalf.'

'What a lovely idea,' Mrs Foley replied. 'I'm sure my husband would be delighted to help. He'll be up at the church all morning. Shall I tell him to expect you?'

'I suppose, if you're sure he won't mind. That's very generous.'

'Not at all. Will eleven o'clock suit you?'

'Well yes, of course, thank you. I'm afraid I don't have the address.'

'It's All Saints, in Great Ashwood. I'll tell him to expect you.'

*

Marcia appeared from the kitchen carrying Alistair's ironed clothes. 'I wondered where they'd gone,' he said. 'I normally do my own laundry. I think I just blundered.'

'Problem?'

'Not really, I suppose. I may have talked myself into plodding through piles of old church records with the vicar of All Saints.'

'That was James's world,' Marcia said with a wry smile. 'If you intend exploring his trails, you'll find dusty old books wherever you go. There's lots of information in parish records. James may have spent hours, or even days, there.'

'Oh don't,' Alistair groaned. 'At least it's an excuse for a ride in the country.'

'I have some personal business to deal with, if we aren't going to Bookworm' Marcia said. 'What time are you meeting the vicar?'

'Eleven. I'll take you wherever you have to go, first, no problem.'

'It's something I must do myself,' Marcia replied. 'I'm only planning to meet one person. I'll be fine till you get back.'

'I'd rather not leave you here alone,' Alistair insisted. 'I know your views on mollycoddling and I'll try not to be like your shadow.' Marcia looked into his eyes but did not answer. 'Those texts and that burnt photo, shunted things a huge step forward yesterday,' he continued. 'We need to take care and stay close together. I'll hang on for you.'

She sighed. 'I suppose it would be nice to go somewhere Caroline had been,' she said quietly. 'I'm probably just searching for a straw to clutch at.'

'Maybe we're both doing that,' Alistair replied. 'I'll wait for you. This is serious, Marcia. Please, take no risks.'

She hurried up to the linen cupboard. A few minutes later, she ran downstairs and shouted goodbye. The front door closed with a thud.

Marcia had been at The Bookbinder's House for just one night, yet Alistair felt an odd emptiness settling over the house after she left. James's reading matter, offered no light relief. Alistair retreated upstairs to the PC in the study. He opened a site in search of basic details on Samuel Rosemont, whose grave was being relocated at St Michael's.

Disappointment struck within seconds as the homepage opened with a statement that, *UK census records were not retained prior to 1841*, almost forty years too late.

Chapter 24

Reid sensed Nash arriving behind him. He leaned back yawned and stretched his shoulders.

'That's the sound of a man with a heavy burden,' Nash observed.

'No, sir,' Reid replied. 'It's maybe the sound of a man in search of one. I got nothing from Caroline Blackham's address book. Her friends won't talk to me.'

'I've handed the books and sketches over to Marcia Blackham,' Nash continued. 'She suggested that little photograph could have been intended for Caroline to use as the original for a portrait.'

Reid retrieved his copy of the 7cm x 5cm photograph from among the papers on his desk. 'Not at this size, surely,' he suggested. 'It's already fuzzy. She would have blown it up to A4 at least to have any chance of working a good likeness from it. There was nothing like that in the folder.' He scanned the picture and enlarged it onto his screen. 'It's not much clearer blown up.'

'Agreed,' Nash replied, 'but it's telling us at least one thing. Look at the dot pattern. That print is a photocopy of an old newspaper picture. If it's from the *Chronicle*, they may be able to trace it and give us his name. Have a stroll over there, Alex. See if they can come up with anything.'

*

The Oxton Chronicle proudly retained on its archive a copy of every newspaper that ever carried its name. Reid logged on to the website and optimistically selected archive. Initial enthusiasm nose-dived when the previous day's edition loaded along with the caption, *Issue Number 3,972*. In the absence of any obvious search term to narrow his trawl, he grabbed his jacket and headed off across town to the newspaper's offices.

Reid showed his ID, asked if he might examine the paper's archive, and took a seat in reception. A pleasant man of around sixty, greeted the detective after a few minutes. They shook hands and the man ushered his visitor along to a windowless room near the centre of the ground floor.

Reid explained why he was there and apologised that he had no idea of timescale or personal details.

'I realise it's probably impossible,' he admitted handing over a copy of the photograph. 'I'm not even sure the photograph was in the Chronicle at all. I just need his name for starters. Is it even possible?'

The man studied the photograph for a second or two. 'It is one of ours,' he confirmed. 'The man's name is David King.'

Reid's jaw dropped. 'That's amazing,' he said. 'How on Earth…'

'Luck and coincidence,' the man admitted with a smile. 'That photograph is from a 1981 edition of the *Chronicle*. I made a copy, possibly that copy, around five or six weeks ago. A young woman came in to search the archive. She knew the period she wanted, so I left her to do the search herself.'

'What was her name?'

'Carol, I believe.'

'No surname?

'Not that I recall.'

'Did she say why she was searching, or ask for the guy by name? Was he a relative perhaps?'

'She didn't say. I thought she might be an author, researching for a book or something.'

'Do you have any idea why she might have been interested in Mr King?'

'Around forty or so years ago, David King was a big man in Oxton. He had a business in the town, antiques, high quality not tourist bric-a-brac. He was an active local councillor, ran a junior football team, taught martial arts in the evening. A very popular man apparently. His wife was murdered. The killer was never caught. King was a broken man. A few months after the murder, he sold up his business, the family home, the whole shooting match and left Oxton.'

'Where did he go?'

'I have no idea, sergeant. I just do local news.'

Reid thanked the man and hurried back to the police station.

Chapter 25

When Marcia returned, to the house, she had clearly been crying.

'What is it?' Alistair asked.

She swallowed a tear. 'I'll tell you later,' she said. 'Let's go, or we'll be late.'

The atmosphere in the car was uncomfortably subdued. Marcia appeared distant, pensive, throughout the entire twenty-mile drive north to Great Ashwood. Alistair left her immersed in silent thought until he parked alongside the village green facing All Saints church.

'Are you okay?' he said. 'You seemed fairly keen earlier on.'

'I'm sorry,' Marcia replied nodding across at the church. 'Don't mind me. The vicar is waiting for us.'

The vicar – who's compact, yet sturdy, construction harmonised perfectly with his church – waved from the porch and bustled over to greet his visitors with warm handshakes. 'Tom Foley, welcome to All Saints. I'm sorry to hear about Dr Hastings. Please accept my sincere condolences. I've sorted out the records.'

Rev Foley led his visitors in through a doorway at the rear of the church, invited them to sit and disappeared into an adjoining room. He returned carrying three large and visibly aged registers in his short arms.

Alistair flicked a despondent glance at Marcia. She bit her lip to suppress a smile. 'Perhaps I should explain,' Alistair said to Rev Foley. 'I found your name in my uncle's diary. I'm guessing he came here in connection with his church project, but, quite honestly, I'm stepping into the unknown and I only have a vague idea what the project was about. My uncle was an academic. I definitely do not share that distinction.'

'Dr Hastings had an interest in a local family by the name of Rosemont,' the vicar confirmed.

'That fits,' Alistair said. 'What can you tell me about them?'

'That they were a respected local family in this area, until the mid-nineteenth century,' Rev Foley replied without opening his records. 'You are most welcome to examine the registers, if you wish, though I'm not sure Dr Hastings discovered anything of major interest in there.'

'Then I'm sorry I've wasted your time,' Alistair said.

'Not at all,' Rev Foley replied. 'I spent some time with Dr Hastings. Would you like me to summarise the relevant facts?'

'A summary sounds perfect,' Alistair agreed, prompting another smile from Marcia.

Rev Foley rested his hands on the records, as if absorbing information through his fingertips. 'The Rosemont family had a large estate quite near to Great Ashwood. I understand they were generally well regarded by both the church and the local communities.'

'Only *generally* well thought of,' Alistair queried. 'Were there exceptions?'

'There are exceptions in every family,' the vicar replied. 'Dr Hastings had a particular interest in one Samuel Rosemont, who left this area as a young man.'

'In which case, I suppose you have little or no information about him?'

'Nothing *official*.' Rev Foley slid a notebook out from between the registers. 'Vicars enjoyed gossip in those times, as they still do,' he said. 'This is a personal journal left by the vicar in Great Ashwood at the time. He records Samuel's move to Lowesley Pryor in the spring of 1800.'

'Does he say *why* Samuel moved away from here?' Alistair asked.

'Not specifically,' the vicar replied with a mildly roguish glint in his eye. 'However, local people weren't sorry to see him go. It appears that Samuel had quite insatiable appetites for alcohol, gambling and womanising. No local family was prepared to see him married to one of their daughters. Samuel was forced to cast his net more widely. Shortly after moving from here, he married some unfortunate girl from the other side of the country.'

Alistair felt a surprisingly pleasant, buzz of interest. 'Does the journal mention whether Samuel had personal or family connections elsewhere?' he asked.

'Regrettably, no,' Rev Foley confirmed. 'Dr Hastings asked the same question.' The vicar opened his desk index. 'He called me a day or two after our meeting, requesting contact details for Rev Austin Leech at St Gilberts Church.'

'Where's that?'

'Some place called Wellandsley, in Lincolnshire.' The vicar flipped through his desk diary and wrote down the contact details. 'Your uncle seemed very keen to meet Rev Leech,' he said, handing over the note.

Alistair felt Marcia's restless shuffle beside him. He thanked Rev Foley for his assistance, slipped the note into his pocket and followed Marcia, who had not spoken except to say hello and goodbye to the vicar, back to the car.

'Let's go home?' Alistair said. 'You're obviously not in the mood right now.'

'James wanted to contact Rev Leech,' Marcia replied. 'It's a possible lead. You ought to give him a call at least. Please, Alistair. I'd feel awful if you missed out because of me.' Alistair looked into her sad eyes. She forced a tiny smile. 'Please.'

He hesitated briefly then called the Lincolnshire number on his speakerphone. Rev Leech answered quickly. Alistair explained his interest and asked if he could visit to examine the church records.

'I'm leaving on an overseas mission tomorrow,' Rev Leech said' I am rather busy. In any event, as I explained at some length to Dr Hastings and his colleague, you may learn much more by speaking to a man named Barnaby Dolman. He is the fount of all knowledge on the history of this area. I'm sure he will be more than happy to take you back beyond the Great Flood, should you so wish.'

'Do you have contact details?' Alistair asked, reaching for the small notepad in his blazer pocket.

Rev Leech gave the address, 8 Seaton Terrace, Swinsdyke, together with a landline phone number. 'Barney doesn't have a mobile,' he said. 'Not one he has ever disclosed to me anyway. He can be difficult to contact by phone. A home visit is probably your best option. Swinsdyke is on The Wash coast. It's very remote. And he often spends days away from home.'

'Why does Mr Dolman come so far to attend your church?' Alistair asked.

'Barney is a historian,' the vicar replied. 'He has an interest in a family with a historic connection to St Gilberts. I cannot be more specific. I tend to avoid discussions with Barney unless I have several hours to spare. I think it's best that you speak to him yourself.'

Alistair rang off and looked across at Marcia.

'Phone him,' she said.

Alistair tapped in the number. The call connected and continued ringing. It did not switch to voicemail. Alistair disconnected, gave a disappointed huff and set off toward home. He had driven almost ten miles when Marcia finally spoke.

'Pull over,' she said quietly.

Alistair drew into a layby. 'Are you okay?' he asked.

Marcia nodded. 'I think we should go to Swinsdyke,' she said.

Alistair stared. 'Fine,' he agreed. 'We'll talk it over at home, and maybe go tomorrow.'

'Now,' Marcia replied. 'We didn't get much from the vicars. Mr Dolman may have the thread you're looking for.'

'Do you realise how far it is to that Swinsdyke place?' He entered the details into his sat nav. 'It's over a hundred and eighty miles and there's no motorway for the final hundred. It's a long way, Marcia. It may be a bit late for visiting by the time we get there.'

'It's a long way from Oxton, so it's probably safer,' Marcia replied. 'I think you'd be on your way there right now if you were by yourself, so that's what we should do.'

Chapter 26

Alistair drove east, through heavy afternoon traffic, until he reached the beautiful Lincolnshire Vales then on through miles of undulating farmland. The land became flatter. Vegetable crops stretched into the distance beneath an enormous sky on either side. Cultivated land finally gave way to reed and marsh until, beyond the Fen hinterland, the vast embayment of The Wash dominated the view. Land became sea and then sky, in a seamless continuum reaching out toward the cold North Sea.

Alistair stopped and lowered his window. 'This is like a parallel dimension,' he said. 'I wonder what James made of it.'

'That vicar only provided James with contact details,' Marcia reminded him. 'We can't be sure he followed them up.'

'He did,' Alistair replied with absolute certainty. 'I can feel him here.'

Marcia shivered and rubbed her arms. 'Then he must have noticed how cold it is,' she said. 'This is a raw and desolate place. I don't like it.'

Alistair raised his window, turned up the heater and pressed on.

Seaton Terrace, a block of four houses plus two pairs of semi-detached companions in a single row, was all that remained of what had once been the small village of Swinsdyke. The weatherworn properties faced out to sea across a flat expanse of mud. Number 8 appeared to be a typically compact two up two down terrace end home. Alistair knocked several times on the peeling front door, without drawing a response. The curtain twitched in the window of number seven. A moment later, the front door opened. A woman emerged. 'He's away,' she said. 'Goes off regular. Lives by himself. He often disappears for a day or two. Never much longer. He'll probably be back tomorrow.'

A freshening east wind had begun sweeping the fine summer day toward a chilly evening. Alistair thanked the woman and returned to his car. Marcia sat gazing through the window, attempting to rub a little warmth into her fingers. Her face remained taut.

'We'd best head for home,' Alistair said. 'You're obviously not happy here.'

'Bad day. I'll get over it,' Marcia replied. 'You're beginning to reconnect with James. It wouldn't be fair to drag you away with nothing to show for your effort. Anyway, I daresay you're hungry. Why don't we find somewhere to stay? The neighbour thinks Mr Dolman will be back tomorrow. We can give it another go then.'

'I'm sure that isn't what you want to do,' Alistair said.

Marcia turned and smiled. 'I'm sure it's what you *need* to do,' she said. 'We'll try here again in the morning. If he isn't back, we'll push off and rely on the phone.'

*

Alistair drove several miles in search of somewhere to stay. Dusk was closing in when he found the isolated Feathers Inn. The manager apologised for the smell of paint and blamed, or perhaps boasted, recent redecoration. The good news, he said, was that although he had only one room available, it was his best. Alistair and Marcia exchanged slightly self-conscious glances, booked into the first floor double and went upstairs.

'At least it's clean,' Alistair said.

'The en-suite is nice too,' Marcia replied poking her head into the bathroom.

They washed a little awkwardly and went down to eat.

A dozen or so male customers sat chatting over drinks in the bar. Two couples and a party of four were eating in the dining room. A friendly waiter showed Alistair and Marcia to a window table.

Marcia chose the lone vegetarian option of goat's cheese and mixed leaves from the limited menu. Alistair selected stuffed chine, a local pork speciality. They didn't order drinks and ate quietly. Immediately they had finished their meal, Marcia announced that she was going upstairs.

Alistair stood to go with her. 'Why don't you have a beer or something?' she suggested. 'I need to be quiet tonight.'

Alistair nodded. 'I'll be here if you change your mind,' he said as Marcia disappeared toward the stairs. He went through to the small bar, perched on a stool and ordered a pint of local ale. His eye wandered suspiciously over the room. Conversation died away. Alistair felt embarrassingly conspicuous. He took a single swallow from his drink, set the glass down and stared into it for a few minutes before he left it and headed upstairs.

When Alistair opened the bedroom door, Marcia was standing alongside the dressing table speaking on her phone. She smiled.

'Sorry, Nick, I have to go,' she said. Alistair began turning to leave. Marcia beckoned him back. 'Yes, yes fine. Thanks for calling.' She rang off. 'He called me,' she said as if compelled to explain. 'We split up over a year ago. He heard about Caroline and rang to check that I'm okay.'

'You don't need to explain,' Alistair replied. 'You're obviously not okay. Those incidents on Gaia and at the shop must have given you a real jolt. There's something else too, isn't there?'

She nodded. 'I went to see Warren Hinchcliffe this morning. I have to arrange Caroline's funeral.' Her lips trembled. 'I couldn't see it through. I'll try again when I'm more prepared.'

'Why on earth did you go alone?' Alistair blurted. 'Sorry, I didn't mean to shout. I would have come with you. I'd have done it for you.'

'It's my job,' she said. 'I have a duty, just like you.' She swallowed. 'It's odd, isn't it? Despite what happened and what I saw, Caroline wasn't really dead, not forever, until I began choosing a coffin for her. My blood turned to ice. The world feels cold and empty, like that place we drove through this afternoon. That's how I am now, cold and flat and desolate.'

'I know,' he said. 'You're saddled with an awful painful burden. My shock can't compare, but I know what it's like for you. I get it, Marcia. I'm here for you and I know you're here for me. Right here, right now. I wonder if I was right or just plain selfish to bring you up here when there may be nothing to find, especially today.'

'Maybe we both needed that distraction you mentioned this morning,' she said. 'A temporary escape. At least we have that. If there's nothing to find here, so be it.'

'We'll give it one more shot tomorrow, then we go home,' Alistair said as he took a pillow from the bed and turned toward the bathroom. 'One of us obviously has to sleep in the bath. Do you need the loo, before I turn in?'

'No thanks, I'm fine,' Marcia replied. 'Are you sure you don't mind?'

'I've slept in worse places,' he assured her. 'I'll see you in the morning. Just try not to have a bath before I'm up. Goodnight.'

Chapter 27

Nash snatched his phone from the bedside table and squinted at his clock. 'Hi Alex, do you know what time it is?'

'Six forty-eight, sir.'

Nash swung his legs out from beneath the duvet and sat on the edge of his bed. 'So, what's up?'

'Dave Hawkins just called me. He was duty sergeant overnight. Rev Chapman has reported an intruder at St Michael's. A dog walker spotted activity in the churchyard and called the vicarage. Rev Chapman is at the church now. Dave is asking if we want to follow up ourselves or send a uniformed team.'

'Did he have any details?'

'Nothing useful except that the guy apparently left in a vehicle of some sort. Rev Chapman didn't provide a description.'

'It's probably minor but we'd best check it out ourselves. Where are you?'

'I'm at my desk, sir; about to have another trawl through the database.'

'Okay, carry on with that. I'll follow up at the church on my way in.'

*

Clive Chapman emerged from the church door as Nash walked down from the car park. 'You must have been quick off the mark to be out of bed and over here before the intruder left,' Nash said.

'I tend to rise early and grab a spell of uninterrupted work before the daily chores take over,' the vicar replied. 'I was at my desk when the call came through.'

'And the intruder was still here when you arrived?'

'He was. I saw him walking away from the church.'

'Where did he walk away to?' Nash asked.

'A car, I think. I heard some sort of vehicle leaving. I didn't see it,' the vicar replied.

'And he escaped before you could get close enough take a description, or maybe even identity him?'

'Well…. My parishioner thought the man was behaving suspiciously. In light of recent events, I informed you immediately. I haven't found any signs of forced entry. No damage at all in fact. It appears to be a false alarm.'

'Good,' Nash replied. 'I presume the building is locked when it isn't in use.'

'It is,' the vicar confirmed. 'There's a list of keyholders in the vestibule and another on the notice board near the gates. Amanda and I each have a set, along with the two church wardens, the organist, and Algy Bains the handyman.'

'No-one else?' Reid asked.

The vicar considered for a moment. 'Just Peter Christy, but he has no official role here.'

'Then why does he need keys?' Nash asked.

'Peter is terminally ill and a devoted Christian,' Clive replied. 'He arrived here in search of comfort and consolation soon after our churchyard work commenced. I believe Peter was the person reported as our intruder. I gave him a set so that he can use the church for private devotions. It seems to be the least I should do in the circumstances.'

'So, Mr Christy doesn't reside in the parish,' Nash observed. 'He arrived here very soon after work commenced on the grave relocation and car park. The nature of those operations may obviously trigger, press interest and some sort of opposition or fringe activity. Are you sure Mr Christy didn't come in search of information? He may have some entirely unchristian agenda.'

'Peter is clearly very ill,' the vicar replied. 'He worships at St Michael's whenever he is well enough to attend. He's very fond of our church.'

'We'll need contact details for Mr Christy,' Nash confirmed.

'I'm afraid I don't have any,' the vicar replied. 'It didn't seem appropriate to ask.'

'Really?' Nash queried. 'Two people who were carrying out a project here have been murdered.'

'I don't understand, Chief Inspector,' the vicar replied. 'You surely don't think that Peter....'

'I advise you to think very carefully before you hand over key sets to strangers,' Nash interrupted. 'Please also instruct *all* your keyholders to avoid carrying theirs unless they have an unavoidable need to do so.' Nash thanked the vicar for reporting the incident, walked back to his car and phoned Reid. 'Nothing to report, Alex,' he said. 'Dawlish's place isn't far away from the church. Charlie One has been covering the house. Give him a call to make sure it's all secure.'

'Done it, sir,' Reid confirmed. 'He reports no-one at home since 17.00 yesterday when the housekeeper left.'

'So, where the hell are Dawlish and Marcia Blackham?' Nash asked. 'There's no point in wasting manpower keeping an eye on the house, if they've cleared off somewhere else. I'll give them a shout and invite them in. It may be time to give their kennels a bit of a kick anyhow.'

Chapter 28

Alistair strolled into the bedroom attempting to coax circulation back into his cramped shoulders. He looked over at Marcia, lying on her back, hair spread across the pillow like a pale gold halo. She opened her eyes and smiled.

'Please don't tell me you slept well,' Alistair said, returning the smile.

'I tried, but you obviously ate or drank something a bit suspect last night,' she said. 'I peeped in to see that you were okay. You were thrashing around and mumbling for ages.'

'About what?' he asked.

'I couldn't make it out, but you definitely weren't happy and you were soaked with sweat.'

'Commissioned ranks don't sweat, they perspire,' he said with a smile. 'You wouldn't have slept any better in that bath. At least I didn't fall out.' He headed back toward the bathroom. 'You got the bed so I'll take first shower,' he said.

Careful timing ensured that they each managed to shower and dress without any major embarrassment. Immediately after an early breakfast, they checked out and returned to Swinsdyke.

*

Morning sun sparkled on the distant sea, suspended like a fine gold chain between featureless land and pale blue sky. Seaton Terrace basked in clear light, streaked with receding strands of sea haze.

Alistair knocked on the door of number eight. No one answered He knocked a little harder, listened for signs of movement inside then gave a despondent shrug. Marcia sighed and they returned to the car. Alistair began scribbling his contact details and a short explanation for the visit on a page from his notebook. His ring tone shattered the silence. Marcia gasped.

'It's Nash,' Alistair said. 'Good morning, Chief Inspector... In my car... Yes, she's with me.' He switched to speaker.

'Perhaps you and Ms Blackham would call in at Oxton Police Station,' Nash said.

Marcia nodded. 'Certainly, Chief Inspector,' Alistair agreed. 'Do you have news for us?'

'I'd like a chat,' Nash replied. 'I was surprised to learn that you two aren't at home. Where exactly are you?'

'Lincolnshire.'

'What are you doing over there?'

'This and that, we'll probably be back around noon.'

'I'll be in my office,' Nash replied. He disconnected.

A smile flickered on Marcia's lips. 'Maybe they have a lead,' she said.

'Best speak to him before we start raising our hopes,' Alistair cautioned.

An ageing salt-caked Volvo saloon drew up behind the Mercedes. The driver, a large man, aged seventy or so, with a sun-bleached beard framing his weather-etched face, approached number eight and inserted a key into the front door lock. Marcia nudged Alistair and nodded toward the house.

'Forget Nash for now,' she said. 'If that's Mr Dolman, I suggest you nail him before he disappears again.'

Alistair discarded his unfinished note and sprang from the car with Marcia in hot pursuit. The man shot round, eyes agape, as the pair ran up behind him.

'Sorry to startle you,' Alistair said offering his hand. 'Rev Leech thought you may be able to help us, if you're Barnaby Dolman.'

The man studied Alistair and Marcia briefly before accepting the handshake. 'I'm Barney Dolman,' he confirmed warily. 'Why has Austin sent you all the way up here?'

'A relative of mine has been researching a family named Rosemont. I believe they were connected with this area,' Alistair replied.

A broad smile lit Barney Dolman's face. 'Then your relative is James Hastings?'

Alistair nodded. 'My uncle.'

'Dr Hastings is a fine scholar. I trust he and his companion are well.'

'Sadly, they aren't,' Alistair replied. 'I'm sorry to tell you that they both passed away recently.'

Barney's eyes widened. 'Both? I'm shocked. How? They seemed so full of life.'

'The police are investigating,' Alistair said.

'I see.' Barney opened the front door and retrieved his key. 'You'd best come in.'

Alistair followed Barney and Marcia through the sparsely furnished, almost Spartan, front room and on past the foot of a bare wooden staircase into the back room. Small heavily curtained windows added only minimal brightness to dark wooden doors, tired brown leather furniture and threadbare carpet.

The visitors sat side by side on the sofa. Their host settled into a sagging chair beside the empty fireplace.

'This is astonishing news,' Barney said turning to Marcia. 'Were you close?'

Marcia stared. Her lips quivered. No sound emerged. 'Marcia worked with Dr Hastings,' Alistair said. 'His companion was her sister.'

'A double tragedy,' Barney said. 'You must both be deeply shocked. How may I help you?'

'My uncle and Caroline didn't manage to complete their project,'

Alistair replied. 'I've inherited the estate. I'd like to honour the bequest by finishing the work, if I can. Unfortunately, it seems that he left no notes. You appear to be our only source of information.'

Barney stroked his beard. 'I don't know anything about the Rosemont family,' he said. 'I'd never heard the name until James mentioned it to me.' Alistair flicked a disappointed glance toward Marcia. 'Did your uncle ever mention the name of Gould?' Barney asked.

Alistair looked at Marcia. She shook her head.

'The Goulds had a daughter,' Barney continued. 'Her name was Eleanor. Around the year 1800, Eleanor moved from this area to Shropshire. Dr Hastings told me that she married a man named Samuel Rosemont.'

'So, there is a connection to Lowesley Pryor,' Alistair said. 'My uncle may have been searching for a book. Did he mention anything like that to you?'

'Dr Hastings was very much a collector of information, rather than a distributor,' Barney replied.

'He obviously came here to gather material on the Goulds,' Alistair continued. 'What sort of family were they?'

'A wealthy and troubled one,' Barney replied. 'Farmers, merchants, ship owners. They have a family vault at St Gilberts, hence my interest there.'

'They sound like a well-heeled bunch,' Alistair observed. 'How come they were troubled?'

'I imagine envy played a large part,' Barney replied. 'There were times when the chances of any family member surviving to old age were very slim indeed. That's possibly why they sent their daughter away.' Barney smiled. 'History only records the what's and when's of the past. The how's and whys circulate in stories. There are endless stories about the Goulds and they vary according to who is telling them.'

'How true are they?' Alistair asked, instantly regretting the question as he recalled Rev Leech's warning about Barney's long discourses.

Barney laughed. 'Who knows? Stories don't have to be true they only have to be believed.'

'Are there any Gould tales that may have led my uncle to a book?' Alistair asked.

'Not directly but there is a story.'

'I thought there might be,' Marcia murmured in Alistair's ear as Barney launched into his tale.

'Most local folk accepted the Bible as absolute fact in the nineteenth century. A few are said to have followed a very different religious path. As far as I've been able to discover, it was a toxic blend of Christian fundamentalism and some ancient Viking religion involving serpent worship.'

'Religious conflicts aren't unusual, particularly if there's a bit of black magic to spice things up,' Alistair said. 'There are silly witch stories doing the rounds in my area to this day.'

'That sect went a bit further than scary tales,' Barney cautioned. 'It isn't difficult to control isolated communities with fear and superstition. The serpent became a powerful symbol of retribution. We don't have many serpents in Lincolnshire, but there are plenty of snakes out on the marshes. People soon got the message that they were constantly being watched.'

'Was the alternative version written down?' Alistair asked.

'Folklore says the group had some sort of book,' Barney confirmed. 'The tale is that there was only one copy and its contents were restricted to a few very carefully chosen individuals. I've never found anyone prepared to confirm or deny its existence. According to the stories, any outsider who looks into the book must pay the ultimate price, so its secrets have stayed hidden.'

'James would scent huge profit in something unique like that,' Alistair said. 'Do you believe the book exists?'

'I have no idea if the *group* ever really existed,' Barney replied. 'One tale tells that the Goulds acquired some of the forbidden knowledge.

I don't know whether they did or not, but they certainly upset some dangerous people. Eleanor died within a year or two of leaving here and her parents suffered terrible deaths. Let me show you something.'

Alistair sensed the approach of yet another story. 'Thanks for your time, Mr Dolman,' he said. 'I'm sure we've detained you from more important matters long enough.'

Barney was already opening his sideboard drawer. He lifted out an old unframed ink drawing and handed it to Alistair.

'That was apparently the fate awaiting anyone who strayed from the path, especially if they questioned anything or saw too much. There were apparently many similar executions over the years.'

The sketch depicted a desolate watery landscape. Scattered islands peeped above dark water. Fog rolled over vast marshes. Two figures, one male one female, with their arms and legs lashed to wooden posts, occupied the foreground in front of a dark building. Flames licked up over their slumped bodies. The victims' eye sockets were shown as black voids. The crude image of a snake was carved into each forehead.

'The Goulds?' Alistair queried.

'Eleanor's parents,' Barney confirmed. 'They were the last of the family. No one mentions the story nowadays. Bad luck they say.'

Marcia seized Alistair's arm. Her fingernails dug deep into his skin.

'Hell fire,' he murmured.

'In every sense,' Barney agreed. 'And like I said, there are stories of many others who died like that.'

An expression of sheer horror had frozen Marcia's face into a living death mask.

Alistair thrust the sketch back into Barney's hand and thanked him for his information as he swept Marcia out of the house and into his car.

'I'm sorry,' he said. 'I shouldn't have let him ramble on like that. He's a hard man to stop.'

'You came looking for information,' Marcia replied shakily. 'You had to listen.'

'He confirmed that Eleanor Gould married Samuel Rosemont,' Alistair replied. 'James already knew that when he came here. The rest was folk tales and guesswork. Maybe that's why the old boy went home and abandoned the project.'

'That sketch was no folk tale, any more than Caroline's was.' Marcia replied.

'Sorry again,' Alistair said. 'That was a shock I definitely didn't foresee. I'll call Nash and put him off. You've had more than your share of stress.' He reached for his phone.

Marcia placed her hand on his. 'Don't,' she said. 'If Nash has something to tell us, I want to hear it. I hate this place, Alistair. Get me away from here, please.'

He punched the gearstick forward and rammed his foot to the floor. Swinsdyke disappeared into a plume of dust and smoke.

Chapter 29

A constable escorted Alistair and Marcia up to Nash's office. Reid joined them from the CID.

Nash invited his visitors to sit. 'Have there been any more intimidating texts or phone calls?' he asked.

'No texts to either of our mobiles,' Alistair confirmed. 'Marcia and I haven't been home, or to the shop, to check the landlines yet.'

'Did your visit to Lincolnshire have any bearing on the situation here?'

'My uncle visited a local historian called Barnaby Dolman there, in connection with his project at St Michael's. I feel guilty that he and I didn't keep in touch. I know it's probably too late now, but I'd like to fill in a few gaps and maybe complete the project for him, if I can. We definitely discovered where Caroline got the idea for those gruesome sketches she made. Barney showed us a disturbing sketch of a two-hundred-year-old death scene, very similar to Caroline's work.'

Reid took down Barney Dolman's contact details.

'Why did you go with the Commander?' Nash asked Marcia.

'Because you asked us to stay close together,' she replied.

Nash nodded and turned to Alistair. 'I'd like to speak with Ms Blackham, alone if I may,' he said.

'Why?' Alistair asked.

'Please go with Sergeant Reid, sir. I won't keep you long.'

Reid walked over and opened the office door. 'This way please,

Commander,' he said.'

Alistair looked at Marcia. She swallowed and nodded.

Reid escorted Alistair to an adjoining office.

*

'Why did you go to your sister's cottage on the afternoon of the murder?' Nash asked.

'I've already told you. I received a text message.'

'From the victim?'

'From Caroline's phone, yes.'

'We have confirmed that you were somewhere near your mooring when you received that call. You had not planned to visit your sister?'

'Not that day. I was at home. I hadn't been going to the shop since James died. I planned to go over and drive her to James's funeral the next day.'

'But you didn't plan to attend the service yourself?'

'Not the church service. I intended to lay a wreath and say a private goodbye.'

'We know that an image of the murder scene was recorded on your sister's phone, sometime between her death and the burning of her body. You are the only person known to be at the cottage during that short period.'

'Other than the murderer,' she reminded him. 'I've told you I received a text. The person who sent it obviously wanted me to witness what I saw.'

'How well did you and your sister get on?'

Marcia's eyes narrowed. 'Very well,' she replied firmly. 'We were extremely close.'

'But you had argued and hadn't contacted each other for several days.'

'Soon after they began researching that grave, James became uncharacteristically timid, fearful of something or someone. He was suddenly reluctant to continue with the project. He even suggested that someone may have been following him. That amounted to a total character reversal for James. My sister sometimes pursued oddball ideas and attracted freaky characters. I worried for her safety and warned her to be careful. We argued and retreated into our shells when James died.'

'Were you involved in the St Michael's project at any stage?'

'I work at Bookworm,' Marcia replied. 'My interest in history is limited to old books. Cal and James were bound together by their compulsion to root out hidden histories. I could have joined them. I wish I had now. It would be nice to have all those memories I declined.'

'Do you and Commander Dawlish have a similar bond.'

'Completely different, I'd say. Caroline and James chose to share their common passion for things they loved. Alistair and I have been ensnared by tangled bonds of grief.'

'How well do you know him?'

'I don't.'

'Do you like him?'

'He seems kind, thoughtful. We're supporting one another through a painful experience.'

'How much have you seen of him over the years.'

'I haven't seen him at all. As far as I know, he left for uni and never returned until he arrived for James's funeral.'

'That will be all for now,' he said. 'Thank you for coming in.'

*

Reid sat facing Alistair across a desk in an adjoining office. 'What does your boss want with Marcia?' Alistair asked. 'That print Barney Dolman showed us gave her quite a shock earlier this morning.'

'How well do you know her, Commander?'

'I don't, not really. Why do you ask?'

'But you knew her sister?'

Alistair frowned. 'Many years ago. I haven't seen either of them since my teens.'

'So, you met for the first time in almost twenty years, at Dr

Hastings' funeral?'

'During the afternoon, following the funeral. I drove over to offer my condolences.'

'And now you're living together?'

'No, sergeant. Marcia is residing temporarily at my home, because DCI Nash thinks, and I agree with him, that she is safer there than she would be living alone at her isolated mooring. There is an inference, deliberate I believe, when you describe our current arrangement as "living together." It is entirely misplaced.'

'But you have just returned from an overnight trip together.'

'We have.'

'I suppose you'll have to return to your work soon, Commander. Will Ms Blackham be remaining at your house and looking after the bookshop for you?'

'I am no longer a serving officer, sergeant. My time is currently my own.'

'Convenient in the circumstances. You're rather young to be pensioned off, surely.'

'Yes sergeant, but quite old enough to recognise loaded questions and comments.'

Reid's desk phone rang. He listened briefly and replaced the handset. 'The DCI and Ms Blackham have finished,' he said. 'I'll wish you good day, sir.'

*

Nash sat looking out through his office window. 'Impressions, Alex,' he said when Reid rejoined him.

'Commander Dawlish is a cool sort of person, sir, though I'd say he has a streak of steel. I suppose that's to be expected, given his background. He's left the Navy, by the way.'

'Was it a planned departure?'

'He didn't say, sir. And he isn't a suspect so I had no grounds to push it.'

'Fair comment. How did Marcia Blackham strike you?'

'As expected, to be honest, sir, I'm not altogether sure why you wanted them in here.'

Nash swivelled around to face him. 'We know that Marcia Blackham was at the murder scene very soon after the event. It's possible that she could have been there throughout, or had an accomplice who was.'

'I suppose it's *possible*, sir. What are your concerns about Commander Dawlish?'

'We already know he isn't quite the upright law-abiding citizen he appears to be. He claims he hasn't been near this area for nigh on twenty years. Suddenly, within the space of a few days, James Hastings dies, Alistair Dawlish pops up itching to claim the loot and Caroline Blackham is murdered.'

'Commander Dawlish has a legitimate reason to be here, sir.'

'I know he does, Alex, and he *might* be kosher,' Nash conceded. 'The point is we don't know if he came back because Dr Hastings had died, or if Dr Hastings copped his lot *because* his nephew had turned up again. We're looking at two murders here. Dawlish has possible motive in one case and Marcia Blackham turned up a bit too conveniently at the scene of the other. I also find it a bit odd that two people, who claim they haven't met for twenty years and hardly knew one another anyway, suddenly seem to be joined at the hip.' He leaned back and stretched his aching shoulders.

'You look tired, sir,' Reid said. 'Why don't you go home and put your feet up?'

'My feet are fine where they are, thank you, Sergeant,' Nash said. 'I'll go home when I'm good and ready.'

'Of course you will,' Reid replied. 'I just meant...'

'When I'm ready,' Nash repeated. 'I know you mean well Alex and I appreciate your concern, but... That house of mine is a bit big for one and it still feels cold without Jen.' He swallowed. 'That sketch Dawlish mentioned sounds like a weird sort of link spanning two hundred years.'

'Aye, sir, so it's unlikely to all be the work of the same killer. That sketch and Caroline Blackham's depict ritual killings, as you said sir. We've already discarded any ritual motive in either of our cases. Burning has always been a popular way to destroy evidence. The threat of it is also a great way to instil fear in a witness or a potential victim. I'd say that's why Caroline Blackham's killer sent that image to Marcia. I believe it also lets her off the hook.'

'I suppose so,' Nash agreed a little grudgingly. 'Nothing else?'

'Nothing obviously relevant. The guy at the *Chronicle* put a name to that wee photograph instantly. He said he made a copy, maybe the actual one Caroline Blackham had in her folder, quite recently. I'm fairly sure Caroline searched the archive and had that copy made. The subject is David King. His wife was murdered here almost forty years ago. The case was never solved. Mr King sold up and left Oxton a few months after his wife's death.'

'Pull the file,' Nash said.

'It's at Div. HQ, sir. Oxton was only around a third of its present size in those days. There was no CID here.'

'It's unlikely to be relevant, but we'd best check it out,' Nash replied. 'Get over there. I'll make the arrangements. And I'll ask the carrot crunchers to keep a low-key eye on that Dolman character for a day or two.'

Chapter 30

Alistair drove away from the police station with Marcia, silent, beside him.

'What do you think that was all about?' she finally asked.

'Fishing trip,' Alistair replied. 'They're struggling to find a lead.'

Marcia huffed and was about to reply when her phone chirped. Alistair heard the sharp intake of breath and began slowing down. Marcia's hand trembled slightly. She looked down at the display.

'Sorry about that,' she said, with obvious relief. 'False alarm, it's Aiden. Carry on.' She hit the green button. 'Hi. Aiden, how can I...? I see... Yes, we're fine... in town... of course... we'll meet you there.' She rang off. 'He's at the shop,' she said.

'What for?'

'He wants to see you. He's rung Bookbinders a few times and got no answer. I suppose he's worried. I'm sorry. I should have asked you before I agreed to meet him.'

'Not a problem. We may as well see what he wants.'

*

Alistair parked beside Aiden Gale's Jaguar in the carriage yard. He stepped out of his car and gave the outstretched hand a cursory shake. Marcia kissed Aiden's cheek.

'I became a little concerned when I couldn't contact you,' Aiden said.

'We're fine, as you can see,' Marcia replied. 'We've been to...'

'To grab a little respite,' Alistair said. 'Marcia said you want to see me.'

'Mainly to confirm that you are both well,' Aiden replied. 'I also wish to renew my offer of assistance here at Bookworm, should you require it.'

'I have your card Mr Gale,' Alistair reminded him. 'I hadn't forgotten your offer or your interest. I realise it must be difficult for you, seeing my uncle's business in the hands of an amateur. You needn't worry. Marcia is piloting the ship very competently.'

'Have you given any further thought to the future, disposal of Bookworm et cetera?'

'I recall what I said when we last met,' Alistair replied. 'I was clearly in a state of shock at that time. When I make my final decision regarding Bookworm, I shall fully respect my uncle's memory. I won't deceive you or dishonour him. I'm sorry, this doesn't seem an appropriate time.'

'I agree,' Aiden replied. 'I remain at your service should you require my assistance. Thank you.'

Alistair watched the Jaguar disappear beneath the archway.

'Aiden has lost his soul mate,' Marcia said quietly. 'He's grieving and he wants to help you.'

'I know,' Alistair conceded. 'Okay, I'm sorry. I'll accept that he may be genuine. He still gives me the creeps.'

'Then I suggest you try to get over it,' Marcia advised. 'I know it's none of my business, but he's a good man, Alistair, and he has exactly the kind of expertise you may need very soon.'

'Don't apologise. I need your input and I'm listening,' Alistair replied. 'Right now, we both need to chill. Coffee?'

She nodded.

*

Alistair prepared the coffee maker, while Marcia fumbled around, searching for mugs and spoons. 'Sorry, I've moved a few things,' he called over his shoulder.

'I haven't seen these before,' she said.

Alistair turned casually and stifled a sudden gasp. Marcia was holding the letters he had quickly tucked away two days earlier. He hurried over and snatched the bundle from her.

'I'm sorry,' she said. 'They were in the table drawer.'

'I slipped them in there the other day,' he said, as if suddenly needing to explain. 'I'd forgotten. Sorry I snatched them from you. They're a bit embarrassing.' He coughed and adjusted his shirt collar. 'Silly childish ramblings, I wrote them for my mother in the days when I still thought she might come back for me. I could obviously never send them. They were my way of talking to her, even if she wasn't listening. They've been hidden under the floorboards in my old bedroom.' He blew away a little of the dust. 'I was worried that Fred Reynolds' guys might find them. I suppose I should have shredded the things.'

'That would be an awful shame,' Marcia said. 'They obviously meant a lot when you wrote them.'

'That was a long time ago,' he said.

Marcia pointed out a vellum envelope tucked into the bundle behind the blue letters. 'I don't think that's one of yours,' she said. 'It looks like James's stationery.'

A flush of pink coloured Alistair's cheeks. 'The old man obviously found my secret stash,' he replied. 'How embarrassing.'

Marcia read the words – *Alistair, for your eyes only* – written on the envelope. 'And how mysterious,' she added. 'He obviously wanted you, and apparently *only* you, to see whatever's in there.'

'I never dreamed he'd find this stuff,' he said. 'You don't suppose he's shown these to anyone do you?'

'They look pretty undisturbed to me,' she replied. 'Why don't you read whatever it is that James wants you to know? It might answer a few of your questions.'

Alistair opened the envelope, pulled out the single page and slowly unfolded it to reveal James's immaculate handwritten italic. His hand quivered as he began to read.

My dearest Alistair,

Firstly, I hope you will accept my sincere apology for inadvertently discovering your secret.

The depth of your loss and longing at your mother's absence from your life are suddenly starkly clear to me.

If the emotions which urged you to write these beautiful and poignant letters, remain with you, as they surely must, they will one day compel you to return and retrieve them. When that day comes, you and I must try to heal the scars of loss and longing imposed by your motherless childhood.

Let that day be soon.

Sincerely,
James.

Alistair stood gazing at the page in his hand.

'What is it?' Marcia asked. He handed over the document.

She read, and reread the short letter. 'What do you think it means?' she murmured when she had finished.

'I really have no idea,' Alistair replied. 'And it's too late even to begin now. I'll never know what he had to tell me.'

'He may not have had anything to *tell* you. I haven't read the letters and they're none of my business. Maybe he thought it was important for *you* to talk about the things *you* wrote, when *you* were ready.' She handed back the letter and held on to his hand. 'I see the questions in your eyes, Ali. I wish I had answers to offer you. Let's go home.'

He nodded. 'Give me a minute to straighten my brain.' He refreshed his mouth with a little water and took a step out into the yard for a breath of fresh air.

Marcia locked the kitchen door and joined him. 'I don't think your mind will be on driving,' she said, handing over all the letters.

He didn't reply, but finally handed over his car keys.

Marcia took a minute or two to familiarise herself with the Mercedes, then drove steadily out under the archway.

Chapter 31

Detective Sergeant Mike Mason had spent years, perhaps too many years, probing the murky shadows of unsavoury lives. Each of those years had written its signature on his face. He showed Alex Reid up to the fifth floor of Wroxborough Divisional Police Headquarters.

'I've put you in a spare office,' Mason mumbled, with the casual disdain reserved for officers from its outlying "local yokel" stations. 'I think I've pulled out everything you need and I must say you're welcome to the job. God knows what you expect to find after all these years. If you need anything else, I'm on 222. The kettle and coffee are in the office on the floor below, help yourself. The team normally chips in to keep it stocked up.' Mason pushed open the door of the abandoned former CID office and pointed to a spare desk with four cardboard boxes stacked alongside it. 'All yours,' he said with a smirk. He turned to leave. 'If you hear the fire alarm, just follow somebody.'

'Thanks,' Reid replied as the door closed.

The office, unfurnished except for two damaged desks and a chair, had clearly lain abandoned for some time. A large sagging brown patch on the ceiling above the allocated desk, suggested a possible reason for the evacuation. Reid dusted the chair seat with his handkerchief, sat down and lifted the first dusty lid on case number UH3-1047/81.

On March 21 1981, the first day of spring, Mrs Deborah King

went out for a walk. Over the preceding winter months, Debbie's walks, when she managed to slip out unnoticed, had become a deepening worry to her husband, David. As her mental state deteriorated, she had increasingly shunned her life as the wife of a successful local businessman and returned to her twelve-year-old self, Deborah Walker. Whenever she could, Debbie would wander in search of her long since demolished childhood home on the outskirts of Franley. Due to the loss of that major landmark and the many other changes over the intervening fifteen years, she no longer had her signposts and would find it impossible to navigate her way home. As nightfall approached that evening, David reported his wife missing. The local police, carried out what had become an all too regular search of the fields and byways between Franley and the current family home in Oxton. They failed to locate Debbie and duly logged a vulnerable missing person report.

Several friends and neighbours, in Franley and Oxton, assisted with the police search for three days, before the matter was transferred for investigation by Wroxborough CID.

The last recorded sightings of Debbie were two days prior to her disappearance, when she accompanied David to Oxton market, where they purchased fruit and sweets. On the day of her disappearance, she was said to have been left alone, locked in the house, for approximately an hour, while David did a little early pruning in the garden.

The demands of David's business prevented him remaining at home as Debbie's full-time-carer, so she normally attended a day centre on five days each week. On the day of her disappearance, Debbie had apparently complained of a stomach upset. David took a rare weekday off to care for her at home. He later said in a police interview that he believed Debbie had fabricated her upset stomach, so that she could "escape" for her walk. That opportunity would have been impossible from the day centre.

Debbie's trail went cold for almost three months, before a spaniel hunting for a lost ball in Stoatley Wood, well off Debbie's normal wandering route, drew its owner to a small patch of shrubbery. The dog's frantic scratching had already scattered enough soil and leaf litter to reveal, a hand.

Police retrieved Debbie's body from its shallow grave. Post mortem examination quickly revealed that she died by being strangled with her own scarf. Five suspects, including David, were interviewed. No-one was ever charged with the murder.

Chapter 32

Marcia drove cautiously over the stone bridge and up the narrow road to Lowesley Pryor. The car approached St. Michael's, where two men wearing yellow hard hats appeared to be in discussion with the excavator driver in the car park. A lorry was reversing to unload materials.

Alistair pointed out a 4x4 parked near the churchyard gate. 'I think that's Clive Chapman's car,' he said. 'I wonder if there's been any progress.'

'I'm not stopping,' Marcia replied. 'Compared to my car, this is like driving a supercharged bungalow. We'll both be safer back at Bookbinders.'

She pressed on through the village, turned with relief into the little lane and parked behind her own car outside the workshop.

*

A young man and woman stood chatting at the roadside a little way from the house. Alistair and Marcia headed toward the front door. Three rapid flashes of blue light brought them to a startled halt. The woman Alistair had seen talking with her colleague as Marcia drove in, stepped forward and thrust a microphone at him. The man scurried around busily capturing images.

'April Maylor from *The Chronicle*,' the reporter said.

'We can't add to what you already know,' Alistair insisted.

April pressed her card into Alistair's hand. 'I'm sure you can,' she said. 'We'll talk later.' The reporter and her colleague walked away.

'April is only local press, but she's trying to make a name for herself,' Marcia said. 'She obviously thinks she's picked up a scent and has a reputation for being a persistent tracker.'

'Thanks for the warning,' Alistair said as they went inside and closed the door behind them.

Nancy appeared from the kitchen. Her smile withered. 'What's wrong, dear?' she asked looking at the keys in Marcia's hand. 'Why have you been driving Alistair's car?' Marcia had no ready answer. Nancy turned to Alistair. 'Please tell me, Ali,' she begged. 'If something is wrong, I'd like to help.'

'We're fine, really. I just need to be somewhere quiet for a little while.' Nancy's eyes did not waver. 'Would you mind making some coffee, please, Marci,' Alistair said. 'I need to have a chat with Nancy.'

He ushered the housekeeper out to the terrace table. They stared across at each other. Alistair pulled James's letter from his bundle and passed it across. 'Do you have any idea what he may have wanted to tell me?' he asked when Nancy had finished reading.

'I don't,' she said. 'He mentions your motherless childhood, so it possibly had something to do with Kate. She had already left when I arrived. I'd heard the gossip around town about her leaving you, of course. That's all I know. I don't recall Dr Hastings mentioning her to me, not once.'

'Nor to me, unless I pushed really hard,' Alistair replied. 'Even then I never got any more than, "we can't change the past, Ali. Always look to the future." Odd comment for a historian, I suppose. That's what I've always tried to do, but being deserted by your mother isn't something that's easily pushed aside. I've never even seen a picture of her. It's as if she never existed as a real person. Now suddenly...'

Nancy nodded slowly. Alistair could not complete his sentence and nor could she. She squeezed his shoulder and walked back to the kitchen.

*

Marcia found Alistair gazing out across the gorge. She stood beside him. 'Nancy has gone home,' she said. 'I don't want, and have no right, to underplay what happened this afternoon, Ali, but both of us are already tied up in dreadfully knotted emotions. I don't think this is a good time to add another thread to the tangle. Don't get hung up about James's letter. That issue has stayed scalpel sharp all through your life. It will keep a little longer, if it has to. The village is quiet. Go for a walk. I'll make dinner while you're away. It will have to be your food. I haven't contributed anything yet.'

'You're contributing much more than you probably realise,' Alistair replied. 'You are welcome to as much food as you want. Unless Nancy has changed an awful lot over the years there'll be plenty to choose from. Sort out a bottle of wine too. Neither of us is driving tonight and we both need to chill.'

Chapter 33

The front door closed with a thud. Alistair headed away toward St Michael's.

A small car cruised by and stopped directly ahead. Alistair moved to the crown of the road. April Maylor rolled down her window as he walked past.

'Do you mind if I ask where you're going, Commander Dawlish?' she asked.

Alistair looked down at her. 'You may ask me anything, Ms Maylor,' he replied. 'I trust you will be happy with my answer.'

'Which is?'

'Which is, mind your own damned business.'

'I'm hearing from my sources that Dr Hastings was murdered,' she said. 'If it's true, two murders in as many weeks probably add up to the biggest story in the history of Oxton. Is it true, Commander?'

'As I told you earlier. I can't add to what you already know. If there are any developments, I'm sure the police will issue press statements in the normal way.'

April shook her head. 'I only want the facts, Commander. Simple truth, that's all. It will come out in the end, it always does. Why not tell me now?'

'Because I can't,' he said with irritation rising in his voice. 'I really have no idea what's going on here. That, I promise you, is the truth.'

'Think about it. I'll be in touch.' She smiled and drove away, leaving Alistair standing alone in the middle of the deserted road.

Chapter 34

Vehicles and construction machinery littered the car park at St Michael's. The vicar's 4x4 remained near the church gate. A man of around Alistair's own age stopped nervously tugging at his wispy beard as the final pallet of materials settled onto its stack. He removed his hard hat and attempted, with minimal success, to rearrange his unruly black hair as he mopped his brow. He replaced his headgear and walked over to Alistair.

'I don't think we've met,' he said with a smile. 'Are you with the contractor?'

'No,' Alistair replied. 'Alistair Dawlish. My uncle was a historian with an interest in the site.'

The man beamed. 'Ah, so you're James's long-lost nephew. I heard about the funeral fiasco.' He held out his hand. 'Ollie Grainger, County Archaeologist.'

Alistair shook the outstretched hand and glanced over at the Council Board. 'I imagined you'd carry out something like a grave relocation behind screens at night,' he said.

'The relocation would have been lower profile if things had gone as planned,' Ollie confirmed. 'Alas, they did not. Have you seen our omen?' He guided Alistair over to a broken headstone near the corner of the site. 'That stone has survived here undamaged through storm, pestilence and two world wars since 1803. The contractors managed to wreck it in less than an hour. That's why site movements

161

and large vehicles make me so twitchy.' Ollie traced the virtually illegible inscription with his index finger. 'According to this, the grave belongs to one Samuel Rosemont, 1779 – 1803, whom I believe was the estranged son of a wealthy family from north of here.'

Alistair's thoughts slipped back to Barney Doman's stories about the Goulds and their daughter. 'Did you mention an omen?' he asked.

'Don't scoff, Commander Dawlish,' Ollie replied with a smile. 'Twixt thee and me, I confess that I share your scepticism. However, several of the good folk of Lowesley Pryor take such matters quite seriously. The grave is widely regarded as their local haunted place. The damage sparked whispers that God himself smote the stone asunder. People are terrified. You must have noticed how quiet the village is. The wave of fear seems to be creeping over Oxton now too. I'm worried that whispered superstition may escalate into something more serious.'

'Why did they bury Samuel outside the churchyard?' Alistair asked.

'I understand he was something of an embarrassment,' Ollie replied. 'The Rosemonts' were quite a prominent family. They would have felt morally bound to erect a marker for their wayward offspring.' He flashed a wry smile. 'Given Samuel's somewhat colourful reputation, Christian decency required that he was located at an appropriate distance from the spiritually unblemished.'

'Is the grave legal?'

'Absolutely. As it happens, the ground is consecrated. In the course of the exhumation, it emerged that our burial took place on the site of the former priory. However, it isn't illegal to have burial sites on private land. Many wealthy families have ancestral tombs and vaults.' He coughed. 'Speaking personally, I find the practice of having decomposing relatives at the bottom of the garden distinctly unappealing. A few years after the burial, the site became a carriage park and finally a car park,' Ollie continued. 'The old place has fallen into disrepair over recent years. Clive Chapman began an appeal for funds to restore the car park. After an encouraging start, the project has been fraught with delays. Work couldn't commence until the old grave was dismantled and its occupant removed. Then the contractors failed to break ground on the agreed date. When they did finally get moving, the old priory emerged, hence my unwelcome interruption. My investigation has pushed things back still further. All unavoidable of course, but poor Clive must be tearing his hair out by now.' Ollie's eyes twinkled. 'James teased him endlessly about the perils of disturbing the departed. I'm sure he had something up his sleeve concerning this place.'

'Do you know what it might have been?'

'Not exactly, but he and Caroline Blackham clearly knew rather more than they were prepared to disclose to me. Before we even began the exhumation, James casually mentioned that our body would turn out to be that of a woman, as the locals have always believed. He also told me, in that impish way of his, that the woman had a story to tell. Both predictions were correct. Our remains are undoubtedly female and the unfortunate lady died of massive head injuries. Half the skull is crushed. That level of damage almost certainly resulted from a deliberate and sustained assault. The police quickly concluded that the bones were too old to be of any interest to them. By elimination that just left me, as the County Archaeologist, to confirm the woman's identity. The strange thing is, immediately after making his prediction James dropped the entire exercise. He wouldn't talk about it, refused to write any more articles and stayed away from the site.'

'Did he mention Lincolnshire?' Alistair asked.

'Not to me,' Ollie replied. 'I didn't see much of him after he stopped visiting the site.' He gathered his thoughts. 'That's the other odd thing. We hadn't spoken for quite a while, yet he had my phone number scribbled on a torn scrap of paper stuffed in his pocket when he died.'

'Do you know why?'

'The police have asked me the same question several times now. I really have no idea.'

Alistair reported his visit to Lincolnshire and confirmed that the Gould's daughter, Eleanor, had married Samuel.

'That fits,' Ollie confirmed. 'So, it's probably safe to assume that she is our skeleton, though I fear the manner of her untimely death may knock the official version on the head, if you'll forgive the pun.'

'Which is what?'

'That Samuel's wife ran off and left him. Overcome with shame and remorse, the poor man took his own life. My personal theory is that she planned to run away from the brute, he discovered her scheme and bumped her off. Samuel could have faked his own death to account for the burial and disappeared leaving behind the story of a heartbroken husband.' Ollie paused. 'I'm surprised her family never came looking for her.'

'They had troubles of their own,' Alistair replied. 'They ended up murdered too.'

Ollie smiled. 'So, maybe Lowesley isn't a unique breeding ground for the dark myth,' he said. 'I must look into Eleanor's story. I haven't spent much time on her up to now. I'm on my own here and, as you can see, this dig has grown some way beyond a simple exhumation. During the English Reformation, Protestants allegedly sacked and burned the original St Mary's Roman Catholic Priory. The church's fine architecture saved it from destruction and it eventually became re-consecrated as St Michael's. I've been given limited time to investigate before the contractors kick me off the site. I admit I've become a little preoccupied with the priory rather than Eleanor. Thanks for the information.' He looked across to the church. 'James may have given Clive a bit more detail, of course. Why don't you ask him?' Ollie pulled a small trowel from his back pocket.

Alistair sensed that the archaeologist was anxious to make the most of his diminishing time on the site. 'I'm sorry I've kept you from your work,' he said. 'I'll let you know if I learn anything of interest.'

*

Alistair left Ollie to his excavation and walked down to the church. Clive appeared at the door. 'I had called in for a quick word,' Alistair said. 'If this is a bad time, I can come back later.'

'No, no, do come in,' Clive insisted. The vicar ushered Alistair inside. 'Come along, we'll talk in the vestry. How can I help you?'

'I'm rather hoping that you can give me an early date for James's burial,' Alistair replied.

'Regretably I cannot. Delay is a constant feature of life here these days. The archaeologist has also raised a potential difficulty with relocating our historic remains. It seems we have a witch on our hands.'

'I may be able to assist there,' Alistair offered. 'Her name is Eleanor Gould. She moved here from Lincolnshire to marry Samuel Rosemont. Her family were pillars of their community.'

'Excellent,' Clive replied. 'The antiquity of the grave grants its occupant the right to a resting place in the old churchyard. A suspected practitioner of the black arts could not possibly be allowed that privilege.'

'This is the twenty-first century,' Alistair reminded the vicar.

'This is also Lowesley Pryor,' Clive replied. 'I would like tangible evidence of Nellie's faith before I move her to the churchyard.'

Alistair left Clive to his duties and walked home to Bookbinders.

Chapter 35

When Alistair arrived home, he found Marcia busy in the kitchen. 'Dinner's sorted,' she said. 'Chicken and ham quiche and salad. I know it's a little bit early. I thought it might be nice to enjoy it out on the terrace, while the sun is still warm. I know it's simple but I still feel uncomfortable rummaging in Nancy's store cupboard.'

'Treat it as your own. And don't apologise, for your version of simple. You're speaking to a man who screws up poached eggs. Did you sort some wine?'

'Sauvignon blanc in the fridge, but if you prefer red, blow the rules I'm easy.'

'White's fine,' Alistair agreed. 'I'll be down in ten.'

He showered and changed quickly. Marcia carried out the food while Alistair followed with the wine and two thoughtfully chilled glasses from the fridge.

'Didn't work, did it?' Marcia said.

Alistair looked at her. 'It looks delicious,' he said. 'Perfect.'

She smiled. 'I meant the walk. Your eyes tell me, it didn't clear your head.'

'Sorry. When I lifted that loose floorboard I opened up a huge black hole.'

'This isn't a good time for more surprises, is it?' she agreed. 'I wonder why James chose to do it now.'

'He may have written that letter ages ago,' Alistair suggested.

'No, he didn't,' Marcia replied. 'It's fresh ink on clean paper. James hardly mentioned your childhood for thirty-eight years. I wonder what persuaded him to bring it up now.'

'Who knows? Maybe he didn't realise it had been a big deal to me, until he found my letters. I suppose he could have felt guilty in some way. I hope he didn't. It must have been difficult for him to suddenly find me dumped in his life. He never complained and he gave me what he truly believed was the best start I could have.'

'It's possible that the project at St Michael's reminded James of his own mortality,' Marcia said. 'Maybe he saw his time running short and decided you should have closure. He only wanted to talk. There may be nothing new to find.'

'Or maybe his time ran out before he'd told me something crucial,' Alistair countered. 'The inheritance makes me responsible for settling his affairs.' He looked into her eyes. 'I want to know him, who he was, what he was about. I have to look, Marci, but I'm scared of what I may find.'

'You and James were really close for half of your life. I've known him for a good chunk of the rest and I can tell you he was deep, private in some ways, but definitely not scary,' Marcia reassured him. 'You won't find anything nasty about James. The worry is, because you two were so close, you might find things about yourself too. I think that's what may be scaring you a little.'

'I can't let go,' he said. 'We both know James and Caroline were up to something. More than ever now, I have to find out what it was. I owe it to him, to both of them. I really don't want this job, but I have to finish it, solve the puzzle and find him, Marci, I must.'

'What happens after you've solved it, and found whatever you find?' she asked. 'I can see why you may want to tie up your uncle's Eleanor Gould thing, but I sense that you also have another issue that has nothing to do with James. It's none of my business, but I think someone needs to say this. We can't choose our own history, Ali. Running away doesn't change anything. Wherever you go the past, *your* past, travels with you. I've seen the nightmares. You have a ghost to vanquish and it goes way beyond what you found today. Your roots were broken before you came back here. I'm not prying. All I'm saying is Bookbinders may be a good place to put down fresh roots. Don't rush to dismiss Oxton and everything you have here from your plans again.'

'I've given up making plans,' he replied. 'I haven't had much to plan for lately. I thought the inheritance was my opportunity to sell up and ship out, with the wind of fortune in my sails. It's already more complicated than I'd imagined. I don't want to repeat an old mistake.'

'Do you mean a "you and Caroline" sort of mistake?'

'I know there's a big difference between feeling drawn together and being thrown together,' he said. 'Grief, loss, maybe mutual need brought you and me here. We only met a few days ago, but it seems much longer. I'm trained to cope with the unexpected, but James's death and then Caroline's, hit me like a tsunami. I'm sure they had a much bigger impact on you. I think being together has helped, is still helping, both of us.'

'I agree,' Marcia replied. 'I like your company and I've felt safer having you around. It's just maybe… I don't know how to say this Ali,' she admitted. 'I had a bad experience.'

'And you don't know me yet?'

'Nor you me,' she said. 'I'd like us to let things roll and see where we go, but I can't help wondering if perhaps….' She hesitated.

'What?'

'When you saw me at James's funeral, you thought I was Caroline, didn't you? Am I your Caroline substitute, Ali?'

He looked into her searching eyes. 'It's been a long time, and you do look like I imagined she might look by now,' he replied. 'You are you, Marci, a bright, beautiful and very special person, a completely *different* person to Caroline. You are most definitely not any kind of substitute.'

'I had to ask.'

'Of course you did. Was Nick the bad experience?'

Marcia smiled. 'No. Nick is the marketing man who helped set up the new office and showroom. He's a good-looking charmer, superficial, self-obsessed. I'd never have been anything more than a temporary amusement to him, a tiny trophy perhaps. The *bad* experience happened a long time ago, a couple of years after you left Oxton.'

'Do you want to tell me about it?'

Marcia looked into his eyes for a long time before she spoke. 'I was a quiet girl in my teens, as I'm sure you remember, stuck-up, or so everybody thought, too fond of books when I should have been moving on to boys.' Her lip quivered. 'Most of the other girls had boyfriends. Caroline had you. I didn't even have a best friend. Nobody likes being an outcast.'

'I know, believe me,' Alistair replied.

'I wanted to prove I'm normal. He'd asked for a date several times so, in the end, I accepted. We went to a pub called The Green Man, in Meadford. I remember nursing my cider as if I'd won an Oscar. I'd never drunk from a bottle before. The froth kept fizzing up my nose. We chatted for a while, and then he said he had to be up for work early next morning so he was going home. He said, if I wanted to stay, I'd have to make my own way back; from Meadford mind you. It's miles. I'd have been scared stiff by myself.'

'What a gent.'

'He had a bit of a macho reputation. I thought his performance was part of the image. Anyway, he had a car so I went with him. He held the door open for me as I got in. I felt so special. We must have gone nearly ten miles when he pulled off the road. He kissed me and put his hand up my dress. I pushed it away and told him I wasn't that sort of girl. You soon will be, he said. He was suddenly all over me like an octopus.' She grimaced and shuddered. 'I managed to fight him off and get out of the car. He just slammed the door shut, drove off and left me there. It's dark out on the hills. It took me over two hours to walk home.'

'What a louse. You must have been terrified.'

'Terrified and ashamed that I'd been so naive. He turned up again next day and stopped me as I was walking home from sixth form. You owe me, he said. You've had your free ride. You owe me one now.'

'He didn't…?'

'No, but he wouldn't leave me alone. It went on for weeks. His car would cruise past my house. He'd turn up outside school and in town, brushing past for a quick grope. He seemed to be everywhere, and he obviously thought he'd bought a free pass to my knickers.'

'That's stalking, Marci. Did the police pick him up?'

'I didn't report it. I felt dirty. People make assumptions, don't they? I'd been stupid and I paid the price.'

'Who? I mean, he was obviously local. I may have known him.'

'Yes, you did,' she replied. 'His name is Clive Chapman.'

Alistair stared in utter disbelief. 'Clive? He's a vicar.'

'He certainly wasn't a vicar in those days.' Marcia's gaze sank back to her lap. 'I swore I'd never tell and I never have, until now.'

Alistair squeezed her fingers. 'No wonder you left Oxton. I assumed you'd just gone off to uni like the rest of us.'

'I did. I went to live the dream. When I got there, I couldn't hack it. Clive Chapman had made me scared of people my own age.'

'I don't know what to say,' Alistair murmured. 'I'm amazed you ever came near Oxton again.'

'I never would have if I'd thought he'd still be around. Amanda had swept him off his feet and whisked him away by then. It was years before they showed up here again. Who would have believed he could ever have the sheer nerve and as a vicar of all things? Fortunately, this place is well away from his patch. It hasn't been too difficult to stay out of his way.' She wiped away a tear. 'I'm not sure which of us was more surprised when we saw one another. He knew, still knows, I could point him out whenever I choose. I fooled myself into believing that little threat gave me some sort of power over him. All it really gave me was another feeble excuse to keep my secret.'

Alistair looked into her eyes. He didn't reply.

Chapter 36

A uniformed sergeant joined Reid, carrying a mug of tea and a microwave ready meal. 'Dave Gibson,' he said. 'I almost checked to see if you were still alive before I brought these up. It's chicken.'

Reid leaned back on his chair and glanced out through the window. The evening traffic had reached its peak. 'Sorry,' he said, stifling a yawn. 'I got wrapped up in this lot and forgot the time. I think I'm about done.'

Dave Gibson cleared a small space on the desk and set the food down. 'This case sparks a few memories,' he said.

'From 1981?' Reid replied. 'Shouldn't you be drawing your pension by now?'

Gibson smiled. 'Not quite. This job just makes me look old. I wasn't born until the next year, but my parents and me lived close to Stoatley Wood, where the body was found. None of the local kids were allowed to play there when I was growing up. The husband was given a hard time, by us and the local finger wagers. Nothing was ever proved, but mud sticks doesn't it? It was a big event locally for a long time. You must have heard about the case.'

'I grew up in Glasgow,' Reid said as the yawn escaped. 'I came south to join the force. If the story ever made it north of the border, it died down before I came into the world.'

Dave nodded toward the tray. 'You might as well hang on and eat this while the traffic gets away.' He left his visitor returning files to their cartons.

Reid finished re-boxing the files and, since he now had a meal to eat and a little time to kill, he turned his attention to the fourth carton, marked UH3-1047/81 – EXHIBITS, which he had not planned to open. He carefully untied the tape and opened the top flaps. The carton contained several clearly labelled sealed white paper evidence bags. Reid carefully lifted them out and glanced at their labels. Each bag contained a single item of the clothing, Debbie King had been wearing when she was murdered. Reid felt an almost personal contact with the victim as he looked through the collection, pausing for a few moments on exhibit 7 – Yellow silk chiffon scarf. He imagined the fine elegant accessory shielding Debbie's neck from the cool spring breeze, until the moment it tightened and throttled away her life. He carefully repacked and resealed the carton.

*

When Reid arrived back in Oxton, the CID stood in darkness, except for the almost perpetual light burning upstairs in Nash's office. He went inside and ran upstairs to his desk.

Nash followed him into the CID room. 'Anything of interest?' he asked.

'No,' Reid replied. 'I've come in to knock up a summary for you. I'm ready for a brew first. Do you want a cup, or are you leaving?'

'Thanks Alex, I'll hang on and catch the news. Let's hope there's nothing to wind things up here.'

They went to the mess room. Nash switched on the TV, while Reid made tea. The local news carried a short report of the Caroline Blackham murder investigation, but did not mention James Hastings.

'Maybe they'll give us a bit of breathing space,' Nash said as he switched off the TV.

'Aye sir, maybe,' Reid replied. He went back to his computer and logged on. 'I'll knock these notes off and call it a day.'

Nash turned toward his office.

'No need for you to hang around, sir. We can't do any more

tonight. Why don't you go home?'

Nash turned and looked at him. 'You know why, Alex,' he said.

'Aye, sir,' Reid acknowledged. 'I know.'

Chapter 37

Alistair turned to answer the phone beside his bed. 'Speaking… No problem. What can I do for you?' He sat up and slid over to the edge of the mattress. 'Yes of course. I'll be there in a few minutes.' He pulled on his tracksuit pants and a T-shirt, and stepped out onto the landing.

Marcia stood in her bedroom doorway, wrapped in the duvet from her bed. 'What's wrong?' she asked.

'Hopefully nothing,' Alistair replied. 'Somebody has apparently damaged the showroom window and set the alarm off. The police want me to go over there.' Marcia disappeared into her room. 'You don't need to lose any sleep,' he called up to her as he ran downstairs. 'They only need me to check for damage inside the shop.'

She appeared beside him in the hall, now wearing a T-shirt and black joggers, almost before the words had left his lips.

*

Dark shadows cloaked the streets of Oxton. Bookworm stood dark and silent. Alistair drove into Radley Street, turned behind a marked police car and stopped beneath the archway. A ghostly blue tarpaulin hung alongside the metal stairway, masking the back door. Blue and white crime scene tapes fluttered in the light breeze. A torch beam swept across the yard as a police officer approached from beneath the stairs.

'Alistair Dawlish and Marcia Blackham,' Alistair announced.

'Yes, sir.'

'You called,' Alistair said.

'Not me, sir, I've just stopped by to move our tape while the area is quiet.'

Alistair frowned. 'You, or someone from the police, phoned to report some sort of vandalism.'

'I've called in to check the property over a few times,' the officer replied. 'I haven't seen any activity.' He shone his torch over the yard and building. There were no signs of damage. Alistair and Marcia followed the officer around to Bishop's Hill. The shop door and windows appeared secure and undamaged.

'Did the caller give a name, or the agreed password sir?' the officer asked.

Alistair glanced at Marcia, 'I didn't think to ask,' he admitted suddenly feeling stupid.

A muffled explosion, followed by the sound of shattering glass, burst from the back of the shop. The trio raced back to the yard. Flames leapt over the upstairs door and windows. The officer radioed for assistance.

'Move your car,' he shouted to Alistair. 'They'll need access.'

'Quickly, Ali,' Marcia urged. 'Give me the shop keys.'

Alistair flung over the keys and ran to his car. The Mercedes screeched backwards across the road and came to an oblique halt on the opposite pavement. Marcia ran up to the showroom door. Alistair caught up as she fumbled with the key and barged inside. He grabbed the fire extinguisher and raced back to the carriage yard, with Marcia at his shoulder.

Sirens wailed in the distance. Acrid smoke rolled down from the mezzanine. Alistair squirted his feeble extinguisher at the flames. Blue beacons flashed somewhere outside the archway. Fire fighters rushed in from the street. An officer wearing a white helmet ushered Alistair and Marcia away.

When Nash and Reid arrived, fire fighters had already

extinguished the blaze. Steam and smoke curled up from the charred office door. Soot black streaks snaked across the walls. Shattered window glass littered the yard.

'Is the stock damaged?' Marcia asked the chief fire officer. 'There are books in the office and the front rooms.'

'You were lucky,' he replied. 'There's just superficial damage, nothing structural. Your books are safe.'

Nash ushered Alistair and Marcia back to the showroom. 'Why are you here at this time of night?' he asked Alistair.

'Your officer, or someone claiming to be an officer, phoned me at home.'

'Not the police,' Nash said. 'You were lucky it kicked off upstairs. It might have been very expensive if it had started in here. This is bound to crank up the tension, especially with so many strangers rolling up.'

'What strangers?' Alistair asked.

'We cancelled that book fair too late to stop people turning up. They're camping over near Stowe. With things as they are, strangers, including you right now, might attract unfriendly attention.'

The doorbell clanged. Reid stepped into the showroom. 'Ambulances have left, sir,' he said. 'The Fire Service will be away in a few minutes.' He turned to Alistair. 'The back doors and windows will need boarding, Commander. I have a set of keys. If you give me your insurance details, I'll get things organised for you.'

Alistair turned to Marcia.

'It's Chieftain Commercial,' she said. 'The details are in my bottom right desk drawer, black wallet under, I.'

'Thank you, Sergeant,' Alistair added. 'We appreciate your help.'

'It's my pleasure, sir. I'd go home now if I were you. We'll see to things here.'

*

Alistair drove past a stationary police car and parked in front of the workshop. A soft bumping sound caught his attention as he and

Marcia hurried along the shrubbery path to the terrace. They stopped as they saw the French door, swinging against its frame. Alistair scanned along the shrubbery and across the terrace. Tiny specks of light shimmered like feline eyes on the glossy leaves of a holly bush. Marcia's fingers tightened on Alistair's shoulder.

Footsteps approached from somewhere beyond the house, then stopped. Sounds of snapping twigs echoed on the gorge side below the workshop. Alistair vaulted the low fence and hurtled down amid dust and flying leaf litter until he crashed against a large tree. Scrambling feet receded toward the river below him. Sounds of angry voices and clattering furniture drew his attention back to the terrace. He scrambled up, using ivies and low branches to haul himself over the loose surface.

'Marci, are you okay?' he shouted. She didn't reply. He grabbed the fence and vaulted over. Marcia knelt holding a slightly built figure, face down, against the terrace.

'Would you like me to take it from here?' Alistair asked.

Marcia released her grip on the intruder's hair and stepped away.

Alistair stared down at the panting figure. 'I'm sure you can explain, can't you?' he demanded. 'Now please, Ms Maylor.'

The reporter glared up at him.

Marcia phoned Reid's direct number. 'Sergeant Reid, we have an Archangel problem at The Bookbinder's House,' she said a little breathlessly.

Alistair waved April Maylor to her feet. 'I'm waiting for an answer,' he said.

The reporter stood brushing dirt from her scuffed cheek. 'I'll admit I was in your garden,' she replied with an exasperated and deeply annoying huff.

'No, Ms Maylor, you *are* in my garden,' Alistair corrected. 'I'm asking where you *were,* before I arrived.'

A uniformed constable appeared from the lane and stopped with a jolt. 'CID is on the way, sir,' he said. 'I've been watching the house from across the road. I didn't see anything unusual.'

'He left as I arrived,' April said.

'Why exactly did you come here?' Alistair demanded.

'I'm a journalist,' she replied as if it should have been obvious. 'The town is buzzing with tales of an avenging witch. The person who lived here has been poking around her grave. Now he's dead and the police are constantly back and forth to his shop. When I saw the constable leaving, I thought I'd take a look around.'

'I did leave for a few minutes,' the officer confirmed. 'My sergeant sent me to another job. I wasn't away long.'

'Plod,' April mumbled.

Alistair rounded on her. 'It's two o'clock in the morning,' he said. 'This is private property and someone has forced my French door open. I demand an explanation.'

'Maybe the constable can assist,' she said. 'When I arrived, somebody had already broken into your house. The intruder might have walked straight past him.'

'The only people who walked past me tonight were Commander Dawlish and Ms Blackham,' the officer insisted. 'If anyone else had approached this property, I would have seen them.'

'You didn't see me,' April replied, turning back to Alistair. 'As I've already said at least once, I came here to look around, that's all. As I arrived on your patio, someone ran from the house and disappeared beside that old shed thing. I thought it was you, Commander, and since you'd been kind enough to leave the door open, I took a peep inside. The mess told me you'd had an uninvited visitor, so I decided to push off before I collected the blame for anything. When I got to the road, the police car was back. The only other way out of here is along the gorge. I didn't fancy that, so I came back to hide until the coast cleared. Then you turned up and I was marooned. When you charged at me, I panicked and ran. I almost broke my neck down there.'

'So you decided not to risk following your partner down to the river?'

'What partner? I certainly didn't plan to die for *The Chronicle*. I came here to find a story not to become one.' April glared at Marcia. 'I would have left without a fuss, if she hadn't leapt on me. I think I fell on my recorder.'

'I'll never forgive myself,' Marcia huffed, sarcastically.

Flashing blue light swept across the shrubbery and workshop. Nash and Reid ran onto the terrace followed by two uniformed officers, who proceeded to scan the gorge with powerful torches.

'Burglary is going to look really good on your CV, April,' Nash said. 'What were you after?'

'A story, what else.' She held up her hands. 'Look, no gloves. I haven't touched a thing. I guarantee you won't find one print or an atom of my DNA in there. You might find my face print on these slabs though.'

'We'll see what the SOCO report says.' Nash nodded to a constable, who took April by the arm and led her away.

*

Several of James's prized books littered the lounge floor and coffee table. Drawers slumped open and disarrayed. Officers reported similar disturbance, together with minor damage to a few photographs, in the upstairs rooms. Oddly, despite what had plainly been a thorough search, it seemed that nothing had been taken.

'Did you check the phone?' Nash asked one of his constables.

'Yes, sir,' the officer confirmed. 'Incoming call logged at 12.51, from Caroline Blackham's missing phone.'

'April didn't do this,' Nash said. 'She's a nosey pest, not a stupid one. We received a report of some disturbance at St Michael's, obviously a false alarm. I'd guess that April saw the constable leave then came around here and disturbed your intruder. My officers will search her and her car. I guarantee they won't find that phone, or anything from your house.'

'I heard someone down near the river,' Alistair said. 'If we discount April Maylor, are we looking for two other people?'

'Not necessarily,' Nash replied. 'We couldn't justify a permanent police presence at the bookshop, although it's a recent murder scene. We've had officers calling by to make random checks. I reckon the fire bomber waited until our man completed an inspection then planted his device and came over here. He got rid of you with that nonsense about vandalism then spun another yarn to lure the constable away. With the house empty and unsupervised, in he came. He hadn't planned on April's arrival, not many people do.'

'You think the Bookworm device was remotely detonated?' Alistair asked.

Nash nodded, 'A simple phone call and whoosh, up went the shop.'

'You think it was just a warning?'

'A minor distraction I'd say,' Nash replied. 'Enough to keep you occupied over there while he had a look around in here, and once again apparently took nothing.' He turned to Marcia. 'Are you quite sure that neither your sister nor Dr Hastings mentioned finding anything recently?'

She shook her head. 'Not a thing,' she replied.

Chapter 38

Alistair's ringtone shattered his brief doze at five-thirty next morning. He reached for his phone and swung his legs out of bed.

'Oh hello, Kelly,' he mumbled.

'You all right. Alistair?' his landlady chirped. 'You sound tired.'

'It's rather early. What can I do for you?'

'I'm sorry to disturb your holiday. Somebody burgled your flat last night.'

He shot to his feet. 'What happened?' he asked, barely managing to control a sudden tide of panic.

'Well, I closed the salon as normal at around seven. I went up and checked the place over before I left, like you asked me to. Everything was fine. Vijay from the shop next door phoned to tell me the alarm was going off just after midnight. Good job too, or your flat would have been open all night.'

'Is there much damage?'

'It hasn't improved the place much, that's for sure. Your stuff was scattered everywhere. I don't think they took much but it's hard to tell now the police have been tramping all over the flat. One of them said the flat smelled funny, cheeky sod. I've never known anybody fussier about cleanliness than you are. Mind you, I stuck my head in for a quick look after they'd gone and there was a bit of a rubbing oil pong. Nothing to do with you. Anyway, I've hung around to keep my eye on things and I've tidied up a bit for you.'

'No don't,' Alistair blurted. 'I'll come straight over. Don't go to any trouble.'

'No bother,' she chirped. 'Everything's under control. The men are coming to fit your new door first thing this morning. There's no need for you to rush over. The thing is, when you do come back, you'll have to turn up while I'm here, because of the new lock and that.'

'I'm on my way. Thanks for letting me know.' He rang off and slammed the phone down. 'I don't believe it,' he groaned.

Alistair's bedroom door creaked open. Marcia stepped in, sleepy eyed and duvet clad. 'Problem?' she asked. 'You sounded upset.'

'That was Kelly, my landlady,' Alistair replied as he headed for the bathroom door. 'She's at my flat. Somebody turned the place over last night. I have to get over there.'

'Calm down,' Marcia urged. 'There's no major panic if your landlady is there.'

'I need to know if anything's missing,' he called from the bathroom. 'Then I must get back to Bookworm. The contractors are coming to repair the fire damage and start the other work this morning.'

'Take your time,' Marcia shouted. 'I can open up. I need to go in and check for damaged stock.'

'No,' Alistair insisted. 'I don't want you there on your own. The stock can wait. If I get a move on, I'll be back in time for the contractors.'

*

Alistair's spirits slumped as normal when he approached the flat. Kelly materialised alongside the car, in all her high-definition vulgarity, before he had released his seatbelt. She greeted her tenant with a scarlet lipped vampire-like grin.

'Sorry I had to bother you,' she said, fumbling between her breasts. She retrieved a key and dangled it from her crimson talons. 'Careful,' she chirped. 'It's hot. They've fitted your new door. The place is secure again. I told you not to rush over.'

'Thanks, Kelly. I really appreciate what you've done but I have to check things out for myself.' He sprinted upstairs.

Every cupboard in his kitchen stood open. Someone, presumably Kelly, had filled a bin liner with damaged bits and pieces gathered from the floor, and packed surviving items into two cardboard boxes on the worktop. Salvaged crockery stood washed and neatly racked in the drainer. The white loose covers had disappeared from his furniture, no doubt into Kelly's laundry basket. More worryingly, his landlady had apparently given the flat a thorough vacuuming. Alistair ran to his bedroom. Gratitude veered toward despair when he saw fresh bed linen. He ran over, reached in a full arm's length beneath the mattress and retrieved a document. His pulse slowed a little. He wandered through the flat, clutching the papers in his hand. The intruder had managed to break in, search and leave unseen, yet the computer and other high value items remained apparently untouched. 'What were you looking for?' he whispered.

He had no time to ponder the question. The contractors would soon be arriving at Bookworm. He folded his retrieved document, slipped it into his pocket and left.

Chapter 39

Reid tapped on Nash's office door and stepped in carrying a printout. 'Fax from Lincolnshire, sir. They've been keeping an eye on Barnaby Dolman, as requested. They followed him last night.'

Nash looked up from his monitor. 'And?' Reid didn't reply. 'Come on, Alex, you can tell me, I'm a policeman. I could use a bit of good news about now. Where did he go?'

'Toward Newark, sir.'

'What's there?'

'The force boundary, sir. They couldn't follow him any further.'

The germinating smile withered on Nash's face. 'Did they pass him over to Notts?'

'No sir. They had no good reason to follow him at all. We can't ignore the man's human rights.'

'He was heading this way.'

'Aye, sir. Unfortunately, he was still eighty miles away.'

Nash took out a handkerchief and blotted perspiration from his neck. 'Barnaby Dolman had close contact with our victims,' he reminded Reid. 'Something about that contact apparently gave Dr Hastings a serious bout of collywobbles.'

'Anything might have made Dr Hastings cagey,' Reid replied. 'Even if something about that trip to Lincolnshire did disturb him, we have no evidence it had anything to do with Barnaby Dolman.'

'You think it was coincidence?'

'I don't know, sir. All I'm saying is it may be.'

Nash glared. 'Okay, so you're right, as usual,' he conceded. 'I'd still like to know where he was going.'

Chapter 40

Fire had shattered every pane in the Bookworm office windows and mezzanine door. Sturdy security shutters cloaked the room in sullen darkness. Clammy odours of charred timber and residual dampness lingered in the air. Soot clung like a grimy smoke spun web to the walls and ceiling. Dust and splintered glass covered James's desk. Alistair switched on the lights, found a soot-soiled hand towel and waste bin in the upstairs kitchen and began clearing debris.

Vehicle doors slammed shut in the carriage yard. Something crashed against the wall. The window shutter creaked and fell down onto the mezzanine. A shaft of dust-filled daylight streamed into the office. A face peered in through the empty window frame.

'Oops,' the man said. 'I didn't think anybody was here. I'm Gary, from Reynolds'. The missing link downstairs is Nigel.'

'I've parked at the supermarket to give you a bit more space,' Alistair replied.

'Thanks. I wouldn't bother with any cleaning up just yet, Captain,' Gary said, nodding to the towel in Alistair's hand. 'You could put the kettle on though, if you like.'

Alistair dropped his towel into the bin and left the men removing shutters.

Incoming draught swept the depressing stench downstairs. He opened the back door to refresh the air, made coffee and took two mugs up to the office.

Alistair glanced out over the yard. The ghostly man he had met briefly on his first visit to the shop, stood gazing up from the shadow of the archway. His expressionless eye scanned across to the window, where Alistair stood watching. They made split second eye contact before the man retreated and disappeared.

Alistair returned downstairs to kill time and maybe spark some enthusiasm, browsing the showroom shelves. Noise, dust and a musical brainstorm wailing from Gary's radio, drove him away to the kitchen within minutes. Soot covered several of the books Marcia had taken to the old desk. Alistair began flicking off superficial debris with paper kitchen towel and quickly gave up, fearing that his unskilled efforts might inflict more damage. He gave the dresser a wipe over and gazed around in search of a different time-filler. *I suppose, if I'm careful, I could have a browse through some of the good stuff*, he thought. *Maybe it will kick-start my enthusiasm.*

He made more coffee and took fresh mugs up to Gary and Nigel. Dustsheets covered every open surface in the office. Breeze drifted in through a gaping hole where the mezzanine door and window had been.

'We'll need to nip out for a few bits and bobs to get a temporary alarm on for tonight,' Gary said. 'We won't be away more than an hour, but you'll need to keep your eyes peeled. Some nosey creep keeps wandering into the yard and this hole is a bit of an invitation.'

Alistair returned downstairs and closed the doors to the showroom and the carriage yard. He swung the dresser aside and entered the strongroom door code. The hiss of air, as the door swung open, triggered an unexpected buzz of excitement. Alistair pulled on a clean pair of cotton gloves from the pack on the centre shelf, selected a box at random and carried it over to the table. Sooty dust swirled in a shaft of sunlight from the window. *Best not risk it*, he thought.

He returned the box to the strongroom, lifted the precious volume out onto the shelf and eased open the creaky leather cover. Superb artistry seized his attention. Illuminated designs, protected from harsh light throughout their long life, gleamed with breathtaking colour. Alistair was instantly engrossed.

A breath of air lifted the page beneath his gloved fingers. Faint, vaguely remembered odour wafted past his nose. The shadow caught Alistair's attention a second too late as the arm seized his neck and squeezed, cutting off the blood supply to his brain. He gasped, tried to turn but was pressed hard against the shelf. The strongroom swayed, resistance ebbed from his body, his brain became a surreal slow-motion whirlpool, consciousness slipped away.

Chapter 41

Vehicle doors clanged shut in the carriage yard. Aiden Gale stepped out from the kitchen as Gary and Nigel disappeared up the mezzanine stairs. He followed them to the office.

'Do you have any idea where Alistair might be?' he asked. 'I expected to find him here.'

'Perhaps he's slipped out for lunch,' Gary suggested.

'It is possible, I suppose,' Aiden said glancing down into the yard. 'His car isn't here.'

'He's parked at the supermarket,' Gary replied, rearranging the dustsheet on James's desk. 'I see he's been poking around in here while he had the place to himself.'

'Poking around?'

'Trying to tidy up I suppose. He does like things shipshape, doesn't he? I found him tarting around with a duster when I arrived this morning. Maybe he's popped out for a pint, to lay the dust. I wouldn't mind joining him.'

'Did he have a woman with him?'

Gary checked with Nigel. Neither of them had seen a woman.

Aiden decided to walk over and look for Alistair or his car at the supermarket, even though he had no idea of the car's registration number. He spoke to several shoppers but, since hardly anyone in town knew Alistair, the effort drew a blank. Aiden gave up and returned to Bookworm.

He paced the kitchen and showroom, tidying, flicking a duster and fretting. When Alistair had not returned after another hour, Aiden called Bookbinders.

'Ah, Marcia,' he said, 'I rather hoped to have a word with Alistair.'

'Try Bookworm,' she suggested. 'He'll be there all day.'

'I am at the shop now,' Aiden replied. 'There is no sign of Alistair.'

'He definitely planned on being at the shop, to open up for the contractors,' Marcia replied.

'Gary Jennings has confirmed that Alistair was here when he and Nigel arrived,' Aiden said. 'He apparently left some time later, while the men were absent.'

'Hang on,' Marcia replied. 'I'll try his mobile.'

A phone rang beneath a discarded kitchen towel on the desk. Aiden picked it up. 'Congratulations my dear,' he said. 'I have the phone. Alas, its owner remains absent.'

'Something isn't right,' Marcia said. 'Why would he leave without his phone?'

'Who knows?' Aiden replied. 'When I arrived, I found the back door and the entire upper storey open to intruders. Surely Alistair would not leave the premises unattended.'

'Ali's flat was burgled last night,' Marcia explained. 'He went over there early this morning. I suppose the police may have called him back. He definitely planned to be at Bookworm all day.'

'But I found the kitchen door open wide,' Aiden repeated.

'Maybe Reynolds' men left it open,' Marcia suggested, sounding uncertain.

'They say not. Do you have a landline number for Alistair's flat?' Aiden waited while Marcia checked through the index.

'Nothing listed,' she said. 'Nancy is out. Give me a few minutes. I'll see if it's been entered on the wrong page. James could be quite haphazard.'

She rang off, flicked the index open again and ran her finger over pages of James's friends, business associates, academic colleagues and several names she didn't recognise. She finally paused at a possible useful number and tapped the digits into her keypad.

A bright young female voice answered. 'Thomas Nightingale and Thomas, Solicitors. How may I help you?'

'I'm an associate of Dr James Hastings,' Marcia replied. 'We have a family emergency. I need to speak with Dr Hastings' nephew, Commander Alistair Dawlish. Would you mind telling me the commander's home telephone number please?'

'I'm very sorry,' the receptionist replied. 'We aren't allowed to disclose information regarding clients.'

'This is an emergency.'

'We must respect client confidentiality. You could be the press.'

'You have Dr Hastings' details on your files,' Marcia replied. 'Phone me on his private number. That will prove who I am.'

'I daren't,' the receptionist insisted. With a final apology that she really could not assist, she terminated the call.

Marcia had fallen into deep despondency when the phone rang. An unexpected voice greeted her.

'Hello, Ms Blackham, it's Owen Thomas. Did you manage to contact Commander Dawlish?'

'No,' she confirmed bluntly.

'I really am very sorry I can't release the commander's telephone number,' the solicitor said. 'Would you like me to try it for you? If the commander is at his flat, I'll ask him to contact you.'

'You're very kind,' Marcia replied with huge relief. 'Please hurry.'

An age seemed to pass before Marcia's phone rang again. Her pulse raced. She connected hoping to hear Alistair's voice.

'Hello Ms Blackham, it's Owen Thomas again. No luck I'm afraid. I've spoken to the commander's landlady. Apparently, he called in briefly this morning and hasn't returned.'

Marcia rang off and hit the Bookworm number. She wasted no time on pleasantries. 'Aiden, is Alistair back yet?' she asked.

'No, I was hoping that perhaps…'

'Never mind. I'm going to phone the police. Can you wait there for them?'

'Of course.'

'Thanks, I'm on my way.'

*

Gary and Nigel had begun replacing their security shutters when Nash's car drew into the carriage yard, Reid ran upstairs to speak with the men before they left.

'We've found the Mercedes on the supermarket car park,' Nash confirmed as he stepped into the kitchen. 'If the commander left of his own accord, he probably isn't very far away. How long has he been missing?'

'He was absent when I arrived at twelve-thirty,' Aiden confirmed.

Reid returned from upstairs and reported that Gary and Nigel left to collect materials soon after Alistair took coffee up at a little after eleven o'clock. 'They left the upstairs door off while they were away,' he said. 'Anyone could have walked in. Gary Jennings mentioned some guy who had already turned up a few times before they left.'

'Any description?' Nash asked.

'According to Jennings, the chap looks as if he's at death's door.' Reid read from his notebook. 'Tall, thin and bald, sickly looking.'

'I believe you are describing Peter Christy,' Aiden said. 'Gary Jennings' observation is sadly accurate. Poor Peter is terminally ill.'

'Why would he be hanging around here?' Nash asked.

'Curiosity I imagine,' Aiden replied. 'He and James struck up a friendship during the project at St Michael's. The man is facing a lonely death. James and I offered a little compassionate friendship. We don't know him well.'

Reid made a note. 'Do you know where he lives?'

'I believe he has a flat in or near Crockerby. I cannot be more precise.'

Nash looked at his watch. 'So, if Commander Dawlish left after taking coffee to the men upstairs, he might have been absent for close on five hours. Why has it taken so long for someone to contact us?'

'I… Several people have been attempting to locate him.'

'You should have informed us immediately,' Nash said striding toward the showroom with Aiden sheepishly following. The DCI gazed around with belligerent frustration in his eyes. 'Just look at this place,' he said. 'Apart from a bit of sawdust on the outside stairs, it's like an operating theatre. Maybe if someone had thought to call us an hour or two before the chippies cleaned up, there may have been some sort of clue.'

'I regret that I have also done a little tidying, to pass the time,' Aiden admitted.

Nash snorted and shook his head.

*

Marcia arrived as the detectives were leaving. Nash thanked her for finally calling the police. 'Do you have any idea where the commander might be?' he asked.

'I don't,' Marcia replied. 'He was very agitated when he left the house this morning.'

'Did you have a row?'

'No. There had been a break-in at Alistair's flat. He seemed anxious to get over there. We know he came back here.'

'Do you think he might just walk away and disappear?' Nash asked.

'Alistair is obviously feeling under pressure, as you may imagine, Chief Inspector.' She chewed her lip. Deep concern dulled her eyes. 'Why didn't he take his car or his phone?' she murmured. 'Maybe he doesn't want to be found. Maybe he can't come back.'

'Let's not get morbid just yet,' Nash said. 'We'll check out all the possibilities.' Reid picked up Alistair's phone. He and Nash left.

'He didn't leave here voluntarily,' Marcia said firmly. 'Something isn't right.'

'You sound quite certain, my dear,' Aiden replied, fixing her with his foxy stare. 'Are you aware of something that may have driven

Alistair away?'

'No,' she replied. 'He's keen to complete Cal and James's research into that grave at St Michael's. There may be nothing to find. We haven't come across any notes, but Ali thinks there's a valuable book in the mix. He'd certainly welcome a trivial distraction right now.'

'James rarely wasted his time or effort on trivia,' Aiden replied.

'He did have an impulsive adolescent streak,' Marcia reminded him. 'It's what made James James. Maybe Ali shares the gene.' She blotted a welling tear. 'Why didn't he leave a note, Aiden? What if he's…? Please don't let him be dead.'

'I suggest you dismiss dark thoughts,' Aiden advised. 'These situations often appear more serious than they truly are. We must not prejudge the outcome of police enquiries.'

'I need to know he's safe,' Maria said desperately as tears flooded onto her cheeks. 'I don't think I could stand another…'

'What are these doing here?' Aiden asked drawing Marcia's attention to the books piled on the desk. 'There are some reasonable items among them.'

She dried her eyes. 'I put them there,' she said. 'Alistair wants the stock checked and valued. I've begun sorting out a few things.' She ran her finger over a soiled book cover. 'I see he's begun cleaning them.' She rested her finger where his had been.

'A distraction might ease your anxiety,' Aiden suggested. 'I would be happy to offer an opinion on the premium stock.'

'Thank you, Aiden,' Marcia replied, forcing a sad smile. 'I will need your help but this isn't the time.'

Chapter 42

Hazy consciousness returned. Alistair forced his eyes open and stared at a wall of darkness. His fingers felt odd. Like they're in gloves, he thought rubbing his hands together. And they are. Why am I wearing gloves? Where am I? He pulled the gloves off and reached out, tentatively groping, stroking.

Horizontal, I'm lying on my right side. Can't stretch. Head and feet crammed against hard surfaces, cold. Space feels around... metre long... half metre deep... half metre high. Box, It's a metal box. His hand touched something a few centimetres above his left shoulder. Corrugated? No, spaces, I feel spaces, and rods, metal rods. He examined, warily. No, not rods... Too thin. Wires, horizontal. It's a wire shelf.

His hand moved more urgently, searching, mapping. He touched something close to his face, metallic, rectangular, slightly raised. He gasped. It feels like... It can't be, mustn't be, but it is. It's the lock cover. This is the strongroom door. Holy shark shit, I'm in the strongroom.

Panic surged. He pushed, once, twice. The door didn't budge. He drew in a breath, prepared to shout then exhaled slowly. Stay calm, Dawlish. Don't shout. Mustn't waste air. No one will hear through a hundred millimetres of steel. Salty sweat trickled into his eyes. The strongroom door ran wet with condensed breath. Ageing books exuded a tomblike odour of decay. Alistair sniffed the stench of smoke clinging to his shirt. How long have I been in here, he wondered? How much air have I used up already? How much time? Breathe slowly. Slow and shallow. Save your air. This could be the big goodnight.

*

Conversation had dwindled to sighs and mournful shared glances each time Marcia returned from another searching stare across the carriage yard. Aiden reminded her that the police had found Alistair's car nearby. They would find him. She finally gave a reluctant nod and agreed they may as well go home.

Aiden kissed her cheek and left quietly.

Marcia watched the Jaguar disappear beneath the arch and closed her eyes, almost resorting to silent prayer before she set the alarms, locked the back door and wrenched herself away. She returned to Bookbinders, and held Nancy's hand through the long and sleepless night.

Chapter 43

Marcia returned early to Bookworm. Grim grey shutters covered a gaping hole in the fire scarred office wall, like surgical dressings. Wounded and forlorn, Bookworm seemed to share her sense of foreboding.

An eerie chill gripped the kitchen. Marcia slumped against the sink and remained there until Gary and Nigel arrived, in depressingly good humour, shortly before eight o'clock.

Aiden tapped on the kitchen window a few minutes later. He stepped inside and set about making coffee, while Marcia phoned the police for an update. There had been no developments.

She ended the call and slumped again. 'He had some big issue keeping him awake at night, even before the shocks of Cal and James's deaths hit him,' she murmured sadly. 'I'm afraid he may have done something awful.'

'Such dreadful thoughts will not assist Alistair or us,' Aiden replied stroking her shoulder. 'We must try to remain optimistic. Perhaps this is an appropriate time to turn our thoughts to those precious strongroom rarities.'

Marcia turned and walked away. 'I really can't think about books,' she said. 'Positive thoughts aren't on my agenda right now. I'm sure you can find important positive things to do elsewhere.'

'None more important than this,' he replied. 'I will not leave you here alone.'

'You're a good friend,' she replied with a shaky smile. 'I appreciate your company. I suppose, if you're willing to give me your valuable time, I shouldn't waste it. Maybe Alistair wouldn't mind.'

She swung the dresser aside, entered the code and turned the handle. The door opened. Interior lights glared into life. Marcia half gasped half yelped. Alistair lay curled, fists clenched, arms folded across his chest like a stillborn foetus. A wave of stale air and body odour flooded the kitchen.

*

Sudden brightness forced Alistair's eyes tight shut. He licked his parched lips. His eyelids slowly parted. He squinted. An image floated in a sea of blinding light before him. Female, pale golden hair, intense sapphire eyes. Could it be an angel? A slender hand reached toward him. Sweet citrus perfume stroked his nose. The hand closed, soft and warm, around his. 'Marci?' he croaked. 'Am I alive?'

'Oh yes,' she replied swallowing a tear. 'I can hardly believe it, but yes, Ali, you are alive.'

A sudden muscle spasm wrenched him from her grip. He tumbled out onto the kitchen floor. Marcia fell to her knees beside him. He half rolled, half writhed, onto his knees, where he remained panting, trembling, flexing his cramped joints, forcing blood to his starved muscles until finally, with Marcia's arm for support, he stood and shuffled to the table.

'Sit down, Ali, please,' she urged. 'Don't try to move. I'll call an ambulance.'

'I don't need an ambulance,' he insisted. 'I'll be fine.' He lurched over to the sink, filled a mug with water and drank it down in a single swallow. He refilled and emptied it twice more before he set down the mug and stood clutching the sink edge.

Marcia ran to support him. 'Ali, please come and sit down,' she urged. 'You've been crammed in there for hours. You must have almost suffocated.'

'Almost, but not quite,' he replied. 'I just need to get moving.'

He turned and forced his legs into robotic motion. Marcia stood hands poised to catch him if he fell. Step by fitful step, he reached the corner of the kitchen rested for a moment and tottered on, clattering against walls and furniture, to complete the circuit. He paused, flexing and testing his joints, confirming that his body would not instantly snap back into its foetal curl. He flopped down onto a chair at the table.

'I told you I'd be fine,' he said, massaging his legs.

'You did,' Marcia agreed as she picked up her phone and called the police.

'Why?' Alistair asked.

'Possibly theft,' Aiden suggested glancing toward the open strongroom.

The precious books, along with their boxes and silk covers littered the top shelf like strewn litter. Marcia clasped her fingers to her mouth and stared.

Aiden walked over to count the books. 'There are twenty-six,' he said turning to Marcia.

'Twenty-six is correct,' she confirmed. 'There's nothing missing again.'

Alistair yawned. 'So, if the intruder is searching for a book, it isn't one of those.'

'Marcia tells me that James may have discovered something in Lincolnshire,' Aiden said.

'If he did, we haven't found out what it is,' Alistair replied. 'Mind you, I must confirm that my knowledge of James's affairs is spectacularly incomplete.'

*

Nash's car drew up in the carriage yard. He and Reid hurried over to the kitchen.

'You've had a close call, Commander,' Nash said. 'You really didn't need to take such extreme steps to attract my attention.'

'I'll bear that in mind,' Alistair replied with a smile. 'He surprised me with some sort of strangle hold. He'd obviously done it before, or I'd have had time to put up more of a fight.'

'You didn't see him at all?'

'No, but I'm sure I recognised an odour, just for a split second. Peter Christy had the same one when I met him here. My landlady reported what might have been a similar smell, like rubbing oil she said, in my flat after the recent break in.'

'This is way up the scale from intimidation,' Nash said. 'A straightforward robber would have just left you on the floor and got on with it. This attacker made sure you weren't missed until he'd had time for a thorough search and a proper escape. This was almost certainly the person who now has Caroline Blackham's phone. We've seen his work. He's organised and he's deadly.'

Reid handed back Alistair's shop keys and phone. All calls to and from the phone had been traced to people with firm alibis.

Nash turned to Aiden. 'I'd like to have a word with that Christy person you mentioned,' he said. 'If he contacts you, or if you happen to discover his whereabouts, I expect to hear from you, *immediately* next time, Mr Gale. Old information is cold information. Have I made myself clear?'

'Abundantly, Chief Inspector,' Aiden replied with deeply uncharacteristic humility.

The detectives left.

'Nash sounded a bit miffed at you,' Alistair commented to Aiden. 'What have you done to upset him?'

'Several hours passed before Marcia called the police yesterday. I should have reported you missing much sooner.'

'I'm just grateful that you were here to raise the alarm at all. Thank you. Why were you here?'

'It seems so irrelevant now,' Aiden replied. 'I came to repeat my offer of assistance. Bookworm is very dear to me.'

Alistair yawned. 'Yesterday I would have said no thank you,' he admitted. 'Right now, I seem to have someone using a jackhammer to escape from inside my head. My legs don't seem to be taking incoming calls from my brain. If the offer is still open, Marcia and I would appreciate your assistance.'

'It will be my pleasure,' Aiden said with a smile. 'Perhaps this is an appropriate moment to begin. If you are quite determined to refuse medical attention, I suggest that, at the very least, you go home and rest.'

Alistair handed over the shop keys that Reid had returned.

*

Marcia supported Alistair across to her car. 'Hop in,' she said brightly. 'Let's get you away from here.'

'Bad idea,' he replied sniffing at his shirt. 'I'm laying a scent trail like a startled skunk. I'll take my own car.'

'Don't be ridiculous. You can hardly stand.'

'Of course I can stand,' he insisted as he wobbled over to the archway barely managing a final lunge into its shadow before he fell against the wall. Marcia ran over and somehow held him vertical until his shallow gasps had slowed a little. His gaze darted from the yard to the street and then to Marcia. 'Just give me a minute,' he said. 'I must get to my car.'

'Forget your car,' Marcia said, fixing him with a firm stare. 'You're in no state to drive anywhere.' He jerked to determined, though barely stable, attention. 'Alistair, you haven't eaten for over twenty-four hours,' she reminded him. 'I can't imagine what your body must feel like. Just wait there.' She relaxed her grip. His legs quivered and then buckled slightly. Marcia ran back to her car, scrambled in and drove beneath the archway. She leaned over and pushed open the passenger door. 'Come on,' she urged. 'Nobody can see you. Get in.' He didn't move. Marcia began scrambling across to assist.

Alistair raised his hand. 'No!' he said. 'I can do it myself. Stay there.' He took a few grim-faced seconds to steady his legs then lurched forward, fell into the car and almost slid into the foot-well. Marcia reached over him, slammed the door shut and stamped on the accelerator. The car bounced out into the road and screamed away.

vehicles littered the hospital roadways.

'Excellent,' Alistair said, checking in his mirror. 'He's still with us. Keep your eyes peeled and nip into the first gap you come to after the next bend.'

Marcia swung left and turned into a space so sharply that Alistair's head struck the side window. 'Thanks for that,' he said rubbing his temple. 'Now keep your head down.'

The grey car raced up and sped on past the mini. Alistair read the registration, fumbled in the glove box for a pen and wrote the number on his hand.

'Right,' Marcia said. 'Let's see how he likes being followed.'

She shot off in pursuit. The grey car disappeared out onto the road as a delivery van turned into the hospital. Marcia stamped on the brake. Her car swung sideways and screeched to a halt inches in front of the van. The driver waited, shaking his head, until Marcia moved over to the kerb. She beat her fists on the steering wheel. 'Shit, shit, shit,' she hissed. 'He got away.'

'It doesn't matter,' Alistair replied. 'We have the registration number and he'll know were on to him now, so he may back off.' He phoned Reid to report the incident and the car's registration details. 'Can we go home now?' he said. 'Slowly please.'

*

Marcia turned off to Lowesley Pryor.

'What about my car?' Alistair asked.

'You're in no state to drive and your car is perfectly safe where it is,' Marcia replied.

As they passed St Michael's, Alistair noticed a newly opened plot near the yew tree. Clive Chapman was standing near James's plot.

'Pull over,' Alistair said. 'The police must have finished with James by now. I need to have a word about the funeral.'

'Does it have to be right this minute?' Marcia queried. 'You almost qualified for your own funeral, a few hours ago. I'm sure it can wait until you've rested.'

'I'm fine,' he insisted. 'It won't take a minute.'

Marcia stopped the car. 'I'll wait here,' she said.

Heavy boards covered James's plot. Clive smiled as Alistair joined him. 'I was coming to see you later,' he said. 'James's body has been released. With your approval, Warren Hinchcliffe can accommodate James's funeral at two o'clock next Wednesday, the 24th. I'm just checking that the plot is still sound.'

'Excellent,' Alistair replied. 'Good news at last.'

'For you at least,' Clive replied. 'I hoped to find Ollie Grainger here. I arranged to open up that plot over by the yew tree, for Eleanor Rosemont, on Ollie's assurance that he would confirm her Christian credentials and release her body for re-interment in a day or so. The poor old tree is standing with its roots exposed, and open graves are a serious hazard. Ollie apparently hasn't been here all day.' Alistair fought to suppress a yawn. 'Are you all right, Alistair?' Clive asked.

'Yes of course, preoccupied that's all. We've had a bit of a fire at the shop, nothing serious. I was on my way home to shower when I saw your car. Would it be possible for me to examine your parish records for 1800 to 1841?' Alistair asked.

'Certainly, they're in three cartons, at your bookshop,' Clive replied. 'James very kindly offered to look after them while work is going on here. I believe he has a large safe on the premises.'

Alistair stifled a gasp. 'Yes, I believe so. Sorry, Clive, I really do need that shower,' he said. 'I mustn't keep you.'

*

Alistair turned up the heat, showered and shaved. The bathroom mirror finally showed a facade of restored normality. He went to his room, dumped his soiled clothes in the linen bin and put on a clean shirt and chinos. A small and depressingly familiar car drew up on the road beyond the lane. Alistair went downstairs.

'She's back,' he said.

'I've seen the car,' Marcia replied. 'April Maylor isn't the type of

'You were exhausted,' Marcia replied. 'You still managed to have a pretty awful nightmare before you settled off. Hardly surprising after your ordeal I suppose. You've managed to get a few undisturbed hours.' She stepped inside, slid the door shut and sat beside him on the bed. He began turning to get out. Marcia rested her hand on his shoulder. 'You don't have to go,' she said. 'Lie down. Ali. There's room for two.'

He looked deep into her eyes. 'Sure?' he asked.

'Absolutely,' she replied.

Alistair lay down. Marcia slipped beneath the light duvet, stretched out alongside him and slid her arm across his chest.

*

The rising sun lit the bedroom. Alistair blinked and turned toward Marcia lying on her back beside him.

Her lips stretched into a broad beautiful smile as she rolled toward him. Their lips met and pressed softly together. 'Every day should start and end with a kiss,' she said quietly.

'Absolutely true,' he agreed. 'It's a pity that normal life has to intrude in between.'

'I can hardly remember what *normal* life is now,' Marcia admitted. 'There's been so much death and disruption.'

He pressed his finger to her lips. 'And we have found a beautiful ray of sunshine to light our way out of the dark,' he said. 'We'll make it Marci. You and I together. We'll make it.' His phone beeped an incoming text. 'Maybe that's normal life butting in as it always does,' he said, fumbling to retrieve the phone from his trouser pocket on the floor. 'It's the bank,' he said. 'As the new owner of Bookworm, they want me to authorise continuation of standing orders. I suppose there might be other bits and pieces to sort out. I'd best go over and check the shop emails just in case there's something urgent.'

'I'd like to stay here for ever,' Marcia said. 'Unfortunately, I have things to do too.'

She climbed out of the bed, grabbed her tee shirt from the floor and disappeared toward the saloon. Alistair showered, dressed and followed the aroma of fresh coffee to the galley.

'I can offer coffee, plus cereals, with or without long life skimmed,' Marcia said. 'Or, we could hang around and chill here for a while.'

'That is a seriously tempting suggestion,' he said.

'Would that be with or without the long life skimmed?'

'Best do normal first and chill later I suppose,' he replied half-heartedly. 'Just coffee for now please.'

They drank their coffee. Marcia kissed Alistair's cheek and jangled her car keys. 'Okay, chill on hold. Let's go,' she said.

'I don't think she mentioned it,' Penny said. 'She had other things in her mind by then, obviously. Everybody loved her, Marci; her and James. This town won't ever be the same again. Is James's nephew going to keep Bookworm on?'

'Work in progress,' she replied.

Penny wished her, 'Good luck. Must dash,' she said. 'I have to open my shop.'

*

Marcia slipped into her driver's seat and sent a text to Alistair. *'Have stuff to go in fridge and freezer, so going home to Bookbinders. Will keep Nancy company and see you there later.* She drove back to the house, gathered her handbag and shopping from the car boot and hurried inside. Nancy was out, no doubt at one of her village activities, Marcia decided. She quickly put away her shopping, switched on the kettle and flopped down at the kitchen table. While she waited for the kettle, she pulled Caroline's phone book from her bag and finally opened it for the first time. She smiled. Each entry consisted of a cartoon, with a phone number written alongside. There were no names. 'Never could manage conventional, could you, Cal?' she whispered as she ran her fingers over the pages.

James appeared as a Court Jester, Aiden Gale a fox, Marcia a bookworm, with eyes of sapphire blue. The multiple chins of Mabel Graham and Dawn Tyler's slightly askew halo, shared pages with several other, unnamed yet instantly recognisable local people. One thumbnail, of a red poppy holding a wine glass toward a tiny image of Caroline's cottage, did not trigger a name.

Marcia began phoning numbers. The few people who picked up either disconnected immediately or refused to talk. Marcia turned to Caroline's diary. Among the reminders of appointments, meetings with James, and get-togethers with various friends, the unfamiliar name of Poppy Johnson, appeared regularly enough to spark interest. Marcia picked up her sister's phone index again, flicked through to the poppy thumbnail and tapped the contact number into her phone. The call rang out. No one answered. She checked, re-entered the number and let it ring for a full minute before disconnecting and slumping in her seat. An address would have been useful, she thought as she stared again at the thumbnail. The vital detail became clear. She sat up and smiled. The floral caricature held its wine glass toward Caroline's cottage, *on the opposite side of the valley.* 'Look and see,' she whispered. 'Consider and connect.' Thoughts of coffee disappeared from her mind. She scooped up her keys and handbag and ran to her car.

*

Marcia drove past Redstone Hill and turned, onto the upward snaking flank of Durston Bank.

The village of Durston straddled the road in hotchpotched disarray for perhaps two hundred metres. Marcia drew into a parking place and ran across to a shop with the word NEWSAGENT written in faded white script across its window.

The newsagent greeted her with a friendly smile.

Marcia explained that she was looking for a woman who lives in the area. 'Her home faces Redstone Hill,' she added hopefully.

'Do you know her address?'

'Sorry, I don't,' Marcia replied. 'But I'm sure she lives here or somewhere nearby. Durston is the only village overlooking the valley from this side.'

'That's true,' the newsagent agreed. 'Would this woman have a name?'

'Johnson.'

'Sorry, it doesn't ring a bell.'

'*Poppy* Johnson.'

Recognition lit the man's face. 'Poppy? Everybody knows Poppy. Nice woman, a bit strange if you know what I mean.'

'That will be the lady,' Marcia replied confidently. 'Do you know where she lives?'

'Carry on up the hill,' he said. 'You'll pass a pub called The Quarryman. Take the next turning left. Poppy's cottage is on a bend needed a scapegoat,' Marcia said. 'So, they pilloried Eleanor with spite and ignorance.'

'Maybe you're right,' Poppy mumbled. 'I only know the stories.'

'About things that happened two hundred years ago.'

'Caroline dug up the same tales, disturbed the same grave and let out the same curse,' Poppy replied with deep fear in each trembling word.

'Myths and curses won't answer my questions,' Marcia replied. 'I need facts, Poppy. Caroline had been promising some big revelation. Did that have something to do with Eleanor?'

'I've said too much already,' Poppy muttered.

'I believe my sister may have discovered some sort of rare book,' Marcia continued. 'Did Caroline find Eleanor's so-called book of spells, Poppy?'

'Nobody's ever seen any book,' Poppy replied firmly. 'There may not be a book. Nobody knows.'

'You seemed fairly certain about it a minute ago,' Marcia reminded her. 'Where is the book, Poppy?'

'I told you, nobody knows. Nobody wants to know.'

'So it might just be another rumour?'

'You asked me what I know and I've told you,' Poppy said with discouraging finality. 'Make up your own mind.'

'There must be more to it than silly gossip about a witch and a wife beater,' Marcia insisted.

'We've all seen what's happened since Caroline and James Hastings disturbed her again,' Poppy said. 'It isn't just gossip now, is it? They should have left Nellie to lie buried.'

'Convicted of being a stranger,' Marcia said. 'The good people of Lowesley Pryor decided she didn't belong, so they branded an innocent abused wife as Nellie the evil witch. Maybe it's time to allow the poor woman a little peace. Thanks for your time, Poppy. I'm sorry to have bothered you.' She stood to leave.

'Caroline was frightened too,' Poppy said. 'I shouldn't have...

Whatever Caroline and me said to one another, has always stayed between us.' Marcia held Poppy's eye and waited. 'Her and James had been digging up the history of that grave. It seems like they found something important and valuable. James wrote about it in the church magazine, teasing folk with promises to reveal something soon. Caroline had started joining in too. Anyway, it got into the local press and some poorly man started visiting James at the shop, for a chat. Well apparently, the man said he had a friend who once lived in Oxton. When he mentioned the friend's name James told him to stay away and gave up writing about the grave. Caroline said that James had known the man's friend and thought he might be dangerous. She thought the man and his friend wanted the thing James had found. He couldn't give it to them and was afraid she might be in danger if he didn't.'

'I'm fairly sure that the man who visited the shop is called Peter Christy,' Marcia said. 'Did Caroline ever mention that name?'

'No, nor the friend neither. I didn't see her at all from a few days before James died. She seemed to shut herself away. We had a few chats on the phone but she steered well clear of anything to do with Nellie or St Michael's.'

Chapter 49

A van rattled into the carriage yard. Alistair flopped back on his chair and glanced at his watch. Two tedious hours had failed to reveal any new facts about the Rosemonts. He strolled over to make coffee as Gary and Nigel disappeared up the mezzanine stairs. Aiden drove in from the archway and parked beside the Mercedes. He stepped into the kitchen.

'Good morning Alistair,' he said. 'I wasn't expecting to see you here today. I imagined you may wish to take a break from Bookworm.'

'I did,' Alistair admitted, 'but I knew I'd never overcome what happened by refusing to face it. I'm sorry, Aiden, I should have phoned to tell you I was coming in. You may have more important places to be.'

'I would have been here to face your challenge with you,' Aiden replied. 'James also preferred to tackle things head on. In light of events, he may have fared rather better with a companion at his side. Please take care, Alistair.' He glanced over at the open strongroom door and back to the strewn parish records. 'Do you believe this is a good idea quite so soon after your ordeal?' he asked.

'It seemed a much better idea when I started than it does now,' Alistair admitted. 'I didn't find a single thing of interest. Mind you, I'm not altogether sure what I hoped to turn up.'

'Do you require my assistance?' Aiden offered.

'No thanks,' Alistair replied. 'I've wasted enough time.' He closed the book in front of him. 'I was just about to make coffee. If you'd like to sort that out, I'll clear away my debris.'

Alistair returned the parish records to the strongroom, while Aiden made coffee and carried mugs up to Gary and Nigel. He returned as Alistair was pushing the dresser back into place.

'Good news,' Aiden said. 'Gary informs me that he will have Bookworm sound and secure by Friday. We may at least see the path to normality ahead for the old place.'

Alistair nodded. 'I noticed you've been busy in the showroom. I appreciate your efforts.'

'My pleasure,' Aiden replied. 'I've also begun casting my eye over the shelf and book fair stock. I'll make some notes on valuation. Do you wish me to appraise any other items?'

'I'm not aware of any,' Alistair replied. He poured out two mugs of coffee and joined Aiden at the table. 'You're happy here, aren't you, Aiden?'

'Bookworm and I understand one another,' Aiden replied. 'It is a pity that you find yourself deposited here in such difficult circumstances. Perhaps when Oxton returns to normal, you will reconsider your plan to leave us again.'

Alistair shrugged. 'I'm never likely to become an asset to Bookworm and I haven't noticed too many welcome mats around Oxton,' he said.

'I perceive a rather large welcome mat at Marcia's door,' Aiden replied with a smile. 'She is clearly very fond of you. Think carefully before making your decision. When I arrived in Oxton, I was not planning to stay. I never regretted changing my mind.'

Alistair adjusted his shirt collar. 'Why did you stay?' he asked.

'Because I found James,' Aiden replied.

'Yet in all those years you never considered setting up home together?'

Aiden smiled. 'We considered the matter many times,' he said quietly. 'You must remember that when James and I first met, the law

Chapter 50

Nash leaned back from his terminal to ease his aching neck. 'I don't know how you manage to do this for hours on end,' he said as Reid stepped into his office.

'Professional dedication and lack of choice, sir,' Reid replied. 'Have you come up with anything on Paul Clifford?'

'Only that Clifford seems to have been totally dedicated to his mother,' Nash replied. 'According to the trial papers, the poor old soul had advancing dementia. Paul wanted to have her cared for in a private nursing home. He torched the family home, hoping to pay for it with the insurance money.'

'Could he not meet any of the costs himself?' Reid asked. 'That house in Cleaver Street was his home too. When he burned the place down, he made himself homeless.'

'Classic Catch 22,' Nash replied. 'He could keep his home and risk seeing his mother dumped in some fleapit, or put himself on the street and have her looked after as he thought she should be. He was pretty much up the creek either way.'

'Why could he not sell the place?'

'Mom had let it go apparently. The property needed serious money spent on it and Paul didn't have any. According to the file, he'd lost his job after taking too much time off to look after the old girl. We can ask him all these questions personally, if we ever manage to get our hands on him.'

'There's a good chance he's in this area,' Reid said. 'If he's on benefits, there'll be an address on file. I'll take a look if you like, sir.'

'I've done it,' Nash replied. 'There's no claim showing up on the system. He seems to have come out of prison and disappeared. He might be anywhere now. All we know for sure is that a car registered to Paul Clifford, followed Dawlish and Marcia Blackham the other day. We have no evidence that he was driving the thing.'

Reid nodded and returned to his desk. He had barely logged on to his database when Nash called from his office.

'Alex. Get in here, matey, and look at this.'

Reid ran in from the CID, 'Problem, sir?'

Nash glanced across from his monitor. 'That depends on how long it takes us to nail this bastard. Until he lost his job, Paul Clifford worked as a technician in the chemistry labs at some college. He's more than capable of constructing incendiary devices like the ones at Caroline Blackham's murder scene and the bookshop.'

'Well done, Sir,' Reid said. 'That puts him well in the frame now, whether he was driving that car or not.'

at risk until he does, or the police find him. We must all keep looking. Our lives may depend on it. I want to sort this riddle out and we won't find anything by just talking, that's for sure. Clive Chapman was looking for you earlier. I'd get in touch.'

'Of course,' Ollie agreed. 'I've held things up for much longer than expected.'

Alistair waved Ollie off and turned to Marcia. 'I'd say James and Caroline came home armed with Barney Dolman's background information, applied their local knowledge and started digging. James knew the tales about Nellie the witch so he could have guessed that Eleanor would turn up in the grave. The whole story fits together now we know about those emeralds.'

'Precisely,' Marcia cautioned. 'The point is it only fits together *because* of the emeralds. I'm not inclined to plunge any deeper into this mess. Do you really believe it would make sense to add another item to our itinerary?'

'Don't you want to know?'

'James didn't simply abandon that project, Ali,' she replied. 'He changed the locks at Bookworm. He became timid and secretive. That wasn't the James Hastings I'd known all my life. Something scared him. It may have killed him and Caroline.'

'That's precisely why we need to find out what that something is,' Alistair said. 'I think this is all about Eleanor Rosemont and her family. Ollie's discovery has thrown up a possible motive for murder. James's research could lead us to the murderer.'

'That research has already focused his, *or their*, attention on us,' Marcia replied. 'This situation is horrific enough for me. More probing from us might just tempt the killer closer. Are you sure you want that? I know I don't.'

'I wasn't planning to charge in like the cavalry,' Alistair protested. 'You could at least try phoning Caroline's friends. She may have leaked more detail about that big revelation of hers to one of them.'

'I've done it,' she replied half-heartedly. 'That's where I've been. I actually managed to track one of them down. I hoped she might have some answers.'

'I don't think you should have… Never mind. No harm done I suppose. I take it she didn't come up with anything.'

'It's all folk tales and gossip,' Marcia replied. 'Poppy Johnson is scared, like everybody else. All I got from her was that Eleanor was a witch and Samuel killed her.'

'Where did this Poppy woman get her information?'

'She doesn't have much *information,*' Marcia insisted. 'Poppy is blinkered by all the usual myths and rumours. Apparently, there's also a book of spells which, you won't be surprised to hear, is as elusive as any other tangible evidence around here.'

Alistair's eyes widened. 'That sounds just crazy enough to be the very thing James and Caroline had up their sleeves, to make a big splash at the book fair.'

'Drowning men often make big splashes,' Marcia said wearily. 'I think they dug up the same tales I've been hearing. James realised it was all superstitious nonsense and dumped it before he made a complete numpty of himself.'

'That book may hold all the answers.'

'There may not be a book. Who knows? Anyway, I tried.'

'James and Caroline would have dug out the facts.'

'James was a bookseller and a historian. He was not a TV supersleuth. Grow up Ali. This is the real world.' She bit her lip 'Sorry, that was rude,' she said, squeezing his hand. 'You almost died in that strongroom. This killer is ruthless and determined. The one piece of actual information I got was that Caroline told Poppy that James had asked Peter Christy to stop visiting Bookworm after he mentioned the name of someone James knew in the past. James believed that person was potentially dangerous, to him and Caroline, though Poppy didn't know how. I think we should leave the investigation to the police.'

'They're just looking for a killer,' Alistair protested. 'I'm certain remains. They seem like an odd thing to bury in a country cemetery.'

'I agree,' Barney said. 'I don't have an explanation, but it sounds intriguing. If you come across any more interesting titbits concerning Eleanor, I'd like to hear them too.'

'No problem,' Alistair agreed. 'As it happens, I do have one bit of local gossip, though it may not do much for the family's reputation.'

'Never mind that. Passing comments sometimes lead to priceless conclusions. Let's have it.'

'Word among our local myth-mafia is that Eleanor was a witch,' Alistair said. 'Nobody's mentioned a broomstick yet, but I've heard that she had a book of spells.'

Barney hesitated. 'Or a book of secrets,' he finally said. 'This is suddenly making sense.'

'To you perhaps,' Alistair replied. 'Would you care to explain?'

'You may have stumbled on something very significant,' Barney said. 'That book I mentioned, the one our old breakaway religious mob was said to follow, was known as, the *Book of Secrets*. If such a thing exists and the Gould's managed to get their hands on it, that could explain what happened to them and why they sent Eleanor away. It's possible that her book of spells was the precious, and allegedly deadly, *Book of Secrets*. Do you think James may have found it?'

'In view of what's kicked off over here, I definitely wouldn't dismiss the idea,' Alistair replied. 'The faintest scent of a book like that would definitely float James's boat. I'll let you know if anything turns up. Thanks, Barney.' He rang off with another tidal wave of questions crashing through his brain.

Is that what happened, Uncle James? Did you set off searching for Eleanor's family background and turn up something unique that you hadn't planned for but could not resist? Were you instantly, fatally hooked? You never considered giving up that project, did you? You probed and foraged and found it. You found the *Book of Secrets*. Did your perfect prize put you in fear of your life? Did it take your life and Caroline's too? Could a book, any book actually do that?

Chapter 54

Reid phoned more than a dozen nursing homes before he managed to locate Esther Clifford at the impressive and beautifully situated Hawfield Lodge. He spoke to the receptionist and drove straight over. A delicious aroma wafting through the foyer suggested that dinner preparations were well underway. The receptionist examined Reid's ID, confirmed that he was expected and asked him to wait.

A carer finally arrived and led him to a well-appointed first floor room overlooking a large ornamental fishpond. Esther appeared entirely unaware of her room, or the attractive features outside.

'About time you showed up,' she said. 'When's our Pauly coming? Bloody papers. He should be here having his tea. Never mind delivering bloody newspapers. He has homework to do.'

Reid looked with deep concern at the carer.

'Don't worry,' she said. 'Esther thinks every male visitor is her estranged husband. He apparently walked out on her and their son ages ago. He's been dead ten years.'

'She remembers her son though,' Reid said.

'Oh yes,' the carer replied. 'You heard that for yourself. She remembers him as a schoolboy. He hasn't visited for some time. When he did come, Esther always thought he was her husband and would spend the entire visit telling him off for allowing Pauly to ignore his homework.'

'Sorry, I've wasted your time,' Reid said. He glanced back,

onto the road and roared off out of sight. She apparently had urgent business somewhere away from Oxton.

A minute later, Reid's car drew up behind the Mercedes. Alistair stepped out. Reid lowered his window.

'Don't bother knocking,' Alistair said. 'There's no one at home.'

'You have a troubled look, Commander,' Reid replied. 'Is something bothering you?' Alistair reported Clive's absence and Amanda's sudden departure. 'I'm sure they have things to do,' Reid said dismissively. 'Have you or Ms Blackham seen anything of Peter Christy in the past day or two?'

Alistair confirmed that he had not seen Christy and nor had Marcia. 'Is he significant?'

'Everybody is significant until we know who we're looking for,' Reid said. 'Have there been any more phone contacts or intrusions?'

'No,' Alistair replied. 'I'm sure St Michael's is important somehow in what's happened. Marcia wasn't involved and didn't attract attention until the two people who were researching that grave had been eliminated. I became of interest as soon as I started asking questions about Eleanor Rosemont and the grave.'

'I have more important matters than a car park extension on my mind, Commander.'

'I advise you to have a word with the County Archaeologist before you dismiss the link,' Alistair said.

'We already know we're dealing with a seriously disturbed adversary here,' Reid reminded him. 'I suggest you keep a close eye on Ms Blackham and leave the detecting to us.' He rolled his window up and drove away.

Alistair walked back to his car. 'Keeping that close eye on Marcia, may not be as easy as you seem to think, sergeant,' he mumbled, as he hit the green button to call her. 'Hi, Marci,' he said. 'I'm just on my way over there.'

'We won't be at the shop,' she replied. 'Aiden has an appointment with a client, so I'm going home. You sound a bit hacked off.'

'I didn't get to speak to Clive,' Alistair replied. 'He's apparently cleared off for a day or two and now Amanda has gone too. Plus, Reid isn't choosing to see any link between that grave and the murders. So you're right. I'm not having a great morning.'

'Cleared off where?' Marcia asked.

'Say again.'

Clive Chapman. Where has he cleared off to?' she repeated.

'Amanda didn't say,' Alistair replied. 'I'll see you at Bookbinders.'

Chapter 57

Alistair drove past April Maylor's car, turned into the lane and parked next to Marcia's empty parking space, outside the workshop.

The reporter stepped from her car and beckoned Alistair to the corner of the lane. 'Hello, Commander,' she said with her customary cocky familiarity. 'Did you know the vicars have done a bunk? Bit odd in the circumstances. I wondered if you might like to comment.'

'How do you…?'

'I'm a journalist. I search out stories.'

'I've heard enough stories for now.'

'You haven't heard this one. I've done a bit of checking into the vicar's pasts.'

'Dig the dirt then sling the mud?'

'I prefer to see it as shining a torch and shedding light. Amanda's father is, or was, a vicar so it isn't surprising that she ended up in a cassock. Clive Chapman, on the other hand, was a very unlikely candidate for the clergy.'

'Are all your stories as boring as this?'

'I'm getting to the hook. There was a murder near Franley during 1981.'

'I'm busy.'

'The case was never solved. Amanda Chapman's father was a curate in the area where it happened. Have you spotted the possible connection to something recent? It gets even more interesting when

Amanda, with that family tie, marries tough guy Chapman and hey presto a repeat performance kicks off in Oxton. Are you still bored with this story?'

'Have you passed this *conjecture* to the police?'

'Of course, Commander.'

'Then I'm sure they'll give it appropriate consideration, Ms Maylor, as I have. Good afternoon.'

*

Nancy ran from the kitchen as Alistair stepped into the hall. 'I'm so glad you're home, Ali,' she gushed. 'I don't know where Marcia has gone.'

'Calm down,' he replied. 'I spoke to her not long ago. She's on her way here now.'

'She's already been here,' Nancy said. 'She came in crying and went straight to the lounge. I was still making coffee, when I heard the front door bang shut and she was gone.'

Alistair snatched out his phone and punched in Marcia's number. She connected but could not force words past her obvious sobs. 'What's wrong?' Alistair asked. 'Where are you?'

'Stowe... Going to Stowe... Must get to Cal....'

'I'm on my way,' Alistair replied already at the front door. He turned to Nancy. 'I've found her,' he said. 'I think she's okay. I'm going to her.' The door banged shut behind him.

*

Alistair's car slid to a halt behind Marcia's Mini in the parking spot. He leapt out and ran down through the wood. Gaia remained with her covers undisturbed. Alistair quickly checked that no-one had been aboard and ran off along the riverbank. The circle came into view. Marcia was kneeling with her head bowed, facing into the space. Alistair approached slowly.

'Marci,' he said quietly. 'I'm here to help, if I can. Tell me what's wrong, please.'

She finally turned toward him. Utter despair gripped her swollen

252

eyes. Her hair hung damp with perspiration. Tear tracks streaked her cheeks. Alistair knelt beside her.

'What's the matter?' he asked. 'You were fine less than an hour ago.'

She turned and looked at him. 'What have I done, Ali?' she said. 'I should have... If only I'd told Caroline.'

'Told her what?'

'That assault, the stalking when I was a girl.' She blotted fresh tears on her sleeve.

Alistair kissed her hands. 'That was a terrible experience for you,' he said. 'You did what you truly believed was right. It took strength and character to suffer in silence, Marci,' he said.

'What strength? What character?' she snapped. 'Everybody knew Chapman's reputation. Only a fool would have accepted a date with him, right? Well, you're looking at the fool who did and I should have known better. Maybe I led him on. Maybe I asked for it. I've kept my stupid mouth shut because I was scared that people might point the finger. That's weakness, Ali, pathetic miserable spinelessness. I didn't even tell my own sister. Now she's dead. If Clive Chapman is involved in these dreadful things, I'll never forgive myself.'

'Don't beat yourself up, Marci,' he urged. 'You were a victim. He degraded you but maybe you've carried the wound long enough. It may be time to let it go and look forward. Despite what he did to you back then, we have no proof that Clive is *currently* involved in anything more than a car park extension.'

Marcia sat bolt upright. 'Look at me, Ali,' she said. 'Do you believe that my sister or your uncle would be dead if they hadn't become involved with Clive Chapman's church?'

'I'm sorry, Marci, I can't answer that question,' he replied honestly. 'One thing I can say for sure is that you aren't to blame for any of this.'

'But I should have told her. I have to explain, have to say... It's too late to say sorry now, isn't it?'

'It's never too late,' he reassured her. 'Say it, Marci. Tell her. Talk to her. Let it out.' A brief glint caught his eye. He turned as a man a little way back from the tree line lowered his binoculars, turned and disappeared among the trees. 'This is a private time, just for Caroline and you,' he said. 'Take as long as you need. I'll leave the two of you alone, but I won't be very far away.'

*

The man with the binoculars had vanished as if swallowed by the landscape. Alistair weaved his way through to the hill beyond the trees and ran to the next ridge. He paused and scanned for signs of movement. A little way ahead, the gable end of a cottage roof peeped out from the lea of the hill. Beyond the cottage, a rough track led down to the valley road. Assorted camper vans, cars and tents littered the hillside. Several people milled around the campsite. A slight movement drew Alistair's attention to a small group of trees a little way ahead. He sprinted down and confronted a tall unsmiling man, with dark eyes and pale features.

'I've seen you here before,' Alistair said. 'You're the birdwatcher, but you've been watching rather more than birds, haven't you? What do you want?'

'I am a keen birder,' the man confirmed. 'And yes, I have been watching, your friend and her lovely narrowboat.'

'So, you admit spying on her? Have you also been sending texts and images on her murdered sister's phone?'

'I admit only that I have checked to see that she is safe and well,' the man replied. 'I have made no other contact with her, nor have I attempted to do so. I saw her obvious distress a few minutes ago and was about to introduce myself when you arrived.'

'Why? Alistair asked. Who are you?'

'My name is Toby Lang, Reverend Tobias Lang. My daughter is Reverend Amanda Chapman. Amanda is aware that I visit Stowe Junction quite regularly, for bird watching. As I am sure you are aware, Marcia's sister and her colleague were working on a project together at St Michael's Church. They discontinued their work amid rumours that something or someone had begun intimidating them. In light of recent events, particularly Caroline's tragic murder, Amanda feared that similar intimidation may be directed toward Marcia and the new owner of her colleague's bookshop. She asked that, when I am here at Stowe, I keep an eye on Marcia and her beautiful narrowboat to ensure that all is well.'

'Marcia's boat was burgled recently,' Alistair said. 'Were you the burglar or did you see him or her?'

'None of the above, I regret to say. Marcia has apparently been absent from Gaia for some days. Do you know where she is staying?'

'Elsewhere,' Alistair replied.

A woman, walking two German shepherd dogs, waved and approached from toward the cottage. The dogs clearly recognised Rev Lang. The woman called to him. 'Hi Toby.'

Alistair waited until she drew closer. 'I take it you know this man,' he said.

'Certainly,' she confirmed. 'Toby has been birding among these hills for years.'

'Thank you my dear,' Rev Lang said, almost managing a smile. 'If you will excuse me, I believe I have completed my duty here.' He turned and continued down the hill, toward the campsite.

The woman turned her attention back to Alistair and greeted him with a broad, intensely white, grin. Her loose fitting sleeveless top exposed deeply tanned arms and shoulders. Frayed denim shorts revealed smooth bronzed legs. Dappled sunlight caught her long loosely curled black hair, emphasising her sun-soaked face and dark seductive eyes.

Alistair offered his hand. 'Alistair Dawlish,' he said.

The woman slipped her hand into his and stroked her long fingers across his palm. 'I'm Dawn Tyler,' she said, holding onto his index finger a little longer than necessary. 'I was on my way over to see if everything is okay. I've been keeping an eye on Gaia while I'm walking Cleo and Sheba. There are strangers camping over near my place. They turned up for the book fair and solstice.'

'Marci is having a little quiet time at the stone circle,' Alistair said. 'She isn't staying on Gaia just now. After what happened to Caroline, the police suggested that she stays at my place for a little while.'

'Sounds cosy,' Dawn said, as she straightened her top, playfully drawing Alistair's eyes from her smile to her body. 'My cottage is a bit remote too,' she said with a sultry sweep of her eyes. 'And I'm usually there all alone. Maybe you could look after me too.' She laughed. 'I'd best get these two back home, now you're here to check things out. I'll keep my eye on Gaia. My cottage is only a little way across the pasture, if you ever fancy a coffee, or something.'

'I'd be careful about making offers to strangers, at the moments,' Alistair advised. 'Marci is grieving for her sister and her friend. Their killer is still at large Things really aren't at all cosy, Dawn.'

Dawn abandoned her flirting and looked into his eyes. 'I know,' she said. 'Caroline carried sunshine around with her.' She paused. 'People are setting up camp on the hill below my cottage, ready for her book fair and the solstice. Full of it, she was. Now, suddenly she's gone. Nobody can believe she won't be around anymore.'

'Caroline had been promising some sort of big surprise at the book fair,' Alistair reminded her. 'Did she ever mention a book that may have belonged to Nellie the witch?'

Dawn's voice dropped to a low mumble. The colour drained from her tanned features. 'I don't know anything about that and I don't want to,' she said.

'What's the problem?' Alistair asked.

'Caroline and James opened up that grave,' Dawn replied. 'That's the problem. People have always been scared of Nellie. That didn't stop Caroline telling everybody the witch might be on her way back. You know what she was like.' Alistair didn't reply. 'Dog with a bone, that was Caroline, couldn't let anything go. Well, she went ferreting around once too often and now she's dead. I'm scared, we all are.'

'Amanda seems to have been the big attraction.'

'I can see how that might work, so what's worrying you?'

'Clive had a reputation as the local hard man, a troublemaker. He'd never been popular here, so I can see why he might want to get away. What's bothering me is, years later he's back as a vicar. That's a massive character reversal. How did it happen and what brought him back?'

'I imagine you have a theory.'

'Our case has obvious links to the church and it kicked off soon after the Chapman's turned up.' Nash's eyes narrowed. 'Amanda's father was appointed as a curate near Oxton in 1980,' Reid continued. 'He worked here until he married and moved to Trugfield ten years later. He was living in Oxton in 1981.'

'Steady on, Alex,' Nash cautioned. 'Clive and Amanda weren't born in 1981.'

'I can't ignore evidence, sir. Deborah King was murdered here. Her killer has never been brought to justice. Those are odd coincidences. The cases could be connected.'

'Possibly to each other, at a stretch,' Nash replied. 'Can you show any link to Clive and Amanda Chapman, or any member of Amanda's family?'

'Amanda Chapman's father was a vicar in the area when Deborah King was murdered. She's a vicar here now.'

Nash shook his head. 'You're flying a pretty flimsy kite,' he said. 'No criticism intended, Alex. There are obvious common features between the murders. Maybe we're missing some connection between the victims.' The phone rang again. 'I'll be impressed, if she's found him,' Nash said as he snatched it up and hit the speaker button. 'Nash.'

'Amanda Chapman,' the caller said. 'I agreed I'd call, if I had news.'

Nash grabbed a pen. 'What do you have?'

'Possibly nothing,' Amanda replied. 'I've managed to speak to Clive. He seems desperate to find Peter. I told him about the alias and the conviction. I'm not sure he believed me. I can still hardly believe it myself.'

'Does he have an address?'

'Not yet. I'm still fairly confident it's in Crockerby. I'll keep trying the local clergy. I just thought you'd want to know that Clive has been in touch. He didn't say what he plans to do next, didn't seem to know actually. He's phoning around the churches, as I am. I must admit I've had concerns about Peter, I mean, Paul, myself.'

'What sort of concerns?'

'He turned up at around the time Clive began drumming up interest in that grave. It was nice to see him interested, but it's become a bit of an obsession really. Now that I've spoken to Clive, I know he shares my concern but doesn't actually know any more than I do. I've agreed to let him know if I manage to locate Paul. If I come up with anything else, I'll be in touch.'

Nash thanked her for calling and threw down his pen. 'I was hoping for something definite,' he said. 'A bit more than bugger all at least.'

Reid cleared his throat. 'There may be a way to show a connection,' he said warily.

'Let's have it then, Sherlock.'

'Deborah King's clothes are still sealed and stored with the case files, sir. If we could lift DNA, it might be possible to establish a connection to our cases.'

'Or eliminate time wasting speculation,' Nash added. 'I suppose we ought to show that we've explored all angles, but I can't waste unnecessary budget. That evidence is forty years old.'

'Aye, sir, but it's sealed, dry and undisturbed. And we don't have many other new angles to explore right now.'

'Okay, speak to the lab,' Nash agreed. 'If they think it's possible to lift a sample, get the stuff over to them.'

Chapter 59

Alistair followed Marcia back to Bookbinders. He felt a huge wave of relief when they parked outside the workshop. They went into the house and Alistair made coffee, while Marcia phoned Nancy to reassure her that she was okay.

'What did you do while I was grovelling at the circle?' Marcia asked when Alistair joined her.

'Well, first of all, I identified the mysterious bird-watcher, and guess who he is.'

'How would I know? Was it the Archbishop of Canterbury?'

'Not quite, but probably closer than you think. It was Reverend Tobias Lang. He's Amanda Chapman's father. Amanda is apparently worried about you, so she asked Rev Toby to keep an eye on you.'

'That's really kind.'

'As long as he's telling the truth.'

'Oh, ye of little faith. Didn't you believe him?'

'Yes of course. Dawn Tyler turned up. She's known him for years apparently.'

'So, you've met Dawn? What did she have to say?'

'Quite a lot actually. She told me where I might get some info on Nellie's book of spells. It's too late to follow up now but I'd like to give it a go tomorrow. Let's not dwell on that. Have a shower and freshen up,' he said.

She nodded and wandered off upstairs.

*

A pleasant breeze carried light perfume out to Alistair, on the terrace. Marcia reappeared wearing black trousers with a long open black silk blouse over a white top. Her hair hung loose. Its pale golden sheen returning as it dried in the sunlight.

'Welcome back to your normal self,' he said.

She half smiled. 'I'm not sure I care for my *normal* self any more,' she replied.

'Well, I care for her a lot,' he said, planting a kiss on her cheek.

'Thanks for shaking me out of my self-pity,' she said. 'Would you like to shed a little of your load now? I think it's time, Ali.' They sat at the terrace table. Marcia reached across and held Alistair's hand. 'You've been a victim too. I've seen the nightmares. I watched you wrestling your demons in Lincolnshire and again on Gaia. The monsters feed and grow in the dark. If you force them out into the light, they die. I'm happy to listen.'

'You have your own…'

'Please.'

He gazed beyond Marcia to a distant painful place. 'It started on an intelligence gathering mission around the Strait of Hormuz, between Oman and Iran,' he began. 'Local interpreters were obviously a vital resource and we had some first-class people working with us. I was assigned a guy called Razban.' He paused and swallowed. 'He knew the potential consequences of assisting us and accepted the risks because he cared about his country. Razban went off for three days leave with his family.' The returning memory almost choked him. His hand tightened into a white fist. 'Forty-eight hours later, his body was dumped outside our embassy in Muscat, Oman. Almost every one of his bones was broken. My bosses obviously couldn't be sure whether he'd disclosed any information, so they aborted my operation. By eight o'clock that evening I was on a plane back to the UK.' He held Marcia with a haunted gaze and swallowed another choking lump.

'What happened?' she prompted.

'London decided that: *"It would not be politically expedient to pursue the matter further".'*

Marcia squeezed his hand. 'I suppose they have to consider the big picture,' she said.

'They wrote him off, Marci, dumped the man like a damaged laptop. I knew when I joined the military that I may have to put my life on the line. That's the deal. It's what people like me do. Razban wasn't military. He and his family weren't even politically active. My interpreter had turned down a place at an English university, to stay at home and serve his people. Razban was a delightful, intelligent man whose sole purpose in life was to make things better for everybody. For harbouring that unacceptable aspiration, some psychopath beat him to death.' He looked into Marcia's eyes. 'I have it pretty much under control now. It's just, when I try to sleep, the anger and guilt, the ultimate futility, gnaws at my brain.'

Marcia stroked his hand. 'Don't interpret humanity as a sign of weakness,' she said. 'You're a good man, Alistair Dawlish. The world needs more like you.'

'The Navy doesn't,' he said. 'And it's all I know.'

'What happened?'

Alistair sucked his teeth as if trying to dislodge a distasteful crumb. 'I was reassigned to a shore post as an instructor. I don't sail a flip chart very well and I don't like to see good people written off and swept aside.' He paused. 'The medics tried to explain my reaction away as Post Traumatic Stress Disorder. I'd handled plenty of trauma and stress. I hadn't been up front in a conflict zone and I wasn't disordered. I was just plain angry. I obviously rattled the wrong cages. Friendly advice escalated up the chain. Things came to an inevitable head and I was ordered to attend a disciplinary hearing.'

'Is that as serious as it sounds?'

He nodded. 'Serious enough, but normally survivable. The real rug puller came after the hearing. One of the board members was

Captain Grant Portman. He and I were at school together.'

'It seems odd to have a friend present in that situation,' Marcia said.

'I said I knew him. I didn't say we were friends,' Alistair replied. 'The loathsome cretin cheated and bullied his way through school. Daddy's generous donations ensured that no one noticed. Those animals don't change.'

'Okay, so he wasn't your favourite person. How did he affect the outcome?'

'Portman sat quietly smirking through the chairman's opening remarks. He had no need to say anything. He knew he would rattle me enough, just by being there. The chairman unpicked my career and tossed it aside, piece by piece. Nobody seemed at all interested in Razban, or how he died for us. Their big issue was my alleged refusal to follow orders and drop the matter when I came home. Such behaviour, the chairman said, demonstrated lack of judgement serious enough to impair my operational competence.' He stared into Marcia's eyes. 'I'd never disobeyed an order in my entire career but I saw no point in arguing the toss. I'd already been shunted from a senior operational role to chalk and talk. I'd been comprehensively bollocked by a rear admiral for the best part of an hour. The whole thing felt like the formal endorsement of a foregone conclusion.'

'What happened, Ali?'

'I left after the hearing, prepared to accept whatever decision the panel might make. After walking for a while to unwind, I called into the Officer's Mess, for a beer. Portman was already there drinking with another panel member. He mumbled something to his companion, gave his habitual self-congratulatory smirk and came over to stand behind me at the bar. As I picked up my pint and turned to walk away, he nudged my elbow. I spilled beer onto by best dress uniform. "Clumsy," he said. "Maybe that's how you lost your interpreter." When I turned, Portman was smirking again. I threw my pint in his face and punched him several times.'

Marcia gasped. 'Why on earth…?'

'Poor judgement, moment of…. Who knows? The navy isn't fond of loose cannons. One way or another, I had to go.'

'By the time you got to that hearing, you must have been like a primed bomb,' Marcia said. 'Captain Portman hit the detonator and you exploded. If you don't want to call it PTSD, then don't. Whatever name you give to your ghost, it's still haunting you. It can't leave until you let it out.' She unknotted his fist and held his hand. 'You can't deal with everything by yourself, Ali.'

He gazed into her eyes. 'I thought I could beat it but… I know you're right.' He gave her hand a squeeze and disappeared upstairs. He returned holding the document he had retrieved from his flat.

'What's this?' Marcia asked. 'I couldn't stand another…'

'It's my ghost,' he said. 'The board didn't want to call it PTSD either and they couldn't let it end there.'

Marcia unfolded a single page bearing the Royal Navy crest. Below the formal heading and personal details of Commander A.K. Dawlish, a single line of bold type seized her attention. She gasped.

'Notice of Dismissal with Disgrace.'

Marcia's hand shook as she skimmed, through a brief preamble to the main content.

Charge 1 – That Commander Alistair Kenton Dawlish, being a serving Officer of the Royal Navy, did wilfully and persistently fail to maintain the standards and competencies required for operational command.

Charge 2 – That the said Officer did assault Captain Grant William Portman, thereby occasioning him actual bodily harm.

Having duly considered all evidence presented before this Court Martial, our verdicts are as follows:

Charge 1 – Guilty.

Charge 2 – Guilty.

Disposal: Commander Alistair Kenton Dawlish shall serve a period of twelve months in custody at the tri-service Military Corrective and Training Centre, Colchester. Thereafter, the said officer shall be discharged with disgrace from the Royal Navy.

Having failed, at the date of discharge, to complete the necessary term of continual service, Alistair Kenton Dawlish shall forfeit his right to immediate pension and shall therefore be granted reserve pension rights, to commence at age sixty.

Marcia handed back the document. 'That sentence seems rather harsh for a few punches,' she said.

'Let's just say I had *retained full operational competence* in that particular area,' Alistair replied. 'It took years to build my career. The Navy gave me opportunities I never dared to imagine and there were more to come. I threw it all away by refusing to let go of something that was probably none of my business anyway. I wasn't a victim, Marci. I brought the entire mess down on my own stupid head. The conviction makes me practically unemployable. I've lived on my savings since I came out. That lifejacket is all but deflated now and I won't get my pension for another twenty-two years.' He forced a rueful smile. 'All I have left of the old life is my fancy Mercedes. A friend, my best I thought, looked after the car for me while I was inside. A few days before my release, he turned up at the centre with the keys and written directions to a car park. He didn't want to see me and I haven't been able to contact him since my release. It obviously wouldn't do his career any good to be associated with an ex-con.'

Marcia kissed his hand. 'It won't do mine any harm,' she said.

The Prioress, who perished along with her nuns that morning, was Eliza Blackham. Local artist Caroline Blackham — an acknowledged expert on ancient beliefs — is a direct descendant of Eliza. An unbroken Blackham family line therefore extends back almost five centuries to that event and, in all probability, through the preceding millennia. This serves as persuasive evidence that repression cannot conquer the human spirit.

'So, the big revelation wasn't just to be about an old book that no-one can even read,' Alistair said.

'Apparently not, but it certainly had plenty to do with St Michael's,' Marcia replied. 'James intended spilling the true story of Nellie the Witch, *plus* a completely revised history of the Priory.' She smiled. 'I wasn't sure about having Caroline laid to rest near the old Yew tree,' she said. 'It suddenly seems perfect.'

Alistair stared at the page in his hand. 'I think James hid this in the barbie cupboard because he planned to burn it,' he said. 'What do you think we should do with it?'

'Your uncle had made his decision,' Marcia replied. 'I trusted his judgement when he was alive and I trust it now.' She looked into his eyes. 'Caroline was convinced that fate had drawn James to this place. Maybe he believed that the Blackham ancestors had brought Caroline back to the priory. I think he wanted to have the family reunited with their secret intact.'

'That would have been the honourable decision,' Alistair said. He kissed her cheek and handed over the page. 'You are all that remains of Caroline's family,' he said. 'You have the right to decide what to do with it.'

Marcia tore the page into two pieces and handed one back. 'I think we should have a barbie,' she replied. 'James loved a barbie.'

They stood beside the barbecue and tossed their pieces onto the embers. The paper curled and blackened. Flames leapt to consume the big revelation. Gossamer thin carbon fragments floated into the air.

'Job done,' Marcia said.

'Not quite,' Alistair replied. 'I still have things to finish off. The biggest day of Caroline's year will be here in a couple of days. You have to celebrate for her and with her. That stone circle at Stowe is your special place, so that is where you must be for the big event. We'll move over and spend the night on Gaia tomorrow, so that you are on hand to celebrate solstice with Caroline, in the appropriate place.'

'And you too,' she said. 'We all belong together. Let's forget the wine and turn in.'

Chapter 61

Paul Clifford hobbled into Bannerman Court and up the filthy concrete stairs to his third-floor landing at the top of the building. Each step now demanded greater effort than the last. In recent days, physical effort, even breathing itself, had become a painful ordeal. He turned the heavy brass key, went inside and closed the door behind him. Fume laden air stung his throat. The atmosphere no longer concerned him. At that moment, his only thought was bed; a chance to rest his body and recuperate from the rigours of another challenging day. He took a few steps toward his bedroom. A loud knock on the front door made him gasp. He didn't answer. The letterbox flap crashed open. A voice hissed in from the landing.

'Open the door, Paul. I thought you were never coming home.'

Clifford crept to the door and opened it a crack. The visitor pushed him aside, stepped into the hall and closed the door.

'I need rest,' Clifford said. 'The pain is unbearable. My muscles are on fire. The drugs and my rub don't dull the agony any more. I'm dying.'

The visitor waved the comments aside with a sweep of the hand. 'Never mind that. I'd like you to tell me why the hell you thought it might be a good idea to start a one-man crime wave in Oxton.'

'I had to make sure my mom would still be properly cared for after I'm gone. I knew I only had a short time to get enough money together. That piece in *The Chronicle* said James Hastings might have his hands on something really major, so I got chatting to him, to find out what it was. He was a canny old bastard, never gave away any details, but he told me he'd found some unique thing that might be worth a fortune. It sounded like exactly what I needed. I planned to take it off him and get you to sell it for me.'

'Why, Paul? Your mother's care is already taken care of.'

'For how long? You'll pay her bills as long as I'm around working for you. How much longer do you think I can be your minder? Look at me. I'm dying. Am I supposed to believe you'll keep shelling out for my mom's care after I've snuffed it?'

'You have to believe it, Paul. You don't have any choice now the only two people who knew where this priceless item is are both dead. Do you even know what the thing is?'

'I think it's an old book. That Marcia woman practically runs the business. I reckon she's bound to know where it is. Her new boyfriend must know by now too. If I get hold of Marcia, I can use her to put the squeeze on him. I just need to stash her somewhere, send him a hair sample, maybe a couple of pulled fingernails, and he'll hand over.'

'Are you totally barmy? This isn't the movies, Paul. You've already been loose lipping about us. We've spent nearly forty years off the radar, practically invisible. Then you roll in and screw it all up.'

'All I said was, I had a mate who used to live in Oxton.'

'You said enough to set Caroline Blackham off sniffing around. It stops now, Paul. You do not go anywhere near Oxton again. You stay here, die here if you want to, but you do not go there anymore and you do not say another word to anyone. If that happens, it will definitely be your *final* word.'

The visitor left. Paul Clifford retired to his bed.

Chapter 62

Nash hurried into the CID room, where Reid sat thumbing through his notebook.

'I was sure I had something relevant in here,' Reid said. 'I haven't found it.'

'Never mind that for now,' Nash said. 'My balls are on the line here. The vicars' cars have turned up. Clive's 4x4 is on a pub car park in Haleford. Amanda's car is at Weaverston rail station. Get over there and see if the transport police have any more details.'

'At last. Something relevant. I'm on my way, sir.'

*

A British Transport Police sergeant met Reid at the entrance to Weaverston railway station and took him directly to the police office.

'I've sorted out the available CCTV,' he said. 'I haven't found any footage to ID the driver of that car.'

'Do you know what time the car entered the car park?' Reid asked.

'The windscreen ticket shows eleven forty-seven yesterday morning,' the officer confirmed. 'I have the platform CCTV ready to roll from that time.'

Reid started the machine and zoomed in on the station entrance. Less than five minutes in, the distinctive figure of Amanda Chapman, dressed in her familiar combat pants and white top, walked along the concourse and onto platform one.

'Pay dirt,' Reid said with a grin. 'Let's see whether she met someone or caught a train.' He turned to the platform camera and fast-forwarded through several minutes showing Amanda sitting on a bench. Four trains drew into the platform and left. Amanda stepped aboard the fifth train, which left the station at twelve thirty-nine.

'Where was that one going?' Reid asked.

'The final destination is Manchester,' the officer confirmed. 'I can call up the en-route footage, but it could take a while. That service stops at several places.'

'If you could make it a *short* while I'd appreciate it,' Reid said.

The officer entered the details and the video picked up the train as it drew into Haleford station. Two passengers left the train, four more got on. Amanda did not appear. The officer moved on to Crockerby. Amanda left the train and walked swiftly out of the station. The image switched to the concourse and picked Amanda up as she stepped into a taxi.

'That's it for us,' the officer said. 'I can't follow taxis.'

'Thanks anyway,' Reid replied. 'I would have been here for days going through that footage by myself.' He returned to his car and called Nash.

'Well done, Alex,' he said. 'She wouldn't get into a taxi unless she knew where she wanted to go. We're fairly sure Clifford has a flat in that area.' He paused. 'Clive parked his car a short walk from Haleford station and it's on the same route. Are you sure he didn't catch that train?'

'Quite sure, sir. I suppose he might have caught a different train. Amanda could have been going to meet him.'

'She sounded worried when she reported Clive missing,' Nash said. 'She claimed she wanted to stop him before he met up with Clifford or maybe someone else. It's also possible that Amanda had business of her own. We need to get the Chapman's in here.'

Chapter 63

Marcia finished her phone call and peeped into the kitchen. 'That was Aiden,' she said. 'He's arrived at the shop, so I'm on my way. Good luck with finding Nellie's book of spells.

'Thanks,' Alistair replied. 'Take care, don't go anywhere alone and I'll see you later.'

'Okay. Will you be arriving by car or broomstick?' She blew a kiss and disappeared toward the lane.

*

Alistair drove out to Sparrow Farm, a small council housing estate on the outskirts of Oxton. Sycamore Croft – a dozen semi-detached bungalows – stood facing a communal lawn at the edge of the development. Alistair parked his car and walked up the short front path to number seven. Lack of use had fused the knocker to its hinge. Alistair tapped on the faded blue front door. No one answered. He knocked again and was about to try a third time, when the door creaked open as far as the security chain would allow. Aged yet fire bright eyes scanned the visitor.

'Are you Hannah Brayford?' Alistair asked. The woman nodded. 'Forgive me for calling uninvited like this. I've heard that you are an expert on Nellie the witch. I'm hoping that you may be able to settle a few queries concerning Dr James Hastings and Caroline Blackham.'

'Are you a policeman?'

'I'm related to Dr Hastings. Caroline Blackham was a friend.'

'Leave me alone,' she said. 'I can't help you.' She began closing the door.

'Please, Hannah, people are dying.' Alistair said, placing his hand against the door. 'I'm family, and I know about the *Book of Secrets*.'

The security chain slowly tightened once again. Hannah eyed her visitor around the edge of the door for a moment. She sighed, released the chain and allowed the door to swing open. Alistair stepped inside, closed the door quietly behind him and followed Hannah through to the lounge.

The sturdy furniture shared its owner's well-maintained appearance. Alistair guessed it had also shared a good deal of her long life. Hannah lifted her black cat from the settee and offered her visitor a seat. She sat, unsupported by cushions, on a small wingback chair beside the empty fireplace. Alistair squatted on the edge of the settee, under Hannah's laser-like scrutiny, for an uncomfortably long time before she spoke again.

'The lady you mentioned was named Eleanor Rosemont,' she said at last. 'Nicknames are so disrespectful. The stories about Eleanor are as old as the grave itself. What more can I tell you?'

'I don't want folk tales,' Alistair replied. 'I came to see you because I need the truth.' He felt Hannah's sharp eyes probing deep inside his head.

'How did you find me?' she asked.

'Your name was among Dr Hastings' papers,' Alistair lied.

'Two hundred years this has been haunting us,' Hannah said. 'I'm sick of it, sick and tired. Stories grow arms and legs over the years. Eleanor's death bred generations of hair-raising tales. Gossip will soon conjure stories about James and Caroline. Are you preparing to fan the flames?'

'I'm hoping that, with your help, I might be able to extinguish a dangerous blaze,' Alistair said.

'I belong to yesterday's world,' Hannah replied. 'My fire-fighting days are long past.' Alistair saw deep weariness in Hannah's eyes and began considering a sympathetic exit. 'I'm the last of the Rosemonts,' she said. Alistair's jaw dropped. 'It isn't a fact I like to boast about,' she added. 'We were a wealthy family in the old days, proper gentry until the family broke up. We lost it all well before my lifetime, as you can see for yourself.'

'Why?' Alistair asked. 'Was it because Samuel had killed his wife? Did shame break up the family?'

Hannah shook her head. 'The family knew what he'd done and they were rightly ashamed, but they had a good reputation and wanted to keep it, so they managed to keep Sam's evil deed quiet.'

'Were there consequences for Samuel? What happened to him, Hannah?' Alistair asked trying to conceal his surprise and sudden excitement at her frankness. 'Did he run away to Lincolnshire in search of something, maybe something belonging to Eleanor or her family?'

'I don't know what went on over there, but I'm quite sure that's where he should have stayed,' she said. 'I think James knew something of it. I imagine you do too, or you wouldn't be here. All I know is that Sam came back.' She reached for the comforting warmth of her cat and began slowly stroking between the animal's ears. The two-hundred-year-old story unfolded as if it were repeating before her eyes. 'Twenty-five years he'd been away then one day, without any warning, up he popped again. Nothing had changed. People were looking for him as usual. When Sam disappeared, nobody gave a tupenny damn where he'd gone. It must have caused a terrible panic when he turned up again, with him being the big blundering halfwit he was. There were tales of the fool's tormented soul turning up near Eleanor's grave at least once. That's how some of the Nellie stories started. People believed she'd lured Sam back from his eternal rest. The family pleaded with him to go away again. He demanded protection. In the end, he left them with no choice. They had to kill him. Maybe that was a kind of justice. Sam was supposed to be long dead already, so it should have been the end of the matter.'

'But it wasn't?'

Hannah continued stroking her cat. 'No, it wasn't. Sam brought something back with him, something he had no right to touch.'

Alistair's pulse raced. 'What did he bring, Hannah?'

She gave a sad shrug. 'All I know is he brought something dangerous. Gold, jewels, valuables he'd stolen from some rich family. It could have been anything. Whatever he brought back, the Rosemonts believed he must have killed to get his hands on it. And he came running back here, leading the Lord alone knows who, straight to his family.'

'Did Sam bring the *Book of Secrets* home with him, Hannah?'

'There is a book,' she confirmed. 'I've never seen it, never wanted to. Sam's thuggery and thieving destroyed the Rosemonts. They buried him on the farm, along with his damned loot. Fear and shame scattered our family to the four winds. They ended up as outcasts. Nearly every one of them died in poverty.'

'Why have you and your ancestors, stayed silent all this time?'

'Some stories aren't for the telling,' she said. 'I wouldn't be telling it now if you didn't already know most of it.'

'What happened to Sam's haul?'

Age gathered into furrows on the woman's face. The cat eyed Alistair with feline mistrust. Hannah continued stroking between its ears. 'It's still hidden away,' she said at last. 'James Hastings said he'd return everything to the proper hands. Maybe now he's gone, it should stay hidden.'

'It's too late for that, Hannah,' Alistair replied. 'The secret is out and people are dying.'

'James thought he'd bagged a wonderful trophy,' Hannah continued. 'It got him killed, just like everybody else who ever touched it.'

'If I can find the stuff and hand it back as James planned to do, I might be able to bring this horror to an end,' Alistair replied.

'James may have moved it already.'

'Sam's loot has been safely hidden for two hundred years,' Alistair reminded her 'Maybe James decided it was better not to risk leading anyone to the hiding place until it was time to hand the goods back. My guess is he'd leave things alone.' The creases deepened on Hannah's brow. 'I'm sure somebody else is looking,' Alistair said. 'That's why Caroline and James were murdered. I need to find the place before another innocent soul pays the price. Please tell me where it is.' Hannah gazed deep into his eyes. She did not reply. 'Please, Hannah.'

'There's a private lake with a chapel on it, near the Rosemont house,' Hannah replied at last. 'My ancestors buried Sam and his loot under the chapel. I've never dared go near it for fear of leading someone else there.'

'Surely you've checked that the stuff is still where the family hid it?'

'If anyone had found it, the news would have been splashed all over the papers,' Hannah replied. 'As far as I'm concerned, it would be good riddance. I decided that, as long as I stayed away, the secret was safe and so was I. It worked until Caroline and James came looking.' She stopped stroking her cat, stared into the empty fireplace then turned to Alistair. 'What will become of me?' she asked. 'I'm old and ready to pass on. If death comes to seek me out now, I have more lives to pay for.'

Alistair reached across and stroked her trembling hand. 'You have nothing to pay for, Hannah,' he said. 'James took the secret from you in full knowledge of its implications. It isn't your responsibility any more and nor am I.'

Pain and doubt had dulled the sparkle in Hannah's old eyes. 'Why must you find it?' she asked.

'Because I have to finish what James Hastings started,' Alistair replied. 'He has resurrected a deadly secret. People died more than two centuries ago and now more innocent souls have been lost, all because of a book and perhaps a few baubles. I don't believe in curses, but I know all about the evil that feeds on fear and death. Believe me, Hannah, I know. This horror won't stop until I honour James's promise to you.'

Hannah gazed into his eyes. 'Then do what you must do,' she said.

*

Alistair left Hannah at her empty fireside and returned to his car. He sat thinking very carefully before he turned the ignition key and started the engine. As he drove away, he glanced into his rear-view mirror. An ominously familiar small car, parked some distance away, caught his attention. He drove a short loop around the estate and returned to Sycamore Croft. The car now stood outside Hannah Brayford's bungalow.

Alistair walked along and opened the front passenger door. April Maylor turned and reached for the recorder on the seat beside her. Alistair snatched it away.

'You don't need this for now,' he said, holding the recorder beyond her reach. 'I dislike being followed, Ms Maylor, particularly when I am simply visiting an elderly friend. There is no public interest here.'

'I think you're wrong,' she said. 'I think that friend of yours knows something of great public interest.'

'I will tell you once more,' Alistair said quietly. 'The resident of this bungalow is frail and elderly. Leave her in peace. Do not dig where there is no dirt.'

April glared. 'Don't you dare give me orders. This is…'

'This is serious advice,' he interrupted. 'Listen very carefully. The police have not yet found the person who broke into my home.'

'That had nothing to do with me.'

'Possibly,' Alistair replied. 'However, if I happen to recall a little additional information, they may wish to speak with you again.'

'You wouldn't lie to the police.'

'Of course not,' he agreed. 'However, I am under considerable stress just now. My recall may be a little patchy, not altogether accurate. I'm sure the police would forgive a minor inconsistency of memory.'

'You wouldn't do it.'

'Are you quite certain of that, Ms Maylor?' She slumped into her seat. 'The story you want so badly, *may* be approaching its conclusion,' he said. 'If you attempt to contact the person who lives in that bungalow, directly or indirectly, or if you instruct anyone else to do so, I shall ensure that when this story breaks you will not be running around asking questions, you will be in police custody *answering* them. Have I made myself absolutely clear?'

'This is my big chance to achieve national recognition.'

'Then I advise you not to waste it,' Alistair replied with a smile. He tossed the recorder back into her car and walked away, hoping he had done enough to dissuade the journalist for a little while.

Alistair drove a short distance from Sparrow Farm, checked that no one had followed him and stopped the car. Before attempting to arrange a meeting with Sir Miles Baverstock, he pulled out his phone and selected Marcia's number. Her mobile was switched off, as it regularly remained, to avoid unwanted calls from Caroline's stolen mobile. He tried Dawn's number.

'I'm walking Sheba and Cleo,' Dawn said. 'Marci isn't on her boat. I've just strolled past to check it out.'

'Thanks Dawn,' Alistair replied. 'She should be at the shop in Oxton today, but she tends to go her own way. She shouldn't be out alone, it's too dangerous. If she turns up over there, ask her to call me. He disconnected and entered the Bookbinders landline number. Once again, there was no reply. His pulse raced to a thundering gallop as he punched in the next number. Aiden answered after two rings. 'Thank heaven,' Alistair said. 'Where are you?'

'I'm at home.'

'Is Marci with you.'

'No. Is there a problem?'

'I can't locate her. Her phone is off. I thought she was at

Bookworm with you. She left Bookbinders to join you there earlier. I've spoken to Dawn Tyler and she confirmed that Marci isn't on Gaia.'

'The contractors aren't at the shop today,' Aiden replied. 'I went in earlier, in case Marcia came to go through more of the stock. She didn't arrive. I tried to phone her, as you did. There seemed no point in remaining there alone, so I came home.'

'Okay, leave it with me. I'll keep looking until I find her.' He headed off, hoping to find that Marcia had shown up at Stowe Junction.

*

Gaia's bow and stern covers were in place. The window blinds were down. Alistair snatched a sheet loose and slipped beneath the stern cover. The galley doors were locked from the outside. Marcia was not aboard. He scrambled out and ran along the riverbank. The circle also stood deserted. His pulse raced. He took off over the hill.

Dawn Tyler was grooming her dogs, in the small compound beside her cottage. Several campers milled around their haphazard site. The dogs barked to warn of Alistair's approach. Dawn turned and smiled.

'Hi, Alistair,' she said. 'Have you come for a coffee and a cosy?'

'Marci still isn't on Gaia,' He said a little breathlessly. 'Are you sure you don't have any idea where she might by?'

'Possibly at your place. She phoned to check on Gaia, said she had something or other to do in Oxton then she was coming home to you.'

'I need to get over there,' he said, already turning. He hurried off back to his car, punching in Marcia's name on his contact list as he ran. The connection failed. He slid into his car, snatched the door shut and selected the landline number at Bookbinders. No one answered. He rammed the car into gear and shot away from the clearing.

*

Marcia's car was not in its place at Bookbinders. Alistair ran around to the kitchen where Nancy was filling the coffee maker. 'I've tried to phone you,' he said. 'Has Marci been in touch?'

'I'm only just back from the village, Ali,' she replied, clearly seeing his concern. 'Is everything alright?'

'I really hope so,' he said as he headed back toward the lane. He stood beside his open car door pondering where to search next. He was on the point of phoning the police when Marcia drove into the lane and parked her car behind the Mercedes. She paused to dry her eyes, and stepped out into the sunshine.

Alistair ran and drew her into a tight hug. 'Thank heaven your back,' he said. 'Where have you been? Are you okay?'

'I'm fine, just a little fragile,' Marcia replied. 'I've been to finalise the arrangements for Cal's funeral. I wanted it all sorted before solstice tomorrow. I couldn't leave her in limbo. When I came out of Warren Hinchcliffe's, I could feel her drawing me to the circle again. I'm sure she wants... You were absolutely right. We need to be together to say our final goodbye.'

'Grab what you need,' Alistair said, ushering her round to the house. 'I'll explain to Nancy.'

He told the housekeeper that he and Marcia would be away overnight but planned to be back sometime the next day. Nancy reminded him that it would be her half day, so she would leave a casserole in the oven for them. Marcia returned from her room with a few clothes draped over her arm. Nancy smiled as the couple disappeared hand in hand toward the lane.

Chapter 64

Night still masked the flat when Paul Clifford woke from his troubled sleep and reached automatically for the painkillers on his bedside table. He quickly swallowed three and fell back onto his mattress. Aside from visits to the bathroom, he had remained there for well over twenty-four hours. The inescapable approach of daybreak now forced him from his bed. Warning or no warning, it was time to face the final challenge and complete his mission. If his mother's care was to continue, he must now seize and hold Marcia Blackham until her boyfriend handed over the item that James Hastings had discovered.

He knew that no damned book could possibly be worth so much pain and death. Killing was never part of the original plan. That plan had simply run out of control. If James had not become suspicious and told him to stop visiting, he could have teased out more information and had the scam wrapped up. If the old man hadn't abandoned the church project, Paul could have squeezed more out of the vicar or his wife. If the archaeologist and the contractors hadn't hung around, he could have had the job done before his time ran out. None of it was his fault, and he had no choice. His mom's care must go on being paid for. He had to finish the job.

He struggled to sit up, fumbled for the syringe beside his bed and slowly injected into each thigh. A few precious minutes allowed the pain killer to take its minimal effect, which now barely enabled him to stand. Before struggling into his trousers, he applied a liberal amount of the muscle rub he had used throughout what had until so recently been his active healthy life. He dressed slowly, staggered along to the kitchen and leaned against the sink, for a vital moment to overcome the agony of breathing.

The final two slices of bread, in a wrapper beside his sink, reminded him that he had not eaten for longer that he was able to recall. After pausing to suppress a fresh wave of pain, he took a small piece of cheese from his fridge, trimmed away the mouldy end and used the remainder to make a sandwich. He had no appetite. Another, more urgent matter occupied his thoughts. He left the kitchen and walked along the short hallway to his outer door. After taking a moments rest, he picked up his car keys and left the flat.

Paul took the now familiar route south toward Stowe Junction where, instinct told him, Marcia Blackham would be preparing for the solstice. His attack plan became a little more confused with each pain dominated mental rehearsal. Each excruciating stab drew the knots a little tighter. Confusion fogged his thoughts. Twice, he veered from his route and took precious time to find his way back. He felt the mission slipping from his grasp, and was finally forced to pull in at the roadside and attempt to refocus. Get to hospital, he thought. Quickly. Get some treatment. One dose. Just enough to get this job done, for mom.

Thanks to the early hour, the roads were mercifully quiet. Concentration and consciousness ebbed and flowed over a fuzzy hinterland. Paul Clifford pressed on toward Oxton General, scuffing kerbs and straddling road marking until he somehow careered onto the hospital site. Pain and exhaustion finally overcame him as he mounted the kerb and came to a halt within a metre of the automatic doors at A & E. He fell forward, unconscious with his chest hard against the horn control.

Chapter 65

Alistair opened the galley doors and stepped up onto Gaia's aft deck. Marcia joined him in the pre-dawn, dressed in a long white silk dress. Light breeze caught her loose hair. Alistair took her hand and they stepped down together onto the cool grass. Marcia took a moment to focus her thoughts before they set off slowly and silently along the riverbank.

They reached the circle. Marcia squeezed Alistair's hand a little tighter. He scanned along the river in both directions. All appeared undisturbed, unhurried, at ease. They turned their backs to the water and stood facing east. The ancient stones, stood like silent sentinels, before them.

Trees hid the parking area beyond the grassy slope to their right. The dawn chorus had begun its overture in woodland to the left. Directly ahead, beyond the circle, a dull glow began lighting the open horizon. Marcia once again tightened her grip a little on Alistair's hand. A tide of anticipation rose inside her.

A slight movement drew Alistair's attention to the hill a little way beyond the trees. Marcia felt his instant response. Fear fizzed in her stomach. Their heads turned in unison.

*

Dawn Tyler appeared on the skyline leading a column of people over the hilltop and down toward the circle. The group gathered behind Marcia and Alistair. Silence held the group as each person took position until they stood, as if placed by some invisible choreographer, united by common purpose exactly as Caroline had planned. Marcia turned, exchanged a smile and mouthed a silent *thank you* to Dawn, as she fought back an insistent tear.

The crowd turned as a single silent body to face the approaching sun. A slow drumbeat sounded, from some point behind Marcia and Alistair, to signal that the celebration had begun. People stood aside to create a path. The drummer walked slowly through to the centre of the circle. With Alistair at her side, Marcia led the crowd forward into the ancient space. The drummer stood, drumsticks crossed above his head, watching and waiting.

At four-seventeen, the first golden ray broke the horizon. For a precious minute, Marcia shone like a pure white goddess in the single spotlight beam. The sun gathered strength until it filled her hair like a pure ethereal glow from within.

As the celebration proceeded quietly toward its conclusion, the perfect atmosphere was shattered. People began flipping up the hoods on their hoodies. An agitated buzz skittered on a sudden wave of tension through the gathering.

Amanda Chapman drove into the deserted campsite and ran over to the hillside overlooking the circle. Two uniformed police officers appeared to be monitoring the celebration with the aid of a drone. Amanda watched, hoping her instinct, that Clifford would be there, had been wrong. The crowd began dispersing.

Marcia was satisfied that, despite the annoying drone interruption, she had fulfilled her duty to Caroline. She sensed and shared Alistair's obvious unease. The airborne intruder might clearly be part of a routine police drug scan. It might also suggest that the police believed a murder suspect might be among the crowd. Yet more sinister, was the possibility that the killer himself had put up the drone to hunt them down. Alistair's arm slid around her waist.

'Time to go,' he said quietly. They slipped away and returned to Gaia.

Amanda followed the couple until they were safely back aboard the boat. She waited until she was satisfied that no-one had followed them, and returned to her car.

Chapter 66

Rev Frank Benson, the fifteenth local clergyman of twenty-six on Clive Chapman's list, remembered Paul Clifford as an occasional member of his congregation. He assumed that Paul's recent absence from worship was due to his illness. Rev Benson did not know Paul's address, but believed he may have been a fairly long-standing member of the Karate Kings martial arts club. He suggested they might have the information.

As the taxi pulled up outside the club, Clive's driver suggested that his passenger should confirm that it was open, at eight-thirty in the morning, before he drove away. 'This isn't a good area to go wandering around in by yourself,' he said.

Clive stepped out, and confirmed that the lights were on inside and the front door was open. He thanked his driver and went into the modern and, to his amateur eye, well equipped space. The walls were lined with good quality gym equipment. Several dojo mats occupied the central floor space.

A stocky and obviously fit man walked over to greet Clive. He introduced himself as Andy Bailey, the manager. Clive explained why he was there. Andy shook his head. 'Sorry,' he said. 'Data protection. I can't release members personal details.'

'But you are telling me that Paul Clifford is a member here?' Clive replied with a smile.

'I never said that,' Andy blurted. 'Just give me a minute.' He walked over, disappeared into an office in the corner and returned after a few minutes, followed by a smartly dressed man who Clive guessed to be in his sixties.

The man offered his hand. 'David King,' he said. 'I'm the owner of Karate Kings. It isn't the biggest club around, but we train to a good standard. I'm afraid Andy is correct. We cannot disclose personal details of our members. Does the person you are looking for have your contact details.'

'He does but…'

'Then I imagine he will make contact if he wishes to meet you.'

Clive's phone beeped in his pocket. 'Would you mind if I answer this?' he asked.

'Not at all,' David King replied. 'It may be Mr Clifford.'

Clive hit the green button, introduced himself and listened briefly. 'I see,' he said. 'Yes of course. I'm in Crockerby at the moment but I'll be there as soon as possible.' He disconnected. 'Mr Clifford is in Oxton General Hospital,' he said. 'Please excuse me.'

Clive called for his taxi, then immediately phoned to update Amanda and advise her to head for home.'

'Done it already,' she confirmed. 'I didn't manage to find Paul's address, but I knew that solstice would be a major event for Caroline. Marcia and Alistair would be almost certain to attend in her memory. I decided that if Paul is involved in the murders and intimidation, he'd probably target them there, so I got myself over to Stowe. He didn't show. I'm about to go home. Where are you?'

'Still in Crockerby. I've just had a call from Oxton General. Paul was admitted a few hours ago and he's asking for me. I'm just about to get off down there now.'

'Okay, sweetheart. Be careful and I'll meet you there.'

Clive's taxi arrived. 'That didn't take long,' the driver said. 'If I'd known you were going to be that quick, I would have waited for you.'

'This might take a little longer,' he said. 'I need to get to Haleford rail station, as quickly as possible.'

'We have a station,' he said.

'I know,' Clive replied, 'but yours doesn't have my car parked a hundred metres away from it.'

Chapter 67

Clive Chapman hurried into the hospital and up to the ward. Amanda was already waiting. She joined him at the nurses' station.

'I came as quickly as I could,' he said. 'Is Paul...?'

'Conscious but very poorly,' the nurse confirmed. 'He's been asking for you constantly since he woke. It's room two, on the left.'

'Very well. I'll go straight to him,' Clive replied.

'Shall I come in with you?' Amanda asked.

'Best if I just do as he's asking first,' Clive suggested. 'I'll call you in if he asks to see you.'

Clive stepped into Paul Clifford's single bedded side-room and approached his bed. The patient lay with his eyes closed, clearly having difficulty breathing. In the few short days since he last left the vicarage kitchen, Paul seemed to have become physically smaller, almost withered. Clive reached out and placed his hand on Paul's skeletal forearm. 'Hello Pe... Paul,' he said quietly. 'I'm sorry it took me so long to get here. We can talk... pray if you'd like to, or just sit quietly together. I'm content to do whatever you wish.'

'I just wanted the information from James Hastings,' he said as if desperate to unload his burden. 'Had to find out exactly what he had, where it was. Had to have it. Should have been simple. Would have been, if it hadn't all gone wrong, out of control. I need to tell you, so that you can tell, whoever needs to know.' The effort became too much. He fought for breath as a fresh wave of pain gripped him.

Clive stroked his arm until the agony appeared to subside a little. 'What must you tell me, Paul?' he asked.

'I never planned to kill anybody. Had to get the stuff and I was running out of time. Had to get it, Reverend Clive. Had to, for my mom. You have to tell them, I never planned to kill anybody.'

'How did you get caught up in it, Paul?' Clive asked.

'The guy who owns the gym I use, did use until I got ill, lived in Oxton years ago. He still reads the local paper online. He showed me a piece about James Hastings finding something valuable. He was jealous. That's all it took to get me going. I wish I'd never seen the story or even heard of Oxton now.'

'I can't disclose anything you say to me, Paul,' Clive reminded him, gently. 'If you did what I believe you are telling me, you must speak to the police.' He sensed agitation.

'Not the police,' Clifford insisted, grimacing as pain stabbed again. 'I don't trust them. You've been there. You know what police interviews are like. They'll twist whatever I say. I know you'll tell it straight.'

'It has to be your words, Paul.' He stared into Clive's eyes, depleted, defeated; clearly believing that his moment of confession and salvation, had been snatched from him. Clive felt his devastation. 'Would you like to make a statement?' he asked. 'If you would like that, I'll type out what you say and, if you agree that it's correct, you can sign it.'

Paul nodded.

Clive hurried out to Amanda. 'Laptop,' he said. 'Quickly, sweetheart, give me your laptop.'

Amanda took the laptop from her shoulder bag and handed it to him. 'Why? She asked. Can I help?'

'No. It has to be me. I'll tell you later.' He disappeared back into Paul Clifford's room. 'Are you sure you want to do this, Paul?' he asked as he flopped down onto his bedside seat.

'Dead sure,' Paul confirmed.

Over the next half hour, Paul Clifford described how failing health and mounting pressure, turned what he believed would be a straightforward passport to his mother's future care, into a desperate and deadly nightmare.

Clive's fingers, diverted from their more familiar routine of church bookings and sermon writing, quivered as they struggled to keep pace with the unfolding torrent of confession. Paul finally completed his task and closed his eyes.

'Look at me,' he murmured. 'Who would believe… I've been a fit guy all my life. Gym every day, if I could. Look at me now. And it took less than a year.'

'I think I've been to your gym, Karate Kings,' Clive said. 'It's nice.'

Clifford opened his eyes. A thin smile stretched his lips a little. 'The gym is more of a side-line,' he said. 'Dave King's main business, him and his partner, Lee, is art and antiques, high end, quality gear. They're pretty straight most of the time, but Lee doesn't worry too much about where some of the merchandise comes from. One or two iffy characters turn up now and again, so they've kept me around as a minder, for the past year or two. I see they don't get hurt and they pay for my mom's care home. That's how it's supposed to work, but I'm not much use to them anymore, am I? Lee threatened to have me snuffed, if I even came over here again. You can put that on your laptop with all the rest, if you like.'

Clive added the note and took the laptop to the nurses' station. A techno-savvy ward secretary established the necessary Wi-Fi link and printed off two copies of the document.

Clifford opened his eyes as Clive returned to his bedside. He introduced Dr Kumar, who had followed him into the room to witness that the statement was properly read and approved. Clifford nodded his approval and Clive read the statement aloud. It concluded with the declaration that the document had been read as dictated and that Paul Clifford agreed to its submission as evidence to the police. The doctor handed Paul his pen and held the document while it was

Chapter 69

Nash dropped Paul Clifford's statement on Reid's desk. 'It looks like our murder investigation may be over, Alex,' he said. Reid read through the document. His eye appeared to hesitate briefly on one point. 'Have you spotted something disturbing?' Nash asked.

'I have sir, if it's the same guy,' Reid confirmed. 'Clifford mentions David King. He was the husband of Deborah King, the victim of that unsolved murder here in 1981. The Kings lived in Oxton and David King taught martial arts. That much ties up.'

'He also dealt in art and antiques,' Nash added. 'There seems to be a nasty smell creeping up from that old case all over again.'

'Aye, sir, and we know Mr King disappeared soon after the murder.'

'Well, it looks like he's resurfaced,' Nash said. 'We could be about to launch another flimsy kite here, Alex, but we have a declared connection between King and Clifford. The basically similar murder methods might be pure coincidence, but personal connection might indicate collaboration. We'd best tick all the boxes before we sign our case off. Did the lab manage to lift any DNA from the clothing you sent in?'

'Not so far, sir. I'm definitely interested to see what they come up with now.'

'If anything,' Nash cautioned. 'It might be worth doing some background checks on Mr King, just to confirm that he is the person we think he might be. And in view of Clifford's allegation that some of the antique dealing might be a bit suspect, you could take a look at King's business partner too. I'll update our files and bring the boss man up to date. You can do a bit more digging, see what comes up. Fingers crossed, eh?'

quite impossible to keep the area clear of debris, which, as the old craftsmen obviously knew, provides the perfect location for a concealed entrance.'

A dark flagstone slowly appeared beneath the leaf litter. Alistair scraped more urgently until he managed to ease his fingers under the edge. He and Sir Miles lifted the flagstone and leaned it against the chapel wall.

Alistair peered into the dark void. 'How deep is it?' he asked.

'A bit more than your head height as I recall,' Sir Miles replied. 'I haven't been inside for many years. There should be a ladder. Wait there. I'll fetch an altar candle.' He disappeared toward the chapel door.

Alistair lowered himself into the pitch-blackness. His foot found the ladder propped a little way below the entrance. He climbed down, carefully testing each rung, to the earth floor of the dank chamber.

Sir Miles clambered down the ladder carrying two altar-candles. He lit them with a cigarette lighter from his pocket and scanned the chamber. The flames illuminated a space roughly two metres square and a little over two metres high. Crude brick pillars supported a timber ceiling. A skeleton lay on a stone slab at the far side of the chamber.

'Sam Rosemont, I presume,' Alistair said. 'If the loot is still here, Sam must be lying on it.' He slid the heavy slab aside to reveal a shallow space. 'This looks promising,' he said, tracing along the top edge of a rectangular box beneath the slab. His fingers located two stout hinges and quickly groped around to the opposite side. 'There's a catch,' he said. 'And it's open. There isn't a lock.'

'No need,' Sir Miles replied. 'No one who got this far would be deterred by a lock. Open it.'

A cloak of near spiritual silence descended on the chamber. Alistair's fingers trembled on the catch. He moistened his lips and lifted the heavy lid. Anticipation plummeted to disbelief.

'It's empty,' he murmured. 'How can it be? This must be Sam

Rosemont and I'm sure the family buried the loot with his body. It looks like that intruder of yours did get to the haul.'

'Unless a more recent treasure hunter found it,' Sir Miles said warily.

'This dust has not been disturbed for years,' Alistair said. 'That box may have contained hugely valuable stolen property. Damn,' he said. 'My phone is in my car. I should inform the police.'

'That may not be a good idea,' Sir Miles replied. 'I think you should accompany me back to the house.'

*

Alistair slid the skeleton and its slab back into place and followed Sir Miles up the ladder. They replaced the flagstone and scattered debris to cover the entrance.

Sir Miles rowed back across the lake. Alistair followed him along to the house and directly to the library. Sir Miles walked over to a bookcase and slid a short row of books aside. 'I have something to show you, Alistair,' he said as he clicked open a panel to reveal a wall safe. His fingers trembled as he entered the code and opened the door. He lifted out a rectangular package wrapped in a silk cloth and carried it over to the table.

'There was once a lock on that chest,' he said. 'I opened it and found this inside.'

He unfolded the cloth, to reveal a book of roughly A5 size, bound in flawless polished leather. The front cover bore an intricately embossed and lavishly coloured image of a dragon. The creature stared up from matching ruby eyes.

Alistair stared at the book. 'Did my uncle know about this?' he asked.

'James examined the book quite recently for the first time,' Sir Miles confirmed. 'He apparently managed to decipher a little of the text but could make no sense of it. Several pages appear to be missing.'

'I'll take his word,' Alistair said, carefully leafing through a few pages of the arcane script. 'The book seems complete, to my untrained eye. If those rubies are genuine, the cover alone must be worth a fortune.'

'That is where your mind and mine differ from James's,' Sir Miles said. 'To your uncle's *exceedingly expert* eye, the text appears incomplete. The book therefore has no academic value. He attached little importance to the cover decoration and embellishments. He advised me not to offer it for sale. I feel responsible for its safekeeping, so I agreed.'

'He was a bookseller,' Alistair replied. 'The book may not have academic value, but he'd certainly recognise potential profit. Even I can see that the book has substantial value. Something isn't making sense here. I need to have another word with someone.'

'Will you reveal my secret?'

'That must be your decision,' Alistair replied. 'That thing has a grave and deadly history. Recent events suggest that it may no longer be a secret.'

Chapter 71

The front door creaked open a few centimetres. 'You know why I'm here, don't you?' Alistair said.

Hannah slipped the security chain off and walked away to her lounge. Alistair followed.

'Did you go to the island?' she asked.

Alistair nodded. 'I went there and I found Sam, but I didn't find stolen riches.' Hannah didn't comment. 'I need the truth, Hannah, the whole truth,' Alistair said. 'And I need it now.'

Hannah slumped onto her seat beside the fireplace. 'How closely related were you and James?' she asked.

'Very,' he replied. 'He was my uncle, and the closest person I ever had to a father.'

Hannah searched deep into his eyes. 'Then perhaps you have a right to know,' she said. 'Caroline Blackham couldn't resist a mystery. She had to know every detail too.'

'She had been teasing her friends,' Alistair said. 'What had she discovered, Hannah?'

'The old tales about Eleanor have circulated for even longer than I've been around,' she replied. 'Myth and make-believe surround every fact. I didn't believe anybody could uncover the true story. I was wrong. James and Caroline had done their research. They had managed to dig out proper details and Caroline had contacts. I couldn't fob them off. James said it was time to reveal the truth.'

'What did you tell them Hannah?' Alistair asked. 'I think you're holding back something important. James was a bookseller and I know he'd seen Sam's book.'

Hannah gave a resigned nod. 'Eleanor kept her book safe, until Sam led the serpent people back here to her. She had promised to guard the book with her life. Eleanor had no family in these parts. The Rosemonts were the only people she could trust.'

'They were Sam's family. Why would she trust them?'

'I suppose the truth is that she had nowhere else to turn,' Hannah replied. 'Anyway, she handed her book over to us for safe keeping and gave her life to keep the secret.'

'So, Sam didn't bring Eleanor's book back home with him,' Alistair said. 'It's been here all the time. I suppose the family thought the book would be safe for ever when they buried it with Sam.'

Hannah studied Alistair for a long time before she spoke. 'I hoped James would believe that story too,' she said. 'I expected him to go and find the book in Sam's grave and be satisfied, same as I hoped you would. He told me he'd already seen Sam's book. James was an expert. He knew there had to be more. I've lived nearly a century, Alistair, and carried a dreadful burden for most of my life. In the end, I told him the truth. You're as near as makes no difference to being his son, so you're entitled to know too. Sam did bring a book back with him. That is the book you've seen. *The Book of Secrets* holds mysteries from the dawn of time. It is a dangerous thing, so dangerous that its secrets could not be written in a single book in case it fell into the wrong hands. There are two books. To unlock their secrets, they must be read together, side by side. Eleanor brought her book here so that it could never find its mate. Sam brought the other book. He didn't know there were two of them, but he knew *The Book of Secrets* was valuable. When he got his thieving hands on a book, he would have thought Eleanor had left her book with the family. That poor girl and her family gave their lives to keep those evil things apart. Sam stole the Gould's book and led the serpent people straight back to where Eleanor had her half

313

of the text. My family inherited a real poisoned chalice. That's why Sam had to die. The family buried his book with him but had to make sure the two parts never came together. They all scattered and my great-great-grandpa hid Eleanor's book in a place only he knew. He lived out his life in that little cottage on the red hill, as the keeper of the secret. When he died, the secret passed to his son, then his son's son and finally to me. Only the keeper ever knows where Eleanor's book is. I'm the last of the line. I have a duty to pass Eleanor's book on for safekeeping. When James turned up on my doorstep, fate seemed to have sent the next keeper to me. I had nobody else to pass the secret on to.'

'Did you tell James where to find Eleanor's book, Hannah?'

'I gave it to him.'

Alistair gasped. 'What did he do with it? Do you know where he hid it?' Hannah didn't answer. 'I can't ask the keeper, Hannah, he's dead.'

'James is probably dead *because* he became the keeper,' Hannah reminded him. 'I don't know where the book is. Only the keeper knows. If you go looking and find the thing, that dreadful responsibility passes to you. Are you sure you want to carry such a burden?'

'I have no choice,' Alistair replied. 'James may have disclosed the whereabouts of Sam's book before he realised its significance. The ultimate prize is Eleanor's book. The two volumes together form a unique and deadly pair. After centuries apart, their mysterious and sinister reputation, could make them almost priceless to some museum or collector. But they are toxic. I have to find James's hiding place and make sure those halves never meet each other again.'

'Where will you look?'

'I really have no idea,' he admitted.

He left Hannah, stroking her cat and staring into her empty fireplace.

Chapter 72

Alistair hit Marcia's number and was pleased when it connected. She picked up on the second ring. After saying how pleased he was that she had switched on again, he reported that he had tidied up his bits and bobs as planned and was about to drive over and pick her up. She sounded bright. With her mental load lifted at last she reported that she had caught up with all her messages, and actually enjoyed doing a few domestic chores for the first time in her life. There was no need for Alistair to rush over and pick her up since she planned to shower and then walk over to Dawn's cottage to thank her for supporting the solstice. 'Don't forget to pick me up though,' she said. 'I can almost smell that casserole Nancy promised to leave for us already. According to James, they are fabulous.'

'He was dead right about that,' Alistair confirmed. 'Take as long as you like with Dawn. If you aren't back when I get there, I'll hang around on Gaia.'

*

Marcia's casserole comment triggered wonderful memories. Alistair smiled as he recalled Nancy's beaming face at the top of the mezzanine stairs, with that same mouth-watering aroma reaching out to greet him whenever he returned home from school. She would whisk away his bag as James instructed, 'Ali is home for a holiday, Nancy, hide his school books in the cubby.' He closed his eyes and relived a few moments of blissful contentment.

The smile slowly turned to an expression of slightly stunned realization. His eyes opened. He stared into space. 'Oh, James,' he whispered. 'How could I have been so stupid?' He started his car and sped away toward Oxton.

*

Marcia enjoyed a leisurely shower and dressed in fresh shorts and shirt. She took a moment to gaze out over the languid river before stepping down to begin her walk to Dawn's cottage. A little way along the riverbank she saw Dawn and her dogs some way off walking toward her. Marcia waved and turned back to prepare coffee on Gaia.

A woman, of slender build with mature though still attractive features appeared from among the trees. She strode down to the riverbank and introduced herself to Marcia as Lisa Daniels, a journalist from the *Oxton Chronicle*. She said that she was hoping to have a chat with a man named Paul Clifford and thought he might be at Stowe.

'This place is well off the beaten track for most people,' Marcia observed. 'Why did you think he might be here?'

Dawn had now joined them. 'I suppose he might have come for the solstice,' she suggested bending to give a few calming strokes to Sheba and Cleo, who's rumbling growls suggested they did not like the woman.

'If he was planning to come here, he didn't make it,' Marcia said quietly. 'I'm sorry to tell you that Paul died in Oxton General Hospital, earlier this morning. I don't know any details.'

'I see,' the woman replied. 'I knew he was ill. How very sad. Those dogs obviously don't care much for me. I'll leave you to get on with whatever you have to do.' She turned and left.

'I suppose I should have offered her coffee,' Marcia said.

Dawn shook her head. 'She looks a bit, up to something, to me,' she said. 'She turned up at the campsite, by taxi, just after we all got back from solstice. She's been pestering folk with questions about that man she was looking for, ever since she arrived. I don't like her.'

She bent to stroke the dogs again. 'And my girls are never wrong, are you babies?'

*

Alistair's car slid to a halt in the carriage yard. He leapt out and clattered up the mezzanine stairs. A frantic fumble with the key finally opened the office door. Alistair stepped inside and closed the door behind him.

James's coats still hung, though now smoke and dust soiled, where the old man had left them in the alcove between the office and the upstairs kitchen. Alistair took a deep breath and pushed the garments aside.

His fingers fumbled along the time worn edge of a perfectly concealed false beam. He located the ancient wooden catch and squeezed gently. The hinged front panel swung open to reveal the cubby, where Nancy had once hidden his school bag and books. The long blue sports bag was still there. A spiral bound A4 pad and a silk wrapped rectangular object lay beside the bag, where they had landed after apparently being thrown into the space. Alistair quickly closed the window blind, locked the mezzanine door and set the stair alarm. His fingers tingled as he reached into the cubby, retrieved the items of interest and carried them over to James's desk.

He unfolded the silk cloth to reveal a leather-bound book, similar to the one he had seen at Ashton Grange. The etched and beautifully coloured serpent on the front complemented Sir Miles' volume in all but one vital feature. The settings for the creature's eyes were empty. 'You removed them didn't you, Eleanor?' he murmured. 'You took its emerald orbs, so that it could never see, never ensnare, anyone who might dare to explore its secrets.' He rewrapped the parcel and turned to the closed notebook. A brief but essential pause steadied his racing pulse before he moistened his lips and looked inside.

The notes confirmed the facts of Eleanor's murder and Sam's escape to Lincolnshire. They ended at the ragged edge of a torn-out page. Alistair smiled, knowing that he and Marcia had found and

317

burned the missing piece, which James had felt compelled to remove?

Alistair had a different matter on his mind. Now that he had the book, James's responsibility as its keeper, had fallen to him. He must find a secure new hiding place. Taking Eleanor's deadly volume with him, he returned to his car. He slipped the package very carefully into the spare wheel compartment, replaced the toolkit to conceal it and left for Stowe Junction.

Chapter 73

Sheba and Cleo lay sunning themselves and keeping watch on the saloon roof. As Alistair emerged from the trees on his way down from the parking area, the dogs sat to attention and began barking. Alistair approached a little more cautiously, until Dawn appeared on the aft deck.

She quietly reassured the dogs and beckoned Alistair. 'Come on,' she said. 'The girls love being on the boat, so they'll be happy to have a seadog on board.'

'Is there a problem?' Alistair asked. 'Where's Marci?'

'She's had a minor upset but she's fine,' Dawn replied. 'I've just hung around to keep her company. I'll be off now you're here. She's waiting for you in the saloon.'

He went aboard and down into the saloon, where Marcia sat, looking a little pensive, he thought. 'I've just spoken to Dawn,' he said. 'What happened?'

'Probably nothing,' she sighed. 'It's just... I thought, with Clifford out of the picture everything might settle back to what's left of normal. I've had a lovely lazy morning, not looking over my shoulder any more. And then some journalist turned up looking for Paul Clifford. Dawn says she arrived in her campsite, in a taxi, earlier this morning.'

'Did you get her name? What did she look like?'

'Slim, shoulder length blonde perm. Just normal. She said her name was Lisa Daniels.'

Alistair took out his phone, searched a number and called *The Chronicle*. The receptionist quickly consulted a colleague before confirming that the paper had no Lisa Daniels on its staff. Alistair suggested that the woman was probably just one of the local nose pokers. Purely as a precaution, or so he insisted, he called Oxton police and passed the information to Nash.

Chapter 74

Nash slammed down his phone as Reid entered his office. 'It looks like your day is going the same sort of way as mine,' the sergeant suggested.

'That was Dawlish,' Nash replied. 'Some woman pretending to be a journalist has turned up at Stowe, looking for Paul Clifford. Probably just a gossip peddler.' He passed the details across. 'I've reported Clifford's allegation regarding possible criminal antique dealing activities by David King and his partner. Crockerby aren't interested,' he said. 'They obviously have the same manpower and budget shortages as everybody else. They agreed to log the information but won't take it any further without firm evidence of criminal activity. How far have you got?'

'I've established a firm trail via property and business registrations that David King of Karate Kings and Prestige Antiques is the same man whose wife was murdered in this area in 1981. He currently lives in a very desirable part of Cheshire. The gym wouldn't provide enough income to support that lifestyle. It seems to be more of a hobby than a business. The main income obviously comes from the antiques business. There's no criminal record on PNC.'

'What about the partner?'

'Aye well that's where I've hit my dead end. I haven't found a thing. Hardly surprising I suppose, considering I don't even have a surname to go on.'

'See what you can turn up on that Lisa Daniels woman who turned up at Stowe Junction today. We know she isn't from *The Chronicle*. I suppose she may be a hack from some other publication. It might be worth finding out if she has a different angle on Clifford or King.'

Nash's desk phone beeped as Reid returned to the CID room.

The switchboard operator reported that she has a caller on the line asking to speak with the senior detective.

'Did he say what he wants to talk about?' Nash asked.

'No sir. He just gave his name as David King and asked for the senior…'

'Put him through, Gretchen,' Nash cut in. 'Quickly, before he changes his mind.'

Nash introduced himself and asked how he could be of assistance.

David King explained that he was concerned about the safety of a man named Paul Clifford who he believed was admitted to Oxton General Hospital, early that morning. The thing is,' he said, 'Paul is a casual employee. I've tried the hospital, but they refuse to confirm or deny that he is a patient there.'

'What is the nature of Mr Clifford's employment with you?' Nash asked.

'I suppose he is a personal assistant.'

'I see,' Nash replied. 'Why are you so concerned about a *casual* employee.'

'My partner instructed Paul to stay away from the Oxton area. She went to his flat early this morning and phoned to inform me that he was not at home. I am concerned that she may have come over there looking for him. She isn't answering her phone. I'm afraid that if she finds Paul, she may confront him and get hurt or do something stupid.'

'Why is your partner so keen to keep Mr Clifford away from Oxton?'

There was a pause before the caller spoke again. 'Many years ago, I lived in Oxton, loved the place until my wife was murdered. The murderer wasn't caught, so all the barbed stared and accusing fingers

you to forgo a huge amount of money, but that thing is lethal. Someone may be looking for it right now. Even if no-one is currently hunting, sooner or later someone will pick up the scent. I don't think you should keep it too close to you.'

'I agree,' Sir Miles replied. 'I've done some rather serious thinking since we met this morning. I now believe that the book may have led to my father's death. Given its history, any financial gain would seem rather tainted. I have decided to offer the book on permanent loan to the British Museum.'

'That is a terrific idea,' Alistair said with obvious relief. 'The County Archaeologist has a contact at the museum.'

'I'm so pleased you agree,' Sir Miles replied. 'I'll liaise with the archaeologist. Leave it with me.'

A huge wave of relief washed over Alistair as he ended the call.

'Excuse me,' a voice called. Alistair turned as a man jogged along the riverbank toward him. 'Sorry to bother you,' the man said as he joined Alistair. 'I'm hoping you can help me. My name is David King. I arranged to meet a DCI Nash at Stowe junction. I'm parked at some sort of campsite over the hill. I thought, wrongly, that it was the place I wanted. I'm told there is another parking area somewhere close by but I haven't managed to find any sign of it.'

Alistair pointed to the path. 'That will take you straight to it,' he said. 'It only forty or fifty metres.'

'I'm looking for my partner. I think she may have been seen in this area,' King explained, as he pulled a small bundle of photographs from his shirt pocket and handed one to Alistair. 'It's a frame from the CCTV at home. Not the best picture in the world, but it's all I have. Her name is Lisa Daniels. She's blonde around five-five.'

'I haven't seen her myself,' Alistair replied, 'but I think she may have been here a little earlier. I'll keep my eyes peeled. If she shows up again, I'll ask her to message you. Nash's car is a dark grey Mondeo. It will probably be the only one, other than mine, parked up there.'

Chapter 76

Nash's phone beeped as he drew into the parking area. He parked and picked up.

'Sorry to interrupt your meeting, sir,' Reid said. 'I thought Mr King might be interested to hear that Lisa Daniels could still be over there at Stowe. I've phoned around the local taxi firms and found the driver who picked her up at the rail station and took her over to that campsite. He says he received another call later on to pick her up and take her back to the station. He attended but Ms Daniels failed to show. Unless she walked out, in which case our patrol would have spotted her by now, it's likely that she's still in the area.'

'I got held up processing that bit of evidence,' Nash replied. 'I've only just arrived. There's no sign of King or his car. It looks like I may have missed him.' David King appeared from the path, looked around briefly and approached the Mondeo. 'Problem solved,' Nash confirmed. 'He's here. I'll see you later.'

David King dropped into the passenger seat beside Nash and apologised for keeping him waiting. 'I'm embarrassed to say, I lost my way,' he said. 'I remember this area, as it was many years ago. It's completely different now.'

'You sounded worried about Ms Daniels,' Nash said.

'I do worry about her,' he admitted. 'She worries about me. That's the way our partnership has always worked.'

'So, you've been together a long time?'

'We first met when she was eighteen. I had just graduated and come home to begin my glittering career. Forgive the pun. I was about to take over a tiny jewellery shop in Oxton. I had a history degree so my interests were more inclined toward art and antiques. I took a chance and rebranded the business. I was lucky. History and nostalgia are popular with local people and tourists. The business grew quite quickly. Lisa and I hit it off instantly and enjoyed a wonderful summer together. That September, she went off to begin her nurse training in Kent.'

'Did you keep in touch?'

'I didn't see or hear from her again for more than five years.'

Nash stared. 'Didn't that strike you as a bit odd? Two hormone loaded youngsters, instant attraction, summer of love. Then thank you and goodbye?'

'It's like that during those short years, isn't it? We break away from home, become independent, get a new career, in a new location, with new friends. It's all a bit pick and mix for a while.'

'Maybe,' Nash replied coolly. 'So where did you meet up again?'

King smiled. 'Back in Oxton, believe it or not. She came into the shop one morning, bright and beautiful as ever, as if she had never been away.'

'Had you met Debbie by then?'

'Met and married, Chief Inspector.'

Nash stared at his visitor. He did not reply.

'I see the question in your mind,' King finally confirmed. 'I loved my wife and we had looked forward to a wonderful life together. Her mental health problem wasn't part of our plan and the decline was cruelly rapid. My lovely Debbie faded and disappeared within our first year of marriage. I became her carer; a loving and willing companion, but no longer a husband. I did my best, my very best, to keep her safe and well, and...' He paused and blinked. 'She needed me, depended on me, and I failed her. The pain subsides a little with time but the wound never heals. Maybe that's why I worry about

Lisa. I couldn't survive another wound like losing Deb.'

Nash could not share the circumstances of David King's enduring pain, but he saw it in the man's eyes, and most certainly shared the unremitting devastation of losing a soul mate.

King swallowed the fireball in his throat and continued. 'When Debbie was... when she died, my world disintegrated. Lisa became my anchor my infallible support. There had been no physical relationship in my marriage for a long time. Debbie had become a child again. A sweet innocent little girl. Intimacy would have felt like abuse, assault to us both. It would have destroyed her trust in me. And so, I confess that Lisa and I, rekindled the old flame and fell back into our relationship. It was born of lust and it began, to my eternal shame, before I lost Debbie. My relationship with Lisa did not change the fact that I loved my wife, Chief Inspector. I loved her dearly and, as I told your colleagues all those decades ago, I did not harm her, would never have harmed her and I miss her to this day.'

Nash immediately turned to Lisa. 'Could you tell me your date and place of birth?' he said.

She looked at David. 'I gave you the details, Chief Inspector,' he said to Nash.

'Yes, sir,' Nash confirmed, 'but there may have been an error.' He turned back to Lisa. She repeated the details. 'Thank you,' Nash said. 'Those are the details my sergeant has checked. They are Lisa Daniels' details. They are not yours, are they?'

'I have my birth certificate at home, if you would like to see it,' she replied.

'Lisa Daniels is dead,' Nash continued bluntly. 'You are not, cannot be, Lisa Daniels, so why have you taken her identity?'

All eyes turned to the woman, who appeared tongue tied for several seconds until she managed to utter a single word. 'Shame,' she said quietly.

David King cleared his throat. 'We were in a relationship,' he said. 'I was a married man. A few... very few weeks after our affair began, she told me that she was pregnant. I knew that I had jeopardised my marriage, my career and my social status. I also knew that, thanks to my behaviour, my lover stood to bear the scorn of an entire town.'

'After I finished my training, I landed a position as a Staff Nurse at the Princess Vic,' the woman said. 'I worked with Lisa's mother, who told me that we shared the same birthday. I didn't work there very long. I'd moved on well before I came back to this area. When I fell pregnant, Lisa provided an escape route for me. I knew her details, so I applied for a duplicate birth certificate and tried to become her. I found a flat in Oxton and paid my rent in cash, so that I didn't need a bank account. After a few months, I moved over to Crockerby, with a good reference from my landlord and a new identity. I've never applied for a driving licence or any kind of official stuff.'

King gave her a hug. 'After Deb died, I experienced the accusations and whispers, plus the personal shame of knowing that I had failed in my duty to her,' he said. 'It became intolerable. In the end, I moved away too. We've been together ever since.'

Nash's phone beeped. He glanced at the screen and asked to be excused while he took the call.

He paced the riverbank for a few minutes of what appeared to be a very one-sided conversation, with the other party doing most of the speaking. When he returned, Nash spoke immediately to David King's partner. 'What is your name?' he asked sharply.

'Is that really relevant?' she asked.

'I try never to ask irrelevant questions,' Nash replied, 'or questions to which I do not already know the answer. Think about it for a moment.' He turned to David King. 'I have just been speaking to Dr Nacio Sanchez, at the forensic science laboratory,' he said. 'Dr Sanchez has been carrying out DNA tests on your wife's clothing, sir. You will be pleased to hear that none of your DNA is present. Samples from two people have been found. Sample one is your wife's DNA. Sample two found specifically on the scarf used to strangle her, is also female.'

He turned back to King's partner. 'There was no matching DNA on the national database,' he confirmed. 'Dr Sanchez wasn't surprised, given the age of the specimen and the limited size of the database in 1981. However, he surmised that my sergeant's request for tests was possibly relevant to our recent investigations. He therefore performed comparisons and found enough matching segments to indicate a strong association between the unidentified sample on the scarf and a sample taken recently by my officers. Dr Sanchez believes that the samples almost certainly belong to siblings. That *recent* sample was taken from James Hastings. So now, will you please tell me your real name?'

David King reacted instantly. He leapt across the saloon roaring with uncontrolled animal venom, 'Evil murderous cow. *You* killed her. You murdered Deb.' He seized the woman by her neck. They crashed to the floor overturning furniture as they fell with Alistair on top of them. He grabbed King's arm, forced the vicelike strangle hold open and dragged him away. Nash brought the woman down as she attempted to escape through the galley. Alistair pushed King to the far end of the saloon and held him hard against the partition wall. Marcia assisted Nash by subduing the writhing woman until he managed to apply handcuffs. He lifted her from the floor and threw her down heavily onto a chair.

'That conniving cow began pressurising me to divorce Debbie the moment she found out she was pregnant,' King shouted. 'How could I even think of dumping her like that? Deb depended on me. I loved her. I suggested an abortion. I knew it was cruel but there seemed to be no alternative. She refused. Said her family wouldn't allow it. So, she had the child, changed her identity and disappeared. When Debbie...' He half choked then continued, stabbing his finger toward the handcuffed woman like a lance. 'After *she* murdered my wife, she became, or should I say *pretended* to become, a supportive, caring, even loving, companion.' He glared at the woman slumped on the armchair. 'How could you keep up that heartless pretence, after what you'd done? How could you?'

'She was in the way,' the woman replied flatly. 'If you'd dumped her and married me, she wouldn't have had to go. You wouldn't even marry me when she had gone. Why wouldn't you? Why David?'

'Because I never stopped being married to Deb,' he said as he turned slowly to Nash. 'Her name is Kate Dawlish, Chief Inspector.'

Nash phoned for two cars to take David and Kate away. He glanced at Alistair who was clearly stunned, though he nodded to indicate that he was okay. 'I'll log the assault on your partner, or former partner now I suspect, as reasonable force to prevent an escape,' he said to an equally shocked David King. 'You should thank the Commander for saving you from facing a much more serious charge. I'll need to interview Ms Dawlish formally and take a statement from you back at the station. Can I assume that neither you nor Ms Dawlish is aware who the Commander is?'

King shook his head.

'Should we be?' Kate Dawlish asked.

Nash opened his mouth.

'No,' Alistair said firmly.

'I could hardly believe the implication of what Dr Sanchez was telling me at first,' Nash admitted when the pair had gone. 'When I asked Alex Reid to call for tests on those old murder file exhibits, I thought it was just a final bit of box ticking to show we'd covered everything. I didn't see any firm link to our recent cases. Now we have another solved murder. And you have… What exactly have I unearthed for you Commander?'

'We can only ever find what's there,' Alistair said. 'It just might not always be what we were expecting to find.' He slipped his arm around Marcia's waist. 'Sometimes it's bad. Sometimes it's much better than we could have dared to hope for.'

'Fair comment,' Nash conceded. 'I'll keep you posted if anything emerges from the interviews.' He turned to Marcia. 'I have something for you,' he said. 'I almost forgot when that little scene kicked off.' He reached into his coat pocket, pulled out an envelope and handed it to her. 'Reverend Chapman spotted it among Paul Clifford's personal effects at the hospital,' he said. 'It's quite distinctive and Clive remembered seeing it when your sister and Dr Hastings were at St Michael's. He thought you would like to have it.'

She opened the envelope and gasped. Tears erupted onto her cheeks as she reached in and took out a mobile phone, covered in tiny, exquisite illustrations of birds and butterflies. 'Caroline's phone,' she gasped through her tears. 'It's wonderful.'

'And it's clean,' Nash added. 'The offending images and messages have all been wiped and uploaded to our files.' He smiled. 'I think I'm done here. And I'm sure you've seen enough of me.' He turned and left.

Marcia stared, almost in disbelief at the phone in her hand. She looked up at Alistair. 'I shouldn't feel so ridiculously happy, after the monumental shock you just had,' she said.

Alistair drew her close and kissed her. 'Circumstances,' he replied. 'You have punished yourself for years over your encounter with Clive Chapman. In the past few days, that phone in your hand has brought you nothing but heartbreak and fear. Now, the man who has been your weapon of self-imposed shame and anger, has enabled that same phone to shower you in tears of joy. I've spent years longing to know my parents, wondering why they abandoned me. I've learned today that I wasn't denied anything of value. James was never a substitute; he was a saviour. Kate didn't change her identity because she was ashamed of her unwanted pregnancy. She had to disappear because she was a killer. My mother, the scheming murderess, stole the identity of a dead child and hid in plain sight, right alongside her victim's bereaved husband, for all these years. I wanted to know the truth about her and now I do. She abandoned me and murdered Deborah King just to get the new life she craved. She didn't want me and I never needed her.'

'Will you tell your father who you are?'

'He wanted to abort me,' Alistair reminded her. 'I doubt if he's ever given me another thought. I can live with that. We can't alter the past, Marci, but we don't have to drag it along behind us for ever. You and I have each other now. Our secrets are aired and shared. We have a beautiful new life ahead of us. Let's make a start on our clean new life. We have a date with the world's greatest casserole.'

Chapter 79

Nash and Reid recorded a formal interview with Kate Dawlish who, faced with firm DNA evidence, made a full admission. She was held in the custody block ready for her remand hearing at the Magistrates Court next morning. David King went home with his innocence finally confirmed, but as a newly confused and lonely man.

'I'll take a squint through the case files before I leave,' Nash said. 'Just to make sure we haven't missed anything.'

'I'll do it, sir,' Reid offered. 'You've had quite a day. Why don't you go home?'

'Because, Alex.'

Nash walked along to his office, glanced toward the stairs then, as always, decided to stay a little longer. He pushed the door open and went inside. The case files seemed to appear spontaneously on his desk, without him having any recollection of unlocking the cabinet or pulling them out.

As expected, he found nothing he had not already committed to memory. He began stuffing the files back into their folders. The Maitland Hotels leaflet fell out of the Barney Dolman report from Lincolnshire. Nash picked it up and read the *'Loved and Lost'* advertisement. He crumpled the leaflet in his fist and swivelled his chair around to face the window. This isn't what Jen would want, Andy, he told himself. Wrapping yourself in work won't solve the problem. You know it. Alex knows it too, that's why he printed this thing. He smoothed the leaflet flat, read it once more and slipped it into his jacket pocket. A familiar routine loomed; cold house, cold takeaway, cold beer, cold bed. He disappeared down to the station yard.

The car seemed almost able to take itself to the Canton Star takeaway. Nash drew up and waved to the familiar assistant at the counter inside. Instead of getting out of his car as usual, he pulled the Loved and Lost leaflet from his pocket and read it yet again. Am I ready for a bereavement support group, he wondered? I guess there's only one way to find out. He slipped the leaflet back into his pocket and drove away toward Weaverston.

*

Alistair drove home to Bookbinders. Marcia was plainly happier than he had seen her since they met and he was determined not to spoil a moment of her joy. They arrived in the lane and sat gazing quietly out into the new world beyond the window.

The aroma, or maybe simply the anticipation, of Nancy's casserole finally drew them out.

The truly delicious meal reawakened heart-warming childhood memories for Alistair. Marcia's glowing expression showed that it completely satisfied her expectations. The pair were still contentedly sipping their wine and gazing out over the gorge when Aiden appeared on the shrubbery path. Alistair welcomed him and fetched another glass.

Aiden joined them at the terrace table and accepted, *"just a tiny one,"* from the wine bottle. He took a sip and reached into his blazer pocket. With a broadening smile, he took out a gold fob watch in the form of a book, with the name *Bookworm* engraved on its front cover.

'This was to have been James's birthday gift,' he said to Alistair. 'The dear old darling was always preoccupied with lofty cerebral matters, and constantly plunged his hands into the sink before removing his wrist watch.' He swallowed. 'Now that you are to take over at Bookworm, I thought you might like it.'

Alistair took the watch and smiled. 'Thank you, Aiden,' he said. 'This is a lovely welcome home gift. I shall treasure it.'

Epilogue

Immediately after breakfast next morning, Marcia announced that she was going out for a short while. 'I've decided to drive over to Franley,' she said. 'I must thank Clive for asking to have Caroline's phone returned.'

Alistair kissed her, and walked out with her to the lane. He watched the Mini head off and went over to his own car. Before driving into town, he made a short phone call.

Oxton had begun returning to its unruffled self. Traders opened up their shops and waved as the Mercedes slipped by. A sign alongside the Meeting Rooms front entrance announced, with an apology for any inconvenience, that the book fair would commence one week later than originally planned.

Alistair drove to the discreet rear entrance of Percival Hinchcliffe & Son – Funeral Directors. He stepped out into the sunshine and carefully retrieved the silk wrapped rectangular package he had concealed in the spare wheel compartment.

Warren Hinchcliffe welcomed Alistair to the chapel of rest. 'I was just about to seal her up, when you phoned,' he said.

'Thanks for waiting,' Alistair replied. 'I think Eleanor deserves a keepsake. Do you mind if I place this in the casket with her? It's just a book.'

'Not at all,' Warren agreed. 'She should take a memento home with her, after all this time.'

Alistair placed the package into Eleanor's casket and watched as Warren sealed the lid down. The two men stood together and bowed their heads for a few seconds.

Bearers loaded Eleanor into a plain grey private ambulance in the yard outside. Alistair watched her, and her book of secrets, set off to be reunited with her family in Wellandsley. He thanked Warren Hinchcliffe for his co-operation and returned home with his duties, to his much-loved uncle and their shared roles as keepers of the secret, honoured in full.

ABOUT THE AUTHOR

Melvin Foster was born, and still lives, in the West Midlands of England. What was planned to be a short early career in engineering, stretched on until he had married and made a home together with his wife, Audrey, and their daughter, Suzanne. When it became clear that future career prospects would rely on education, Melvin began studying for his degree. After graduating from the Open University, he was appointed and remained for several years as an officer of H.M. Customs & Excise (now HMRC). He was privileged in 1991 to be appointed as a magistrate in the City of Wolverhampton.

Printed in Great Britain
by Amazon

80047053R00200